THE KEYS

THE KEYS

a novel

RAFAEL SILVA

LIMBIC
PRESS

Published by Limbic Press
Portland, Oregon, USA
infodesk@limbicpress.com

ISBN 978-0-991-28674-4 (paperback)
ISBN 978-0-991-28675-1 (e-book)

Library of Congress Control Number: 2019944612

Edited by Janice Obuchowski
Copyediting by Jennifer Zaczek
Proofreading by Laura Whittemore
Cover and interior design by Lance Buckley
Interior photo background by Oralia I. González Reyes
Interior photo overlay by Oleggg (Shutterstock Inc.)

Printed in the USA

This book is dedicated to the Greatest Generation. To the men and women from all the nations who contributed to the Allied effort during World War II. To those who—with or without a uniform—sacrificed their lives or loves so that three-quarters of a century later, we have the freedom to write our chosen stories.

...she asked that I not contact her...implored me to find happiness with another, as we would surely kiss again, by the river—in another life.

—GUSTAVO MARTEL, *THE KEYS*

THE KEYS

PROLOGUE

A loud hiss lingered. The brakes had just released their excess air. With a soft rattle below the passenger compartment, the westbound commuter came to its final stop.

The cabin was only about a quarter full. Passengers had been gradually getting off at the preceding stations. A few of those remaining, some in wrinkled shirts and with undone ties, were already in the line that inevitably formed behind the exit door. This was their last obstacle to freedom after a long, hard day of work. Other passengers sat patiently, or perhaps just less desperately, in their seats. Almost everyone was talking, texting, or staring at their smartphones' colorful screens.

Sam felt the train stop and heard people bustling around him. He opened his eyes and looked pensively out the window. He'd been mostly successful in forcing himself to sleep—not only during the train ride but also during the preceding five-hour flight to Boston. Before his departure, Sam had purchased some magazines and a booklet of crossword puzzles, hoping they would distract him enough.

He'd wanted to avoid thinking about the last few hours and, for that matter, about everything that had transpired in the last year. But once in the air, the more he tried to read an article or apply his wits to the empty grid of rows and columns, the more he was reminded of the people and places he'd come to know in such a short period of time. The friendships he'd forged in the big city and his experience in that remote mountain village had meant so much to him. The history he'd learned about his own family affected him deeply. Above all, Sam thought of those compelling eyes—beacons of a sophisticated yet down-to-earth presence—that had always thrown him into a blissful trance. If only he'd done things differently that fateful morning.

While contrived, sleeping had helped, albeit temporarily, to tamp down his brooding. Sam knew he'd never forget. But he didn't want to think about it. Not now. Not for a long time. It was disconcerting and painful.

Sam remained seated with the more sensible passengers who waited a little longer to detrain. His railcar was at the end of the commuter, which had come to a halt along the railway platform a good distance from the station. This allowed passengers on his side a splendid view of the dove-white east tower of Worcester's Union Station. The muted sun hitting the tower created a peculiar shimmer. Its setting rays formed a shadowy outline of the stately building. A pristine evening completed the scene.

Under different circumstances, Sam might've appreciated the almost ethereal sight. But he didn't want to feel too much. He was trying to keep his awareness and judgment intact while purposely detaching his heart from his mind. His usual vitality was presently impaired. He was heartbroken.

Sam shook his head and smiled resignedly. He thought, *At least I'm home.*

At first glance, Worcester might've appeared somber and undesirable. Outsiders passing through might've felt inclined to hasten through its stark, industrial façade. But to Sam and most of its nearly two hundred thousand inhabitants, the city was homey and comfortable, even charming in its modesty and simplicity. This was a place with diverse, unpretentious, and sincere people. It had a storied history. Here, in 1926, Robert Goddard launched the first liquid-fuel-propelled rocket and thus ushered in the Space Age. It was the birthplace of the iconic happy face, the smiling yellow symbol Harvey Ball designed in 1963. It was a modern hub for the healthcare and biotechnology industries. It was where Sam had been born—at the old Saint Vincent Hospital—and where he'd lived, happily, for three decades. His sister and her family also lived in, and loved, the town. Most of his childhood friends, with whom he kept in constant touch, still lived nearby. He'd gone to college in Worcester and currently had a job in the city. It was home to the American Hockey League's Worcester Sharks. It was an easy ride from Worcester to Fenway Park for Red Sox games or to Gillette Stadium for New England Patriots football or Revolution soccer matches. Samuel Gleeson had everything in Worcester. He'd never thought of his life or future existing outside this most agreeable spot in central Massachusetts.

But he would have given it all up—unequivocally and in an instant—for her.

How did I get to this point? Sam wondered. How had he fallen so fervently in love, knowing it was all an improbable fairy tale? How could he have dry eyes but also feel a weeping emptiness in his heart? When did this strange affair first start?

Did it begin with those unexpected letters from the law firm? Was it the pair of keys? Perhaps it was Sam's determination to do the right thing. Or was it simple curiosity when he thought there was nothing to lose?

As he turned and saw the last person in line leave the train, he felt the keys against his chest, hanging from the makeshift necklace around his neck. He grabbed his backpack and headed for the exit. He stepped off the train and into a pleasant evening breeze. It was the last day of summer.

Once on the platform, Sam stopped and sighed. A faint and more logical facet to his musings suddenly entered his thoughts. Sam finally realized the precise moment that had started the flurry of recent events. With that in mind, he left the train station and walked home.

It didn't begin with those letters, he'd concluded. Instead, this had all originated about seventy-three years ago, on May 20, 1942, when a German U-boat sank the *Faja de Oro,* a Mexican oil tanker, off the Florida coast. This was improbable, incredible, but true. It changed Sam's life forever.

One summer ago, when the first letter arrived...

ONE

Sam lived in a middling apartment just off Park Avenue—a name that evoked a sense of sophistication and exclusivity. But this was Worcester. His place was behind Dalat, a Vietnamese restaurant. This eatery was flanked by a check-cashing establishment and an auto body shop. A Taco Bell and a fire station stood across the street. An endless array of small businesses—a nail salon, a convenience store, a tax-preparation office with a placard of services written in both English and Polish—could be seen in either direction.

He turned onto Pembroke Street, disappearing through the narrow alleyway that led to an unpaved parking lot. The two-story apartment building framed the lot in an L-shaped configuration. The small complex, which had sixteen units, was reminiscent of a '70s-style motel. Perhaps if seen at night, it might have seemed slummy and even scary. But it was well maintained, with comfortable and efficient one- and two-bedroom units. It had a mix of single tenants and some families, many of whom had lived there for years. Most people knew one another. They shared a sense of community and friendship.

Sam stopped by the mail booth below the stairs. As was his custom, he sifted through his mail and discarded anything he deemed useless. There was a covered trash can at arm's length where he threw out flyers from local businesses, the Price Chopper's specials and coupons section, the inevitable credit card offers, and other items. With that thicket of unwanted mail went an unopened, ordinary-looking envelope from Taylor and

Haas LLP—a law firm in San Antonio, Texas. He thought it was junk mail.

He walked upstairs to his apartment and went about his evening.

The second letter from Taylor and Haas appeared a month later. Sam's roommate, Tony, collected the mail. Tony seldom did that; he didn't even have a key to the mailbox. But he happened to run into the mailman one afternoon. Despite most of their mail being addressed to Sam, Tony opened all the correspondence, whether it was his or Sam's. He took mental note of a few things, then left it all in the ceramic soccer ball bowl on the coffee table. He cleaned Vin's litter box and refreshed the pets' water bowls. After changing into workout gear, he took Nic, Sam's dog, for a run.

They shared a small two-bedroom corner unit, which opened into a living room with a bedroom on each end. To the right of the entrance was an open kitchen. An old but sturdy wood table with four matching chairs stood a few feet from the kitchen counter. In the living area they had a long leather couch facing a flat-screen TV resting on a low stand. The stand also held other devices, from an Xbox to wireless speakers. A custom cover emblazoned with the New England Patriots' logo was fitted over a plush armchair. Two long windows at the far end of the living room provided natural light during the day. A peculiar wooden shelf stood over the windows, running the length of the wall. The shelf connected the top of two multilevel, carpet-lined cat condos standing in either corner. From that lofty vantage, Vin, the cat, blithely groomed himself and observed the activity when Sam came home later that evening.

As soon as he opened the door, Nic jumped and literally adhered himself to Sam's chest. Sam supported the dog's rear end with his hands while still holding on to a plastic bag from Boston Market. With a firm grip on Nic and his face now thoroughly licked, he walked to the kitchen and set the take-out bag on the counter. Sam reached for a stainless-steel container, and as soon as he took off the lid, the sixty-plus-pound mutt detached himself and sat expectantly on the floor. Sam produced a treat, which Nic gently took from his hand. The dog then rushed to the couch to hastily consume the chewy bone.

The only bathroom was just outside Tony's room, through a short hallway, a few feet from the TV. Sam walked in that direction and bellowed toward his friend's room, "I got meatloaf and all the fixings."

"Did you have them scoop the sweet potatoes from the bottom?"

"Yeah, dude. Why do you have to ask the same question every time? I know you don't like the marshmallow topping." Sam partially opened the bathroom door. Almost immediately, he sprang away and crashed against the opposite wall, as if he'd been ejected by some force within the bathroom.

Tony came into the hall, asking, "What the fuck was that?"

"What the hell, man! It stinks in there. How many times do I have to tell you to turn the fan on when you take a crap?" Sam said, half laughing, half completely grossed out.

Amused and wearing a wide grin, Tony replied, "Sorry, Sammy, I just went. I didn't think you'd get here so early. I had a burrito for lunch, and I think I overdid the salsa. It twisted my guts all up. I just couldn't stop, though; it was really good."

"No shit. Now I gotta wait to take a leak. It's toxic in there," Sam said, sliding his arm through the mostly closed bathroom door, feeling the wall for the exhaust fan switch, and turning it on. Then he closed the door.

"Speaking of burritos, it turns out the joint is right across from Kevin's new place. It looks like he started mailing flyers. Did you see? One of the flyers is with the rest of the mail," Tony told him. "They seem to be working, because I saw like four or five guys go in and out while I sat there eating my burrito."

"I haven't seen today's mail, but yeah, I've seen the flyers. I'm glad they're working for him. By the way, I hope you're not stalking him," Sam said.

"No, I'm not. I mean, I still think it's shitty he did the whole thing behind our backs," Tony said.

"Hey, it's not a big deal. We would have been fine with it. In fact, we would have helped him set up his new barbershop."

"That's why it sucks. We were his friends. He should have trusted us."

"'Were'? Come on, Tony. We're still his friends. He knew he'd be competing with our shop, so he felt bad about telling us he wanted to go out on his own. There's plenty for everybody, man. Cut the guy some slack," Sam told him.

"Yeah, I know, I know," Tony said. They were both now at the table, eating dinner. Reaching for the corn bread, Tony changed gears and said, "By the way, there's a letter for you from some lawyer in Texas. It says you should call."

"I don't know anyone in Texas. I'm sure it's junk mail."

"It looks kinda legit, Sammy. It doesn't have that generic look of bulk mail. It's on nice thick paper."

"Oh yeah? Let's see. Well, let me go pee first. I hope your stink is gone," Sam said. On his way back, he went to the coffee table and picked up the letter. Applying redactions, Sam read aloud: "Blah, blah, Taylor and Haas. Dear Mr. Gleeson…blah, blah… second attempt at contacting you…blah, blah…hope this letter finds you well. I represent the interests of a special client and a peculiar case, of which you are the beneficiary. I urge you to contact me at…blah, blah…Central Standard Time so I can explain the matter and arrange a meeting. When contacting my office, please ask to speak with me and provide this code: PCP1. If we do not hear from you in the next…blah, blah…we will contact you by telephone. Best regards, Lena A. Sander, principal and blah, blah." He gave Tony a puzzled look mixed with a skeptical smile.

"I told you it sounded real," Tony said, beaming.

"What are you talking about? This is weird and a total crock of shit. I bet it's one of those scams where you call and they try to get you to send money before you can 'claim your prize.'" Sam crumpled the letter and put it in the to-go bag—destined for the trash.

Tony shook his head. "Maybe it's some inheritance. What if it's about a relative? Don't you want to know? I would."

"Hey, man. I know it's the ultimate dream for all of us who grew up in the system to hear from long-lost parents or a rich uncle, but you and Lilly are my only family. We don't need, and have never needed, anyone else."

"Speak for yourself, bro. If anything like that came my way, I'd be all over it. I wouldn't mind knowing about my parents or any other family I might have. Even if it was something crappy, at least I'd know."

"Sorry, Tony. I get it. It's just a stretch, you know? Besides, we're doing just fine. We always have, haven't we?"

"Yeah. It's just that I thought about the possibility, and it seemed nice. Since I'll probably never have a clue about my own folks, I wanted to feel good about you. But I know, it's a freakin' fantasy," Tony said. Then, in a more animated tone, he asked, "So, what are we gonna do tonight?"

"Let's finish eating," Sam said. "I'll take Nic out in a bit, and then we can catch up on some *Key and Peele.*"

"I'm up for that. Those guys are awesome," Tony replied, nearly finished with his dinner.

Later, Nic demanded proper petting as he stretched out on the long sofa, putting his head on Sam's lap. Vin came down from his perch and sat on the armchair's thick armrest next to Tony, who was slouched with his feet on the coffee table. They spent the rest of the evening watching TV.

TWO

The following morning, Sam lay asleep with his two pets by his side. It was Tony's turn to open their barbershop. He was as quiet as he could be while rummaging in the kitchen. He planned to get a breakfast muffin and coffee from the Dunkin' Donuts on Main Street, just a block from the shop. In his quest to forgo a tasty yet bowel-igniting burrito for lunch, he decided to make a sandwich. He placed the sandwich, a small ziplock bag of chips, and two peaches in a metal Red Sox lunch box. He cleaned up the counter and pressed the garbage can's foot pedal. Just before disposing of dirty paper towels and an empty cheese package, he saw last night's take-out bag. The law firm's letter was visible through the translucent plastic. He glanced toward Sam's closed door. With sudden conviction, Tony salvaged the letter. He put it in his back pocket, discarded the new trash, and left for work.

He didn't know exactly what he'd do with the letter. But he felt he *had* to do something. He knew Sam was right about the constant but surely improbable wish shared by most people who had grown up in the foster care system: knowing something, anything, about a blood relative. Tony loved Sam as a brother. As such, he wanted to investigate the possibility that this letter might lead to something that could make even a tiny part of this wish come true—for Sam and, by nearly fraternal association, for himself.

At the barbershop, Tony turned on the lights and the neon Open sign. Sam had cleaned up everything at the end of the previous day. Now Tony just had to turn on the TV, eat his breakfast muffin, wait for customers, and think about how to proceed regarding the letter. He decided he would wait until Lisa, one of their two employees, arrived so he could carry out his plan without clients interrupting him. Sam had a project to finish that day for his side job as an IT consultant and would then go to the field in the late afternoon. They were both volunteer coaches for local youth soccer teams. Tony knew it was unlikely that Sam would stop by the shop that day.

It was a slow morning. He'd worked on only three customers before Lisa came in. They sat and made the usual small talk. After a few minutes, a young mother showed up with two pre-school-age boys in desperate need of haircuts. Tony knew this would be a good time to step away and get his plan rolling.

"You good with both kids while I take lunch?"

"Of course, no problem," Lisa answered.

In their tiny break room, Tony grabbed his lunch box from the fridge. He took the shop's cordless phone with him. This way, he could answer calls while Lisa was busy. And he thought calling from the shop rather than using his own phone would be better. Sitting at a small plastic table that abutted the wall, he ate some of his sandwich and took a gulp of soda before closing his eyes and sighing deeply. He looked at the letter on the table and dialed.

"This is Samuel Gleeson. I got a letter from your office asking me to contact a Lena Sander. I have a code."

Before Tony could offer the code, the receptionist told him, "I will connect you immediately, Mr. Gleeson."

After the thirty-minute conversation, Tony was dumbfounded. He rushed out of the break room to their front-desk computer. What he'd just learned could be related to one of Sam's relatives and could even have some material value. But it seemed a bit too good to be true. The first thing he wanted to do was to confirm this law firm's legitimacy.

Sure enough, the firm was real. Their website described it as one of the most respected and established law firms in Texas, doing business since 1946. They had offices in various cities in the US, Canada, and Mexico and in some European countries. He read Lena Sander's impressive biography. She had attended the University of Texas and Columbia Law School. She had won important cases on behalf of major corporations and held leadership positions on the boards of various institutions, as well as on philanthropic organizations. Tony also saw many references to the law firm on other websites and in online news articles.

It all had to be real, he concluded.

Now, he just had to convince Sam to take a leap of faith and see where this might take him. Given the arrangement he'd made with Lena, Tony had to tell Sam soon. He thought the best time would be Saturday, after the Revs game. They were playing the Philadelphia Union, which had been struggling that season. He figured Sam would be in a particularly good mood if they won the game.

As Tony had predicted, the Revs beat Philly 2–0. However, the celebration following the game precluded him from addressing the law firm's issue with Sam. After the drive back from Foxborough, along with four of their friends, they continued the victory bash at the Wonder Bar on Shrewsbury Street with an abundance of pizza and beer. Tony didn't remember much after that and didn't wake up until late the next morning.

He looked at the time, hastily cleaned up, got dressed, and rushed to the field. Sam was already there, running warm-up drills with the kids. Tony said hello to a few of the parents and then signaled the two goalies over. He and Sam acknowledged each other with a smile. Tony then ran his pregame drills with the two goalies.

After the game, which they won 6–2, they took some of the foster kids on the team to lunch. Once their commitment to the soccer team was over, they headed to Sam's sister's house. They found Nic, who'd been boarded there since the previous day, playing with Sam's two young nieces and their own dog. As usual, they spent a pleasant Sunday interacting with Lilly and her husband's family. Once they got home, they were both exhausted, and Tony didn't feel it would be a good time to tell Sam anything.

On Monday night, Sam was preoccupied with a project he had to finish for his IT job, so Tony thought to pass on addressing the issue then too. On Tuesday, he almost told him while they both took a break from clients at the barbershop, but then a handful of customers entered in quick succession. And that night, Sam hosted a meeting at the apartment for Worcester Animal Rescue League volunteers to discuss plans for an upcoming fundraiser. It ran late. Once again, Tony could not tell Sam anything.

Wednesday was do or die.

It was just after seven in the evening. All the customers and employees were gone. Sam and Tony were finishing up the cleanup for the day.

"Sammy, you know how you always say it's good to listen to people and process what they say in a logical way before passing judgment?" Tony asked as he wrung the mop.

"Well, it depends," Sam replied with a facetious smile. He had just taken out the trash and began to straighten out magazines and chairs in the waiting area.

"Dude, I'm serious."

"All right, yeah, of course. That's how it should be. What's this about?" Sam said. "I think we're done here. Nic, you ready?" He gave a short, sharp whistle.

Behind the reception desk, Nic jumped off his bed and rushed to the door, pacing and happily wagging his tail. Sam was about to turn off the computer when Tony loudly and impulsively said, "Wait, don't turn that off. I have something to show you."

He rolled the mop bucket into the nearby closet, then came over to the desk.

"I'm hungry, man. Let's go. I thought we could pick up some stuff from New England Roast Beef."

"That's fine, Sam. But first you gotta see this. Move over." Tony brought up the law firm's web page and said, "Here, check it out."

"Shit, Tony. Really?" Sam said, then pointed at the dog. "Look, Nic is as desperate and as hungry as I am. Can we bust out of here?"

"I need you to take me seriously right now. Sit your ass there," Tony told him in a benign but commanding tone, lightly pushing Sam onto the stool next to him. "Listen, I called this chick the other day, told her I was you, and got the skinny on that letter you threw away." He pulled the letter from his back pocket and gave it to Sam. "I know you'll want to use your geek-computer-engineer brain on this one, but if you really are my brother, you'll believe I've done enough legwork and you should just trust me. Can you do that for me, Sam?"

Save for some rough patches along the way, Tony was generally a happy-go-lucky, class-clown sort of guy. Seeing Tony's determined stare and hearing the seriousness in his voice, Sam realized this was important to his friend. He settled firmly on the stool and told Tony, "Yes, I trust you. Let it rip."

Sam had apparently inherited a key, Tony said. Lena could not divulge more information about the key over the phone. But she'd conceded it was part of an inheritance. And it also had to do with one of Sam's family members, about whom she was not at liberty to discuss further unless they met in person. Lena told him that it wasn't her intention to conceal anything; she was simply following her client's explicit instructions. "In fact, this is all very genuine and even more unique than it sounds," she'd added. Tony had said she must realize this sounded odd and asked how he could be assured that this wasn't a scam. "I absolutely understand your reservations, Mr. Gleeson," she'd said. "I probably would dismiss something like this myself. But I'm fulfilling not only an obligation to a client but also a personal desire to see the matter come to a positive conclusion—one many years in the making. I know this is hard to digest, but I can promise you that all you have to lose is your time. In fact, this case is so dear to me that my firm will pay for all your expenses. I'm confident that once we meet, you'll appreciate the entirety of this bequest."

"She said all that?"

"Yeah, Sammy, she did. And I totally looked her and her law firm up. I also discovered she's an animal lover. She's a board member of the San Antonio Humane Society. You know they only let real upstanding folks on those boards. That's saying something. I mean, this lady is for real."

"So, now what?" Sam inquired.

"About that," Tony said with a don't-kill-the-messenger grimace. "I've already made arrangements."

"You did what? Are you kidding me?" Sam asked, momentarily stunned. Yet he promptly cracked that peculiar smile he'd used over the years when it was obvious that Tony had gotten himself, or both of them, in a predicament.

"You leave tomorrow!" Tony declared with a sheepish grin and a shrug of the shoulders.

THREE

A single airline served Worcester's regional airport, making connections to Texas difficult. So, Tony had asked for tickets out of Providence, Rhode Island. This was a more versatile and convenient gateway—even more so than Boston.

On the early morning shuttle ride to the airport, Sam still had trouble believing he was actually doing this. But his friend was right. He didn't have much to lose. It would be like a mini vacation. He knew Tony would take proper care of the pets, and the trip would be short enough that they could forgo telling Lilly about it. Sam didn't want to worry his sister or tell her anything until he knew what this strange affair was about.

At the gate, he checked the itinerary one last time. The flight to San Antonio would connect through Houston, where he'd have plenty of layover time to get lunch. Save for the vague purpose of the trip, everything seemed simple and straightforward. Sam jokingly cursed Tony one last time in his mind. With a mellow sigh, he decided he'd make the most of whatever *this* turned out to be.

Upon takeoff, Sam heard the thunderous engine come to life. He felt the peculiar sensation of forward momentum and sank slightly into the backrest. The wheels' rugged friction against the runway quickly transitioned into a buoyant lift as the plane became airborne.

He didn't know it yet, but Sam's perception of life and love had also begun its own transition.

In Terminal B's main arrivals hallway, a few steps beyond the overhead "Welcome to San Antonio" marquee, Sam noticed a USO lounge. He decided to use the perks of his prior military service and inquire there on how best to get to his hotel.

Manning the reception desk was a friendly black man wearing a garrison cap adorned with military lapel pins. Sam didn't recognize any of the buttons, but he could tell the gentleman's hat was from the US Marines.

"Hello, young man. Returning home or visiting our beautiful city?"

"Just visiting, actually," Sam answered. "I was hoping you could tell me the best way to get to the Hotel Contessa."

"Oh yes, of course. It's one of our city's best hotels, right on the River Walk. I reckon you're not renting a car. How would you like to get there? There are taxis, shuttles, and public buses."

"What's the difference?" The man detailed the cost and time for each option. Sam then said, "Thirty minutes and a dollar fifty? The Five VIA bus sounds just fine. Where do I catch it?"

The helpful fellow explained and traced a route on an airport map. Similarly, he handed Sam another map and said, "You probably have some phone app for directions, but on this one, I've marked the downtown bus stop and drawn a path to your hotel. It's just a few blocks from there—no sweat for an athletic young guy like yourself."

"Thanks, I really appreciate that."

"That's what we're here for, soldier," the man said, smiling. "By the way, I assume you're a soldier. I didn't even ask."

"I was. I served with CECOM. Finished up a few years ago."

The gentleman raised his brows admiringly. "Aren't all you boys officers there?"

"I think so. I went in and out as a second lieutenant. But most of us had no actual command. Just the 'geek squad,' you know?" Sam replied humbly.

"Ha, yes. I've heard that. The *real* geek squad, not the one from Best Buy, huh?" He smiled. "You know, they didn't have your kind when I was in the service. All we had for coms in 'Nam were radiomen and the Military Postal Service. *Computer* wasn't even a word anybody used back then. Boy, times have changed! Anyway, I won't take any more of your time, Lieutenant…?"

Recognizing the man's inquiry, Sam quickly offered, "Gleeson, Sam Gleeson."

"I'm Bill Stafford, Fifth Marine Division, Twenty-Seventh Regiment, long time retired. It was nice meeting you, Officer Gleeson. I hope you have a pleasant stay in the Alamo City."

"Thank you. I appreciate your help, sir." Sam offered Bill his hand.

Later that evening, Sam gave Tony an account of everything: his interaction with the old marine veteran, the upscale hotel with a room bigger than their whole apartment, and the river that seemed to run down the middle of downtown.

"Is the river like the one in Providence?"

"Yeah, but bigger and probably a lot longer. It's lined with hotels, restaurants, bars, and shops. Plus, they have tour boats up and down it. Tons of people are walking around having a good time. I guess that's why they call it the River Walk. I'll check more of it out later."

"Any hot chicks?" Tony couldn't help himself.

Sam laughed. "Why am I not surprised you'd say something like that. Don't you think of anything else?"

"What else is there to think about, Sammy?"

Still smiling, Sam said, "Yeah, I saw a lot of good-looking women. All hot and all naked. That's how they roll here in Texas."

"Right! Even if the girls are not walking around naked, I'm sure they're plenty cute. So, Sammy, please get your ass out to a bar and get laid. You've got the whole weekend to work on it, dude. Wait, hmm, you can't. You can only do it when I'm your wingman." Tony burst into a chuckle on the other end.

Cracking up himself, Sam said, "Fuck you, Tony."

After their laugh, Tony said, "No, seriously. It all sounds wicked awesome. Too bad we don't look alike, you ugly punk. I coulda grabbed your license and gone there as you. Shit! You owe me, you know?"

"Owe you? I doubt that. I still don't know what you actually got me into this time. What if I happen to look like some crime boss they're trying to put away, and they planned a switcheroo—I go to jail and the real perp eventually changes his face with plastic surgery, then gets off clean?"

"Dude, they have the death penalty there. You're screwed!" Tony said.

They continued their banter for a little longer, until Sam told Tony he was going to grab dinner. At check-in, Sam discovered the law firm had left him an envelope containing a welcome letter from Lena Sander. It confirmed their appointment, with directions to her nearby office. Also enclosed were three gift cards for restaurants Lena believed would be to his liking for dinner, covering each of the three evenings he was in town.

"Which are you gonna try first?" Tony asked.

"I don't know. Bohanan's seems to be steak. Houston Street Bistro says it's New American and seafood. And Biga on the Banks says it's American. I guess I'll go alphabetical and try Biga."

"Hold on," Tony said. "I just looked that up. It says here it's one of the top five restaurants in Texas. I bet the other ones are just as good. Holy shit! You really owe me, Sam."

"Yeah, seeing as it's gonna be my last meal, it better be good. If I don't call you by this time tomorrow, it was nice knowing you. Take care of Vin and Nic for me. And have a great life, okay?"

"Fuck that! If you become a disappearing act, I'll round up the guys and we'll go bust up this Lena character until she coughs you up safe and sound. Don't worry, Sammy. I got your back."

"Ha, ha. Thanks, bro. All right, talk to you tomorrow."

"Bye, Sam. Good luck."

FOUR

From his occasional trips to Boston and New York, Sam was no stranger to tall, grand-scale buildings. But standing before the Weston Centre on Pecan Street, he felt an odd uneasiness. Subconsciously, he knew it wasn't the imposing thirty-two-story building with its shiny, russet exterior and polarized windows. Once inside, it wasn't the extravagant marble-floored lobby through which many people in office attire walked. His apprehension stemmed from knowing he *had* business there that morning. However, considering his generally unencumbered, predictable, and happy life as of about twenty-four hours ago, he felt he had *no* business being there.

Sam fleetingly considered walking out and going home. Yet a hint of curiosity, perhaps bolstered by fate's prevailing winds, prompted him to press the number thirty-two button in the elevator and forge ahead.

An attentive receptionist greeted Sam and ushered him to Lena's immense penthouse office. She asked if he'd like anything to drink as she politely gestured for him to sit in a comfortable chair—part of a living room set that stood between a large glass-top desk and a twelve-seat conference table.

"I appreciate that, but I'm fine, thank you."

"You're welcome, Mr. Gleeson. Mrs. Sander will be with you momentarily."

Sitting down, Sam looked through the floor-to-ceiling windows overlooking downtown. To the south, he noticed a tall tower with a spaceship-like structure at its pinnacle. It reminded him of a massive air traffic control tower.

"That's the Tower of the Americas," Lena said, walking in. He stood and turned in her direction. He saw a svelte woman in her late sixties. She was dressed in an impeccable gray suit. She wasn't youthful, but even with minimal makeup, she was beautiful. Her shoulder-length salt-and-pepper hair was elegantly styled. She had minimal accessories: a diamond ring and an Audemars Piguet leather watch. Despite her striking and assertive presence, her demeanor was welcoming and friendly. "I'm Lena. It's a pleasure meeting you, Mr. Gleeson," she said, shaking his hand.

"The pleasure is mine," Sam replied, feeling calmer owing to her cordial disposition.

She invited Sam to walk closer to the window. "The tower is in Hemisfair Park. It's an observation tower built as the main attraction for the 1968 World's Fair. I actually witnessed it go up. It was a proud moment for the city. While not the tallest building in the country, it was the tallest structure of its kind until the late nineties. Along with the Alamo, it's one of the emblems of San Antonio." Still addressing Sam, Lena turned and walked to her desk. "That's the extent of my prowess as a tour guide. So, Mr. Gleeson, now to the matter at hand. Please, make yourself comfortable." She took a small black leatherette box from her desk and then sat on the couch closest to Sam. "I'm certain you have many questions. And soon, you'll have even more. But the best way to begin addressing these is to cut to the chase." She pressed a button on an intercom atop the coffee table. "First, an apology. According to the wishes of our client, this should have transpired a little over five years ago, when you were twenty-six. Unfortunately, I got sick."

"I'm sorry to hear that."

"Thank you. I'm healthy now, except for the chronic malady of old age." She smiled. "At the time, we were also restructuring the firm and moving the main offices to this building. Your case

fell through the cracks. Fortunately, here we are, at last fulfilling my firm's obligation. Now, I'm positive you're Samuel Evan
Gleeson of Worcester, Massachusetts, born January 21, 1983. But
I hope you brought your birth certificate and driver's license or
passport, as I indicated when we first spoke."

Tony had instructed Sam to pack those documents. "Yes, of
course. I brought all three," Sam said and produced his birth certificate and passport from his iPad case and his license from his
wallet. He handed them to Lena. She glanced at the documents
briefly and passed them to her assistant, who'd been previously
summoned by the push of the intercom button.

"Kim will make photocopies of your documents." Lena then
gently waved the small black box and said, "With that out of the
way, *this* is why you're here." She extended her hand and gave
Sam the box. "Go ahead, open it."

Sam looked inside. "A key?"

"It's a key to a safe-deposit box at Frost Bank—formerly Frost
National Bank. Thus the engraved *F.N.B.* above the number. As
you can probably tell, the key is very old. It was last used in 1945."

"Wow!" Sam said quietly. "Who would leave this for me? As
far as I know, I don't have any connections to this state. Mrs.
Sander, I'm afraid you have the wrong person."

"I know this is strange. I believe I know the answers to many
of your questions. However, per our client's instructions, I can't
divulge anything else until you've retrieved the contents of the
safe-deposit box. Now, I don't know exactly what lies therein. But
it's my understanding that it contains objects of material and
subjective value. Vague, I know. What you find inside will eventually answer most of your questions. Also, I'd like to assure you
that you *are* the correct beneficiary of this bequest."

Lena's assistant came in briefly and handed her Sam's documents. As Lena gave them back to Sam, she said, "I had to ask that
you bring these for the sake of dotting the i's and crossing the
t's. With that out of the way, let me give you some background.

For seven decades, my firm has employed private investigators to determine the whereabouts and contact information for you and pertinent, preceding members of your family. This has culminated in you being here. I've known about you and your sister since before you were born." She offered a lingering smile. "That must prompt even more questions. Therefore, Sam—if I may address you this way—I'd suggest you head down to the bank. It's just a few blocks from here. Once you've retrieved the contents of the safe-deposit box, I can fill in any blanks you may still have. Besides, a portion of the bequest requires a brief transaction of documents before you return home. How does that sound?"

Sam smiled. "Honestly, it still sounds a bit weird. But intriguing. I guess I'll head over to the bank and put this key to work." They both stood and walked toward the door. Just before leaving, he said, "By the way, I'm not sure it matters, but for the sake of full disclosure, I wasn't the person you initially talked to on the phone. It was my roommate, Tony. He took it upon himself to find a way to get me here. He meant well, pretending to be me."

"Yes, I know," Lena conceded affably. "He slipped a few times and talked about you in the third person. I could tell he was doing it out of love for you. That's why I went along. You're lucky to have him."

"I know. Just don't ever tell him that. It would go to his head."

"I'll keep it to myself, then," she said, smiling. "Sam, it was a pleasure meeting you. I'll see you again soon. Here's the bank's address and my cell number." Lena handed him the sheet her assistant had previously prepared.

"Thank you, I'll be in touch." He waved goodbye.

FIVE

rost was the largest Texas-based bank. It was founded in 1868 by Col. T. C. Frost in San Antonio. Since the early twentieth century, it had been a backbone of San Antonio's and Texas's economies. The institution had not only survived, but through its mission of responsible banking—a rarity in modern times—it had also thrived through two world wars, the Great Depression, the oil crises of the '70s and '80s, the real estate bubble burst of 2008, and the recent banking industry collapse. It was the first bank in the country to decline government bailouts.

Sam sat in the lobby of this acclaimed bank. Five minutes after he'd registered at the information desk, a short, chubby twentysomething representative greeted him.

"Hello, Mr. Gleeson. My name is Jim Hutto. I understand you need access to your deposit box. May I see your key?" Sam opened the small case and showed him the key, which had a flat bow and hollow barrel stem. Jim looked puzzled. "That's not a deposit box key. Not one of ours, anyway."

"Really?" Sam felt perplexed. "I just inherited this key. It's supposed to be for a safe-deposit box established at Frost National Bank in 1945. Maybe I got the wrong bank."

"No, this used to be a National Bank. May I see the key again?"

Sam handed him the key. Jim examined it closely and noticed the three-letter acronym. The key seemed to be made of smooth silver, though it was a bit tarnished.

"It's a beautiful key," Jim said, handing it back to Sam. "From the inscription, it probably was a key from the old Frost Bank. But after all that time, I doubt the account still exists. Unless accounts are kept current, boxes are eventually opened and their contents are transferred to the State Treasury. I'm sure that happened in this case."

Sam smiled reflexively. He wondered if this trip had been a whole lot of nothing. He considered either going back to Lena to tell her the key was a bust or cutting loose, going home, and calling her later on.

Jim interrupted his train of thought. "Mr. Gleeson, let me ask my supervisor about your key. Maybe she knows something I don't. Would you mind waiting a couple of minutes?"

"Not at all. I'll wait right here." He sat back down on the lobby couch. A few minutes later, Jim came back with his supervisor—a middle-aged blond woman.

"This is Mrs. Garcia, my supervisor. May I show her your key?"

Sam handed her the key. She clasped its stem with her index finger and thumb. Turning it back and forth, she examined the bow. Her eyes lit up. "This is definitely a key from the Frost National Bank. It doesn't open any of our boxes, though. It's just too old. But I can look up the key's number and see what turns up. Would that interest you, Mr. Gleeson?"

"I've come a long way for this. So, why not?"

"Great. Please, follow me," she said.

In her open-view cubicle, in the lobby's far corner, Sam sat next to her desk. Mrs. Garcia set the key beside her and glanced again at its number. She typed on her keyboard and read silently from the screen. Sam could tell from her raised brows, alternating with squinting eyes, that whatever was popping up enthralled her. She picked up the phone and exchanged numbers, codes, and dates with whomever was at the other end. A moment later, Mrs. Garcia hung up and turned to Sam with a dazzled look.

"Mr. Gleeson, I'm amazed. The account associated with this deposit box has been kept current all these years. Because of its age, only a handful of people, way beyond my pay grade, can address this account. In fact, the president of the bank is on his way down."

"Wow. Okay!" Sam said.

"May I get you something to drink?"

"How about a beer?" Sam replied in jest.

"We only offer those past noon," she countered with a grin. "At the moment just water, coffee, iced tea, or a soft drink."

"Thank you, Mrs. Garcia, I'm fine."

Following a short lull, she asked, "Are you from San Antonio?"

They had a brief and pleasant conversation. Sam offered an abridged chronicle of where he came from and why he was there.

"You really don't know anything else about that key?"

"Nothing at all," he answered.

"Well, I see Mr. Dahl on his way here." She stood up, and Sam also rose. They shook hands. "I hope your key opens something wonderful for you, Mr. Gleeson. I'll leave you in our president's hands."

The distinguished older man, wearing a tailored suit, came over. He'd heard Mrs. Garcia's last remark. A personal assistant, the vice president of operations, and two burly security men trailed just a step behind him. Sam became nervous, particularly in light of the two musclemen. He recalled last night's conversation with Tony. *Shit*, he thought, *my pets are gonna become orphans.*

But his fear dissipated when Mr. Dahl smiled and warmly offered Sam his hand. The entourage was just standard procedure. The bank president introduced himself and the people around him. He asked to see the key. Sam offered it.

"Oh no," the man stated, putting his palms up as if signaling Sam to stop. "Until you instruct us to close your account, that key is yours and we can't touch it. I know some of my people have, so I apologize." He smiled again. "Just a quick look will suffice."

Sam held it by the stem.

Mr. Dahl stooped and squinted over the rim of his glasses. "Yes, it's authentic." He straightened. "Mr. Gleeson, I checked the activity on this account. Its inception predates your age—and even mine, for that matter. However, the maintenance fees for the box have always been paid since 1945." He glanced at a sheet. "Let's see, they were paid by Landon S. Taylor, Esquire, until 1957; Taylor and Associates until 1969; and by Taylor and Haas. Probably the same company, just different names. Lillian J. Gleeson was added to the account in 1981."

"That's my sister. She was born in 1981," Sam exclaimed.

"I see. In 1983, her name was taken off the registration card and yours was added. I suspect when you were born," Mr. Dahl said, and Sam nodded. "If I could see a photo ID, it will be my pleasure to escort you to your box—still as intact as it was on the day *that* very key locked it."

Sam reached for his wallet. Satisfied with the license, Mr. Dahl invited Sam to walk with him. He told Sam the vault for the deposit box was at an off-site location, a five-minute drive down the street. Two black Suburbans were idling on the street, their sidewalk-facing doors open. The bank president and Sam took the back seat of the first SUV, with one security guard taking the front. The other three boarded the second SUV. They reached their destination before Mr. Dahl had finished explaining they'd driven to avoid being drenched in sweat from the now late-morning summer heat.

The Suburbans parked at the edge of Main Plaza. *Odd*, Sam thought. He saw what was essentially a park. The two closest buildings were the large, colonial-style San Fernando Cathedral and a twelve-story government building. The entourage headed for the latter.

"This beautiful building, Mr. Gleeson, was the original Frost National Bank, built at the turn of the last century. We still own the structure, but we rent it to the city. It is the town's seat of government." They walked through a hallway with signs pointing to the city council chamber. "In the late sixties, management tried to contact a number of our deposit-box clients when we'd just begun plans to move to our current headquarters. Unfortunately, many clients were unreachable. Although, as in your case, their box accounts remained current. In other cases, clients were up in arms at the thought of their valuables being uprooted. Given that some of these people were among the most powerful in Texas, the board decided to keep this vault."

They'd reached a private elevator in a hallway beyond the municipal offices and away from the main elevator banks. They'd also been cleared by a guard. In the elevator, Sam noticed no buttons on any of the panels. The assistant swiped a card through a slot to the right of the doors. The elevator descended. When the doors opened, they walked into a luxurious room reminiscent of a library in an old, opulent mansion. Portraits of important-looking men hung from the walls. There were a few leather armchairs and a table made of fine wood. Opposite the elevator, two additional guards manned a desk.

"Mr. Gleeson, welcome to our original vault—one of the still existing structures from which the term *safe deposit* originated. Miss Jones will show you to your box beyond that door. There's a comfortable sitting area just outside the vault. You're welcome to spend as much time there as you'd like. When you're finished, you're free to continue storing your valuables in this vault. If you'd like to retrieve its contents, we'll terminate the account. But because we hope to close down this place in the next decade, you'd be welcome to take the key with you. A souvenir of sorts. My assistant will wait for you out here until you instruct her on what you wish to do." Mr. Dahl gave Miss Jones a quick nod and turned back to Sam. "And with that, I conclude my service to you in this transaction. You're one of only a few clients I've had the privilege of bringing here in my almost thirty years working for this institution. It was a pleasure, Mr. Gleeson. As Mrs. Garcia said earlier, I do hope you discover something wonderful in there."

SIX

S am stood before a large array of old but meticulously kept safe-deposit boxes. Each keyhole and box number were plated in gold and protruded slightly from the box's front. He identified the correct box, then effortlessly inserted and turned the key. Once the door opened, Sam discerned a peculiar smell. It reminded him of flipping through the pages of an old book. He pulled out the inner tray and walked to the adjacent cubicle. He placed the tray on the countertop and sat on a chair.

The tray held two stacked items. On top was a sapphire-blue velvet case with a silver logo for Van Cleef & Arpels, Paris. Sam picked it up and unlatched the small clasp. He felt a rush of excitement and suspense, akin to opening a gift on Christmas morning. Then he became bewildered, staring at the case's sparkling contents: a white-gold and diamond jewelry set. An exquisitely thin chain necklace with five evenly spaced diamonds encircled matching dangly earrings and a ring with a single diamond on the bezel. The case also contained an old but run-of-the-mill key in the right lower corner of the satin surface. A copper thumbtack through the hole of its flat bow held the key in place. *Strange*, he thought. The key seemed completely out of place.

Sam had no doubt the jewelry was valuable. But he really wondered about its origin—how and why those items came to be in that box, isolated from the outside world for nearly three quarters of a century. Above all, he asked himself what this new discovery had to do with him.

Sam closed the jewelry case, put it on the counter, and retrieved the next item: a leather-bound notebook. The manufacturer's label, embossed on the flap, consisted of two inverted Fs within a circle and *Fendi—Roma—1925* just below. It was tied shut with a raw-leather cord. He loosened the cord, pulled the flap, and popped the brass snap. Then he opened the front cover. He saw an unaddressed, thick parchment envelope lodged between the cover and what was obviously a journal. It was evident that whoever had left these items intended for the recipient to read the envelope's contents first. In his quest for answers, Sam did just that.

28 December 1945

Dearest Friend,

I hope these words find you well. I don't know if you're a young man or a young woman. Regardless, my greatest hope is that time has transpired as I currently envision on this most bittersweet of days.

I trust the recent victory has endured and that you find yourself in the wonderful country that anchored the Great War effort. For without the resolute and tenacious people of the United States, my own nation and most of the world would have succumbed to the tyranny of a few.

I realize this letter and the other contents herein are a revelation to you. On that account, I ask for your patience as you read these lines, written in the best possible English my education and experiences have afforded me. I implore you to understand my motive and accept all its components without rancor toward the member of your family—endowed with unblemished character—in whose honor I have made this bequest. I count on your appreciation that this ostensibly random act derives from good faith and that this gift, which now belongs to you, is rooted entirely in love.

If my wishes, through the efforts of my trusted friend and counselor, Landon Taylor, have come to pass, you are the youngest second-generation descendant of Alessandra Blake. And you are reading this on or close to your twenty-sixth birthday—the age I was, only a year ago, when I met and swiftly fell in everlasting love with your grandmother.

Certainly, this rests on my assumption that, after fate truncated our future together, my dearest Alessandra went on to live a joyous life and begin a family. Consequently, while I wish you were my grandson or granddaughter, you are not. My only relation to you is limited to the brief time I had the fortune to share with Alessandra. A time and a relationship so dear, so enduring to me, that I want it to transcend time. I want it to resonate in your life so that someone on her side may keep a faint memory of this love for as long as possible.

The enclosed journal chronicles the details of my unforgettable adventure. I have spent the last few days translating my entries and arranging them so that you may read my account with ease. I hope one day you will read my words in their entirety to understand the tokens of love now in your possession. Until then, I will tell you the relevant part of my story below.

My name is Gustavo Enrique Martel Lavoignet. I was one of the two medical officers who, along with thirty-one aviators and nearly three hundred support personnel, came to Texas in the summer of 1944. We were to receive final training before shipping off to one of the war's

theaters to contribute to the struggle against the belligerent Axis Coalition.

I don't know if the history books in your country will
include a section about us. So, you may not know about
my small but very special unit—the 201st Squadron of
the Mexican Expeditionary Air Force. Our American
friends called us the Aztec Eagles.

Two years ago, Mexico officially declared a state of
war against the Axis powers after Germany sunk several of my country's oil tankers off the Florida coast.
Stemming from those hostile events, and at the request
of President Roosevelt, our government agreed to
send nearly three hundred thousand people north to
alleviate the shortage of labor American men created
as they shipped off to battle. Shortly thereafter, both
governments decided Mexico should also participate
militarily in the war.

Thus, my unit came into existence. We were tasked
with representing our humble nation with distinction
and honor, and to contribute to preserving human dignity and freedom around the world. As I sit here writing,
just over three months after the Empire of Japan surren-
dered and the war came to an end, I can proudly tell you
our small squadron did precisely that.

Before our departure to the Pacific Theater, my unit
was stationed in San Antonio. While some members,
particularly the pilots and ground artillery men, got sent
to training fields as far as Idaho, New York, and Florida,
I remained here—at the Brooke General Hospital within
Fort Sam Houston. It was on the hospital grounds where
I met your grandmother. Referring to her as such is
strange. Although, I must say—with a smile on my face—I

fell for an older woman. She was two years older than me. But I didn't care about that. I only cared that Alessandra was extraordinary.

Soon thereafter, we shared a blissful love. Before I shipped off to war, we had nearly eight months to enjoy, develop, and cement the bonds of our affection. Imagining a positive outcome for the war, we had begun to dream of a life together. Eventually, my squadron and I sailed off to wage battle against the Japanese for five arduous months. Along with our American counterparts, we prevailed.

I, and most of my unit, had the good fortune to return from the Orient at war's end. The moment our ship lifted anchor from Philippine waters—basking in the exhilaration of victory—my greatest longing was to begin a life with Alessandra.

When we returned to Texas, all the powers that be honored us. We even received a communiqué from General MacArthur on the day we officially detached from the American 58th Fighter Group. In those few glorious days, I was able to rejoin my beloved Alessandra here in San Antonio. We spent most of our days hand in hand, walking along the river. Our joy was like no other.

My squadron returned to Mexico in the late fall of 1945. I had assured Alessandra I would come back to San Antonio promptly and she should be prepared for a most special Christmas celebration. Meanwhile, our people showered us with laurels at every turn for days on end. Finally, a victory parade in the capital took place. In a grand ceremony, we returned our battle flag to our president. And with medals pinned to our lapels, we officially received our nation's gratitude.

I spent an agreeable time with my loving family. My mother, who'd been adamantly opposed to me joining the military, repeatedly burst into tears of joy for several days after my return. The first thing my father muttered, however, was a question. He asked if I was ready to go back to work at the hospital, as there were many patients awaiting my services. This was his way of expressing satisfaction, pride, and immense relief that I was not only alive but in one piece.

The support and love of my family was essential for me to embark on the independent life I'd envisioned the moment I met Alessandra. After a number of inevitable questions, my father had no qualms about me forging a life in San Antonio. As long as anything I proposed was logical, my father would eventually endorse it. There were four basic elements to my reasoning: One, Alessandra and I loved each other. Two, I could be a doctor in Texas, but she probably could not be a pilot in our capital city, which would be unfair to someone of her talent. Three, Mother could make all the arrangements for us to marry in Mexico. Four, Mother could visit us in San Antonio as often as she wanted. Knowing this, my mother, too, bestowed me with her blessing.

Once my family's bearings were set in the right direction, I communicated with my friend Landon in San Antonio. I asked him to arrange the purchase of the house by the river—a lovely residence Alessandra truly adored, and which I was determined to acquire for her.

The last few days before my return to Texas, I set out to purchase the tangible symbol of my love. I visited several jewelers and decided on what I thought was a beautiful engagement ring. I wanted it to be worthy of the woman I'd tendered my heart to. Because I also wanted to be certain Alessandra would relish the ring, I visited my cousin to get a woman's perspective.

Maribel is nothing less than a fashion princess. After she made me tell her every detail of my story, she, too, fell in love with Alessandra. Then she offered her conclusive opinion regarding my recent purchase: I'd selected the most grotesque piece of metal she'd ever seen. Maribel told me that if I loved Alessandra that much, she deserved not only an engagement ring but also a complete engagement set. Thus, she promptly summoned her driver, and we set off to right my wrong. We entered the establishment of Berger Joyeros—a new but excellent purveyor of fine jewelry. One of the owners, Maurice Berger, personally tended to us. He directed us to the jewelry that would eventually come with me to Texas.

The jewelry and the key to the house by the river were intended as Christmas presents for Alessandra. But the ever unpredictable and often bitter winds of fate had a different plan.

When I arrived at San Antonio's Greyhound bus depot five days ago, I expected to see Alessandra and feel her arms around me once again. Instead, my friend Landon was there looking at me with angst. He presented me with a note Alessandra had impetuously left in his care. In it, she professed her eternal love for me. But she also explained she had no choice but to return home to Massachusetts. She apologized for not waiting and offering an explanation in person. She was afraid she'd not be able to fulfill her obligation if she were in my arms again. For the same painful reason, she asked that I not contact her. Alessandra implored me to find happiness with another, as we would surely kiss again, by the river—in another life.

It is thus I find myself on this cold winter day, consumed with loss. My mind is a paradoxical mix of rage and understanding. Yet there is no confusion in my heart. There is only love.

As you can see, the jewels and the key to the house were meant for, and always belonged to, my beloved Alessandra—your grandmother. Therefore, they now belong to you. Please accept them. And please, if you can spare a corner of your mind, do save a small memory of us.

Fondly and forever yours,

Gustavo Martel

SEVEN

S am turned the page, looking for more information. But the letter was complete.

Behind the letter was a bill of sale. In a combination of typed and handwritten disclosures, the document detailed a transfer of residential property to Gustavo E. Martel and Alessandra J. Conti. There was a half-page description of the house, including the land it sat on and its furnishings. The property was specified as house number one at the corner of West River Bank and Woodward, sixty-five yards north of the Guilbeau Street junction.

Sam thought about opening the old notebook to learn more about his grandmother. Why did Gustavo refer to her as Alessandra Blake but the sale document referred to her as Alessandra Conti? What did he mean when he said she'd been a pilot? He also wondered about this house. Did it still exist? If so, would he find more information about his past there?

Sam tried to access Google Maps from his phone, but he had no signal. The vault was deep underground. Unable to learn more about the house, he untied the leather cord and opened the notebook. After thumbing through a few pages, he paused and took a deep breath. Realizing he needed to collect himself, Sam looked at his watch and closed the journal. There was no need to spend more time in the vault. The next step would be to calmly find out if this property still existed. After that, he could return to his hotel and read the notebook.

Sam informed the Frost Bank representative waiting for him outside the vault that he had permanently retrieved the safe-deposit box's contents. As the bank president had previously instructed, she had him sign the appropriate documents to terminate the account and reiterated to Sam that he was welcome to keep the key. Along with the bank guard, she accompanied Sam outside.

He spotted an empty bench in the park across the building and headed in that direction.

Except for his military dog tags, Sam had never worn a necklace. That changed when he sat on that bench. He took the notebook's leather cord, the safe-deposit box key, and the key thumbtacked within the jewelry set. He threaded the cord through the holes on both keys and tied it around his neck. After tucking his newly fashioned necklace under his shirt, Sam grabbed his phone and began to look up the whereabouts of this house. He first tried "1 West River Bank" and discovered there was no street in San Antonio with that name. He then entered "1 Woodward." The Google app asked, "Did you mean Woodward Place?" Sam tapped yes and a red-location tag appeared on the map. He zoomed in and saw the location tag appear next to the river. It was north of a street named Old Guilbeau. That had to be it. He stood and set out in that direction, which was just a few blocks south from where he'd been sitting.

On his way there, Sam imagined an old, abandoned property. Walking along Dwyer Avenue, he came to the intersection with Woodward Place and turned left. As he walked, he noticed the address numbers were in the one hundreds and progressively got higher. Yet he continued in the direction indicated on Google Maps. Eventually, he reached a cul-de-sac. The house on its end was at the river's edge. The water was visible through the colorful gardens flanking the property. The residence had the number 135 on its door. Sam was at a loss. Based on the map and the old description of the location, he was in the right place.

To his left was a bed-and-breakfast, the Inn on the Riverwalk. He decided to inquire there regarding his quandary. Inside the two-story sky-blue and white Victorian house, the innkeeper was at the reception desk. Sam introduced himself and explained his circumstances.

"Actually, I think you are in the right place," said Letty, a gracious older woman. "I started running this place several years ago. The property came with a number of papers that have been handed down to its different owners over the years. As you can imagine, that has been helpful from an advertising perspective and as a point of interest for our guests. This house and the one across the street, which is also part of the inn, were built in 1916. In the old paperwork, the two houses didn't have a precise address. But they were described as houses two and three on the corner of Woodward and West River Bank. So, I suspect the white house next door, right on the river, was number one. I believe they were renumbered in the sixties."

"It looks like the house is occupied. Do you know anything about your neighbors?"

"Sure, a little. When I first came here, a nice, young, professional family lived here. They were renting it. They moved out about three years ago. A corporation owns it. A law firm, I'm pretty sure. Ever since that family left, they use it to put up clients or employees from out of town. Many of them end up here for meals or drinks, which is nice for us."

"Wow. I think that *is* the place I'm looking for," he said.

"Oh, nice. Are you buying it? I didn't know it was for sale," Letty replied.

"No, no. It's…a long story. I think an old relative of mine lived there at some point."

"Well, if you ever want to talk about it, feel free to come by sometime. We do a prix fixe dinner with drinks on Thursdays through Saturdays. And the first drink is always free to tall men with magnetic good looks," she said with a playful, well-intentioned wink.

"I'll keep it in mind. Thank you, you've been extremely helpful," Sam told her. "I'm going to go look around for a bit."

"Have a lovely day," Letty said with a friendly wave.

Sam stood in front of the two-story Victorian next door. It was a medium-sized property with stately curb appeal. The house was painted white. The shutters and front door were black. The landscaping was an attractive array of globe amaranths, gazanias, moss verbena, and summer snapdragon. Red-gravel walkways lined each side of the house and went a short distance into a sloping bank that led to the green river. Through the partially open blinds, he could see furnishings and paintings but no people. There was no driveway. No garage. Sam surmised the main structure had been kept intact since the turn of the previous century. Save for the small parking lot belonging to the inn next door, no cars were on the street near the house.

Sam decided he'd ring the bell. If someone answered, he'd explain himself and perhaps gather more information. Only if no one answered would he try the key from the jewelry case. Sam was prudent enough to consider the old key may not work, and he didn't want to give the impression he was forcibly trying to enter someone else's home.

A few seconds after he rang, Kim, Lena's assistant, opened the door.

"Hello again, Mr. Gleeson. Come on in. Mrs. Sander is on the rear balcony," she said.

Sam was surprised but glad. Lena, seeing him through the balcony's open French doors, stood. She'd been working on her laptop, sitting below a canopy of lofty trees. A gentle breeze blew parallel to the slow river current.

"I had a feeling you'd find your way here." Lena gestured to the house, its gardens, and its picturesque view of the river. Just beyond the balcony, people were walking leisurely along the riverside walkways. The tall and beautiful Tower Life Building was visible at a distance. A pleasing scent of flowers permeated the air. The structure, the land, and the surroundings were charming. "Like I told you earlier, I didn't know the exact contents of the safe-deposit box, but since the house is an important component of the bequest, I knew they'd point you in this direction. As you can imagine, the lock has been changed many times over the years, so I thought working from here would be a good idea, in case you knocked. I'm glad you did. Come, let me give you a tour of your lovely residence."

Lena showed him every room in the house. Architectural details, furnishings, and artwork all seemed to blend perfectly. Each space had a century-old quality but seemed comfortable. Where appropriate, modern and functional updates had been added. The property could've easily graced the pages of any interior design magazine.

They returned to the balcony, and Lena asked him to make himself comfortable. Sam politely declined the snacks Kim offered but helped himself to a glass of iced tea from a pitcher on the table. Lena sipped iced tea as well. "Sam, back to business. I trust you found an explanation for why this house belongs to you. Before I mention the other part of this bequest, do you have any questions?"

Sam wondered what she meant by "the other part." Maybe there was a catch here. Yet at no point had Lena given him a negative impression. So, he put aside his cynicism.

"Let me tell you what I found," he said.

"I have always wondered about the contents of the box. You're not obligated to tell me, but I appreciate it."

Sam told her about his experience at the bank and the details he had learned from Gustavo's letter. Lena was amazed when she saw the jewelry. She confirmed that Landon Taylor was her father. He had died a decade ago, but she knew of his friendship with Gustavo Martel and the story behind this bequest. Sam then understood why the case was personal to Lena.

"I suspect any further questions I may have about events prior to the date on Gustavo's letter will be answered in his journal. What I hope you can help me with is learning more about my family after that date. Something in me still doubts I'm the actual beneficiary. But assuming that I am the right person, what do you know about my parents and grandparents?"

"As I said before, our firm has only been able to investigate and legally inquire about the identity and whereabouts of Alessandra Blake's direct descendants. Of course, my father and I did learn some other details from our investigators, so I'll share those too. Alessandra had two daughters: Barbara Blake, your mother, and Paula Blake. Your aunt Paula was born with a congenital problem that required constant care, which your mother provided for many years. Your mother married a Milton Gleeson. They had your sister, Lilly, and a couple of years later, you. When you were four, your mother was diagnosed with late-stage cancer. Shortly thereafter, your father left your mom. I can't tell you more about him, only that he seemed to have abandoned your family. In his absence, even before your mother died, you, your sister, and your aunt were turned over to the state of Massachusetts. That means there mustn't have been any other family members from either of your parents' sides able to take care of you. You are the youngest second-generation descendant of Alessandra. Therefore, we've followed you and, serendipitously, your sister, through your many different foster families until Lilly turned eighteen and claimed you several months later. By the way, when your mother passed, my father inquired about any property or valuables he could advocate for on your behalf so they could be returned to you and your sister when you came of age. But neither your mother nor her parents owned any property or significant valuables. That's all I know about your family members, relevant to the case."

"I was hoping to learn something about my father," Sam said. "One of our foster parents did mention he'd left out of the blue.

I just never wanted to believe it. Sometimes not knowing the truth feels better. That's life, I suppose. On the bright side, I now know my maternal grandmother was a good person—worthy of esteem and love.

"I knew a little about my mother's side. We knew about my aunt. She had cerebral palsy and died right after we left the system. I was only sixteen. Lilly got notification of her death and was asked if she wanted to pick up my aunt's belongings. We basically picked up a cardboard box with some trinkets that didn't help us learn about our past. Anyway, some of what you've told me about my grandparents, particularly my grandmother, is new and interesting. I really can't wait to read more about her in the journal. Do you know what happened to her?"

"Yes," Lena said. "Alessandra and her husband died in an unfortunate car accident before your mother married. Although my father had no direct contact with her after 1945, he was very distraught when he learned about the accident. He'd considered Alessandra a good friend."

"History doesn't seem to bode well for me. So many premature deaths in my family," Sam said lightheartedly. Lena conceded a smile too. "Do you know why this was left to me in particular? I mean, why the youngest second-generation descendant of my grandmother?"

"From what I understand, Gustavo didn't want to leave this inheritance to Alessandra or her immediate family while her husband was still alive. He didn't want her immediate family to know about their relationship and have that reflect negatively on her. In regard to the stipulation that this should belong to the youngest descendant on their twenty-sixth birthday, I think his purpose was twofold: specifying a single beneficiary avoided any potential disagreements within your family. Also, Gustavo was twenty-six at the time. He probably reasoned that someone his age would be sensible enough to understand his intent," she said, a contrite expression subtly forming on her face. "Once again, I do apologize for fulfilling my firm's obligation a few years late."

Sam smiled. "No worries. Five or six years ago, Tony and I weren't living in the same place. So, I may never have agreed to come here." He briefly pointed at the leather-bound journal on the table. "Now that I've made this implausible yet fascinating discovery, are you sure you've got the right guy?"

"Yes, absolutely certain. That brings me to the last part of the bequest," she said, reaching for some documents from her briefcase. "This part wasn't what Gustavo Martel had in mind. I don't think it was in anybody's mind at the time. However, my father did what he thought was best."

Her tone had turned rather businesslike. He subconsciously braced for the bad news.

She laid out some papers. "The house was paid in full in 1945. Then, from 1946 to the present, my father, various partners, and I have always ensured the place received appropriate upkeep. That anything in need of refurbishing or reconstruction was taken care of appropriately. And, of course, that taxes and city services dues were paid. In order to fulfill this obligation to Gustavo and eventually deliver this house to you in good condition, my father realized the house needed to be put up for rent. So, it has. Our firm has collected rent, on your behalf, for about seventy years. The rent has ranged from forty-five dollars per month in the forties to two thousand four hundred dollars now." Lena thumbed through a set of papers and offered Sam two packets. "This is a running record of all tenants and rents collected over the years. This thicker one is a record of all the expenses that have been incurred." Sam nodded and read the title page of each set of documents. Lena then placed her fingertips on a thin binder. She slowly slid it across the table toward Sam. "Sam, when subtracting all the expenses from the rent we've collected every month since, there has always been a substantial amount left over. That surplus has been deposited in a trust fund, now in your name, which has been collecting interest. Frost Investments has managed your account. They've done it conservatively, but very well. In light of your visit, I had them prepare this for you." Lena opened the binder and pointed to a spot on the first page. "This is the current value of your account."

Sam squinted and leaned forward. Then he gazed at Lena with a puzzled expression.

With her eyebrows slightly lifted, and a gentle nod, she confirmed what Sam had just looked at.

Sam stood and walked to the edge of the balcony. He surveyed the scenic view. He was trying to make sense of everything.

Sam turned to Lena and smiled graciously. He took his seat again. "I can't possibly take this. Coming here has gone from weird to surreal to impossible. Even if I am the person for whom these gifts were intended, it just doesn't make sense. I have virtually no relation to Gustavo Martel. I wasn't even sure I'd accept the jewelry box. But this amazing home? And five million dollars?" He shook his head.

"Five million three hundred twenty thousand seven hundred fifty-two dollars and eleven cents. And there's a little more in an active, discretionary account," Lena said with a jovial tone.

"Yes, that. As much as it would change my life, I can't take it, Mrs. Sander. It doesn't feel right. It would be like stealing a winning lottery ticket from someone."

"Since you mentioned the lottery, the logistical part of this portion of the bequest is a bit like that. If a winner wants the lump sum, they only end up with a portion of the original jackpot. In your case, there will be a tax burden, so the liquid principal will be less—if that's any consolation," she said, trying to infuse some humor into their discussion.

"You have no idea how much I appreciate this. Not so much the material part, but the gesture—the act of love that this case represents. I'm grateful you and your father have gone to these lengths, over two generations, to fulfill this promise. But I have to decline these gifts."

After a thoughtful lull between them, she said, "I anticipated you might feel this way. Sam, if I may. I'd like to show you something. This is something that perhaps can help you come to terms with this inheritance, which, as you said, is not really about its monetary worth." She stood up and invited Sam into the house. "Let's take a short drive. Kim will stay here and package up that paperwork for us. You can leave your belongings here. We'll return shortly."

Kim said Ruben had arrived, and the car was ready outside.

An attentive man in business-casual attire was holding open a red Suburban's rear door. Sam offered Lena his hand as she stepped up inside. He followed suit, and Ruben closed the car door behind him. Seconds later, they drove away.

EIGHT

"Holy shitballs, Sammy. We're rich!"

"Hold your horses, dude. It's not that simple," Sam had said. They'd spoken the previous evening, following Sam's overwhelming encounter with Lena Sander.

"Just take the fuckin' money, thank your lucky stars, and drag your ass back here" had been another of Tony's eloquent comments.

Sam had, in fact, considered that. There was so much he could do with the money: pay off the loan on the barbershop, help Lilly pay off her house, secure college trust funds for his nieces, and help renovate Worcester's animal shelter. And, why not, he'd even considered a new car and buying season tickets for the New England Patriots and the Revs—it was always such a hassle finding individual tickets online or resorting to scalpers.

Sometimes, Sam wished he could see life as simply as Tony did. But because he didn't, he found himself this morning in a lounge at the San Antonio airport, waiting to board. He was anxious, but he'd made a decision. With coffee in hand, he contemplated the rest of his experience with Lena.

Ruben had driven them to a peculiar neighborhood. Old, opulent homes in Greek Revival and Victorian styles lined the streets. Soaring trees with abundant foliage provided a sense of detachment from the adjacent downtown area. San Antonio's King William District was a beautifully preserved community from a bygone era. It was established by German settlers in the mid-1800s and named in honor of Wilhelm I, King of Prussia.

Most of the homes were private residences. A few comprised various professional businesses—law, architectural, and design firms. The car pulled into a driveway. Ruben got out, opened Lena's door, and helped her step down. Sam also got out and walked around the car to meet her. She gestured to the sidewalk. Sam offered his arm, and she led him to the front of the one-story dwelling. It was old, beautiful, and well kept. But it was tiny—almost out of place.

"Sam, this is the current site of our human resources department," she said. "Compared to other houses in the vicinity, it's very small. It was the servants' quarters of that mansion there." She pointed. "My father bought it in 1945. He got it essentially at the same time that he helped Gustavo procure the house by the river. This little building became his first office. It's where my prominent multinational law firm started. Come, let's go sit on the porch. You need to hear this story. I'll keep it short."

As soon as they sat, Ruben emerged from the office with a tray and offered them ice-cold lemonade. Once comfortable, Sam noticed the wooden shingle next to the front door. It read *Landon S. Taylor, Esq.*

With refreshment in hand, Lena began.

"In 1943, my father was in his last semester of law school at St. Mary's University. It was the only law school in San Antonio and the second oldest in all of Texas. Unfortunately, his money for tuition ran out. He was forced to withdraw. At the time, nearly all of South Texas was rural. There was little to no industry. He came from a family of farmers. To contribute to the war effort, they had to lower produce prices such that they scarcely made enough to get by. They couldn't help him pay for school anymore. But my father was determined to raise enough money to finish his education. He went out and got a job. Two, actually. His main job was at Brooke Army Medical Center, formerly Brooke General Hospital. He coordinated the doctors' schedules, patient appointments, and patient care in the surgery department—the same department Gustavo was assigned to when his unit came to the base. For several days they interacted most mornings, primarily in passing and in a work-related capacity.

"One evening, Gustavo and three of his unit members went to a local eatery for dinner. A customer came up to their table and told Gustavo they needed to leave because two of his friends were Mexican and they were in a white-only establishment. Gustavo told this fellow all four of them were Mexican and he didn't see a sign anywhere stating they weren't welcome. This man briefly tried to continue his hateful rant when my father, who'd noticed the situation, came up. For months, he'd been working there as a manager in the evenings. He told the belligerent guy there were no restrictions on who could be in the restaurant. Furthermore, my father told this character that he knew the men at the table. He said they were soldiers about to ship off to war and fight for everyone's rights and liberty, including his own. And if he had a problem with that, *he* was welcome to leave. Apparently, this man quickly left. From then on, my father and Gustavo became good friends. With and without their respective girlfriends, they shared many great moments together. Gustavo particularly admired my father because he worked two jobs and somehow still helped out at his family's farm. At some point, my father mentioned he was doing this so he could go back to law school. Without a second thought, Gustavo offered to 'loan' him the money for tuition. Gratefully, my father accepted this gift and started his last semester in the fall of 1944.

"At the end of the war, Gustavo and his unit returned to San Antonio for several days before going back to Mexico. Then, my father and his girlfriend—who would eventually become my mother—along with Gustavo and your grandmother were walking leisurely down this very street. They noticed this little house. It was in ruins, but for sale. My father had just finished law school and was clerking for a local judge. Your grandmother said she thought this house would be perfect as an office for my father. Everybody agreed. My father had no capital to buy the property, so he joked the place was on the wrong side of the tracks. Maybe in a few years, he said, he'd be able to rent an office on the South Side, where he belonged. The South Side was the area closest to his family and, at the time, a poor section of the city.

"Well, Gustavo took notice. Weeks later, when he asked my father to begin the process of buying the house by the river, he also told him to do the same for this house. He insisted my father do it, that it would be another 'loan.' He wouldn't take no for an answer. And the rest is history.

"In 1950, Gustavo and some members of his unit returned to the US. They received belated recognition from the army regarding their contribution to the war in the Pacific. My father and mother attended that ceremony. Once the festivities ended, they enjoyed some time together. On that occasion, my father tried to repay Gustavo for his tuition and office. The firm had been doing well financially, and he'd secured a home equity loan.

"Gustavo would not have it. He insisted they had never been loans. He'd only said that so my father would take the assistance. Gustavo was adamant that my father's friendship was worth more than anything material. My father urged him to accept the funds—to no avail. That was perhaps the only argument he ever lost. Gustavo told my father that in Mexico, there is no debt between friends. He said he'd take offense if my father kept insisting.

"Their friendship continued over the years. My father realized how special Gustavo was, and that he truly offered those gifts without expectation." Lena inched forward, her free hand gently pointing at Sam and back at herself. "As you can see, you and I have much in common. We are the beneficiaries of Gustavo's generous heart and steadfast character."

"I don't know what to say. That's incredible. Who does that?" Sam exclaimed.

"Not many people. No matter how wealthy they are. That's for sure," she answered. "Sam, this is why you *can* accept this bequest. It's an extension of Gustavo's love. Similar to my father's case—a reflection and extension of their friendship. It just seems overwhelming because of the magnitude of the gifts, which Gustavo Martel had the means to make.

"My father always used to say that when it comes to giving, poor people give small gifts and rich people give big gifts. But their value can be measured in meaning. If those small gifts or big gifts come from the heart, their value is the same." Lena sipped her lemonade. "Sam, I hope what I've said and what I've shown you helps put your mind at ease. I really don't have anything else to add, save for reiterating you're the beneficiary of an ordinary gift for an extraordinary reason."

Sam considered Lena's statement. "Some would argue it's an extraordinary gift for an ordinary reason," he said. "But the sentiment rings true and does make me feel better. It gives me this sense of belonging to something special. It helps me accept that I do have this worthwhile family history. I just can't shake this inexplicable sense of uncertainty." He took a deep breath and exhaled. "I wonder if it's the magnitude of the gifts that's bothering me. If I could be sure they didn't belong to anybody else, that would help. From a legal perspective, they're mine. But maybe ethically there's another rightful owner. Shouldn't this gift belong to Gustavo Martel's descendants? Obviously, he was well off in 1945. What about his family now? What if something untoward has happened and they're in need of this inheritance? I couldn't bear the thought of that."

Lena had concrete answers regarding Gustavo's family. But she just listened to Sam patiently, thinking he should reach his own conclusions.

"I wonder if I should try to find his family, tell them about this bequest, and maybe just give it to them. I feel this is more theirs than mine. As much as this gift could do wonders for my family, I'd be satisfied knowing the contents of Gustavo's journal. Nothing more."

Again, Lena didn't say anything. Inwardly, though, she was delighted and, in a motherly way, proud of Sam.

"Do you know Gustavo's family?" he asked.

Lena knew Sam had to accept the gifts. They had to be disbursed to him. Over the years, from a distance, she'd come to feel affection for Sam. While she wished for him to benefit financially from this bequest, it wasn't her decision to make. Sam could do with his inheritance as he wished. Her obligation, in the end, was to Gustavo.

Fortunately, she did know a great deal about Gustavo's descendants. Some of them, she knew well. They all shared one essential characteristic: integrity. Knowing this mitigated her apprehension and made it easy to answer his question.

With a well-intentioned lie of omission, Lena said, "I know a little bit about them. I think what you said might be a good idea. Perhaps meeting Gustavo's family could help you sort through your dilemma." She set down her lemonade. "After all, you did bring a passport."

"Ladies and gentlemen, in a moment, we will begin boarding Aeromexico Flight 3453 to Mexico City."

Sam stood up, flung his backpack over his shoulder, and holding his boarding pass, got in line for the jetway.

NINE

Sam had read Gustavo's notebook for a few hours the previous night. He wanted to continue reading on the short flight to Mexico. Not only did he wish to learn more for himself but Sam also wanted to be prepared to answer any questions he might be asked. Additionally, he was preoccupied with whether he'd be able to find the contact Lena had given him. If he did, what would he say? Where would he start?

He spent the flight time mentally rehearsing possible narratives, so he didn't read as much of the journal as he wanted. Nearly two hours passed in the blink of an eye. A flight attendant announced their descent into the city.

Through the double-pane window, he glimpsed at the sprawling metropolis below. An ocean of urban development stretched endlessly in every direction. On the final approach, the jetliner circled over architecturally diverse and colossal skyscrapers.

Sam wondered what he'd find in that formidable city of twenty million souls.

The first thing Sam discovered was a convoluted method of getting a taxi from the airport.

The system was set up to standardize service and to enhance the safety of those needing transportation. Customers identified their destination, matched it to one of numerous tariff zones, and paid accordingly at a centralized concession area.

Sam had a hotel reservation, but he wanted to utilize his time and increase the probability of finding the person Lena had suggested he contact. Using the airport Wi-Fi, he looked up his first destination, Galería Alpheratz—an art gallery. After determining the proper transportation zone, he purchased his ticket and walked outside. He was in line for only a few minutes before his turn came to board a taxi. The efficiency with which a small group of ushers got passengers into what seemed like never-ending rows of taxis astounded him.

Sam leaned forward to show the cab driver his destination from his phone. The jovial fellow told him, "No problem," entered it into his navigation system, and off they went. The driver then asked Sam where he was from, and Sam said the US.

"Ah okay. I don't need coin from United States. I like asking for small coin for a collection, you see? I do for eight years now. You want to see?"

Sam wasn't quite sure what the smiling man was asking, but it seemed pretty harmless. "Sure," he replied.

From a small chest on the passenger seat, the man pulled out a three-ring binder, which he handed to Sam. Sam slowly went through its contents. Glued to the thick pages were a multitude of coins and some currency notes organized by country and dates—presumably when he'd received a particular coin or bill from a traveler. The country names were in Spanish, but Sam recognized most of them. The man had currency from Algeria and Argentina to Uzbekistan and Zambia to many others in between. Although some of the euros were the same, they were cataloged under different countries. After a few minutes, Sam passed the album back and told the driver it was impressive. The fellow smiled and named all the different countries he still needed coins from. Sam asked him if he had a favorite country. The cabbie answered, "No. I love all. I not go to there probably. But all the world come to here. With coins, I touch it, you see?"

Sam reflected on the man's optimistic outlook on life. "I hope you eventually get the ones you're missing."

"Yes, I hope too." He slipped a CD into the car's stereo. "Okay, I play you some music, yeah? You like U2?"

"That sounds good," Sam replied.

To classics including "Beautiful Day," "I Still Haven't Found What I'm Looking For," "Pride," and "Where the Streets Have No Name," Sam studied the city as it passed slowly or hastily by, depending on the traffic.

A half hour later, the cab stopped on the southwest corner of the Plaza Río de Janeiro Street. It was in the heart of Colonia Roma Norte. This was an old, mixed-residential and business district. Sam would later learn that for three decades, the area had been undergoing gentrification. Young and dynamic professionals with progressive spirits were reviving its former elegance. These residents embraced everything from socially responsible businesses to the arts. Chic shops, restaurants, and galleries lined its streets. Among contemporary homes and condominiums stood many old European-style dwellings that displayed the Porfirian architecture of the late nineteenth century. Structures were made with imported Italian marble and cast iron, as well as European granite, bronze, and stained glass. They were designed to be reminiscent of Paris or London.

"Served, my friend," said the cabbie, pointing to a gray concrete building with two Greek columns flanking a glass entrance door. Large display windows with dark brown awnings were on either side of the door. A residence with multiple floor-to-ceiling windows and doors, each with their own balcony, stood on the floors above. Only close inspection would betray the building's fairly modern origins. It blended in with the well-preserved mansions, erected during the Belle Époque, on either side.

"Great, thank you very much," Sam replied, giving the man the peso equivalent of about a ten-dollar tip. The driver thanked Sam and with a friendly wave went on his way. Sam entered the building through its open door.

Lena had told Sam she knew of Ari Martel, one of Gustavo's grandchildren. He was an architect but ran an art gallery. She told him Ari was about Sam's age, would probably get along with him well, and he'd likely be able to provide Sam with insight or guidance regarding the matter at hand.

"Hi. I'm sorry I don't speak Spanish. I'm looking for Mr. Ari Martel Fernandez," Sam told a handsome man slightly shorter than himself.

The fellow had a pleasant demeanor. He wore a muted-orange John Varvatos shirt with partially rolled-up sleeves and tailored pants. "Hello," he replied in perfect English. "Who may I say is looking for him?" He was behind a reception counter at the center of the expansive art space. Near the reception desk, a freestanding wall displayed the gallery's beautiful star-constellation logo.

"My name is Sam Gleeson. I'm here on a family matter, I suppose."

"You suppose?" the man asked in a witty but friendly tone.

Sam smiled. "Well, it's hard to explain. But I'm certain it would interest Mr. Martel."

"Mr. Martel was about to go to lunch," he said, walking around the counter and then extending his hand. "Call me Ari." They shook hands. "I'm just waiting for my assistant to return. We're shorthanded today, so we alternated our lunch breaks." He gestured so Sam would walk with him through the exhibition space. "Let me show you some of the works from our currently featured artist. I hope you haven't eaten, because once my assistant returns, we could go to this fantastic café just across the plaza and talk. The sandwiches and coffee will knock your socks off. They'd knock mine off too, but I'm not wearing any." Ari lifted his pants just above his penny loafers and then stood before a painting. "Take a look at this one—my favorite. It's called *Marionettes*. The three shimmering blue-purple figurines remind me of Hidalgos from *Don Quixote*. Some think the one with the big hole through its chest makes it a sad painting. I think it adds to the often painful realism that humans must invariably encounter in their quest to attain justice in the world. Anyway, the artist takes old glass windows from homes being torn down or remodeled and paints on the backs of them. It's amazing: he not only has to paint backward but also in reverse of the depth he eventually wants to achieve. His work is visually splendid but also socially provocative. His name is Ryan Birkland, from Portland, Oregon. I was visiting that gem of a city a few months back and ran into him selling his work at a street fair. I ended up visiting his studio and knew I had to make his work available here."

Ari showed Sam three other works from the same artist before his assistant returned. Shortly after, they took a table at the nearby Buna Café Rico.

Sam wasn't used to having coffee with lunch, but he was happy to follow suit. Ari had been right: the coffee was excellent—like no other he'd ever had. Ari told him that the manner in which they infused notes of Assam tea, chocolate, and caramel into the espresso was top secret.

When the small talk subsided, Sam began explaining his purpose for being there. He started with the moment Tony read Lena's letter.

After sharing a substantial portion of the story, Sam told Ari there was a little bit more, but he didn't want to take more of his time in case he needed to get back to the gallery. Ari told Sam not to worry; his assistant would take care of everything at the gallery. Ari was enthralled. After a shared bottle of mineral water and a second round of coffee with pastries, Sam finished.

Ari sat back, looking more reflective than surprised. He said, "That's very interesting, Sam. I hope I'm not being too forward, but would you tell me about yourself? Where and how did you grow up? What's your family like? What do you do, or what do you want to do for a living?"

There were only four people with whom Sam had shared this information. One was a past girlfriend—the only serious relationship he'd ever had. The second was his bunkmate while deployed in the Middle East. Finally, Lilly and Tony. Yet something about Ari made him feel strangely at ease. So, he opened up to this virtual stranger.

Sam talked for another hour, during which they both enjoyed brief moments of laughter, particularly regarding Tony. Ari learned a condensed version of Sam's childhood and teenage years in the foster care system, about his time in college, his time in the military, his past job, and the current state of his barbershop.

Ari became emotional when Sam discussed his cat, Vin. The kitty had been a stray who'd lived in the compound with Sam's crew while he was on his last deployment to Afghanistan. Every day for a year, the cat had slept on the pillow next to Sam's head. Sam couldn't bear to leave him when it came time to return home. He smuggled the creature on a personnel transport plane to Germany. His superior had known but looked the other way. Once in Germany, Sam had schmoozed with a local veterinarian and finagled a health certificate, and he'd eventually gotten the cat home on a civilian airline.

It was almost four o'clock when Sam shrugged and said, "After all that, here I am."

Ari had mentioned how beautiful the jewelry was. He joked that Sam shouldn't flash the Van Cleef & Arpels case in public too much. When Sam said he had no idea how much it was worth, Ari conceded he also had no clue. But if Sam was interested, he could take it to the Cartier store on Presidente Masaryk Avenue and get it appraised.

Sam had briefly mentioned Lena Sander and Landon Taylor earlier but now directly asked Ari if he knew them. Ari shook his head but conceded he'd occasionally heard the name Taylor mentioned at family gatherings. Now knowing it was a law firm, he told Sam it probably handled legal matters for some of his family members when doing business in the United States.

"Well, Sam. It should be my turn to tell you about me and my family, especially my grandfather. But I won't say much at all. Not now. I have a feeling you'll have occasion to learn plenty about my clan. Now, about this definitely singular inheritance: based on what you've told me, it belongs entirely to you."

Sam felt surprised. *Really? I just offered this guy millions of dollars*, he thought. For an instant, the possibility of keeping the money flashed again through his mind. Unsure what to say next, he just reiterated it made him uncomfortable to accept that bequest, which he believed should go to Gustavo Martel's direct descendants.

"I can understand that," Ari said. "It's admirable, you being here to offer my family this inheritance. But let me say this: my grandfather had four brothers and a sister. And when you take into account all their children, my extended family is really big. But since none of them are direct descendants of my grandfather, they wouldn't have a claim to the inheritance.

"My grandpa only had two children: my dad and my uncle David. The direct descendants would be me, my older siblings, and my uncle David's only daughter, Gabriela."

Ari sighed. "I'll take the liberty to speak for my brother and sister. We're extremely close. I'm certain they would feel exactly as I do. So that leaves my cousin. We're also close, and I suspect she'd agree that the bequest belongs to you. Despite that, I can't speak for her. Perhaps the most appropriate thing to do is to have you meet her and explain this situation."

"I'd like to do that," Sam replied. "I wish this bequest had been limited to a small box. That way I could've just sent it and not given you or your cousin the option to decline it." They both smiled. "Although being here, meeting you, and now checking with your cousin does make me feel better."

"Great, I'm glad. Let's go back to the gallery; I left my phone charging there. I have to make a few calls to find out where Gaby is." As they left the café, Ari asked, "Do you want to do that today, or do you want to settle into your hotel and maybe meet with her tomorrow or Monday?"

"For my peace of mind, if it's possible to do that today, I'd really appreciate it. If she's interested in any part of this inheritance, I can start looking into how to transfer it to her. If not, I can start coming to terms with what this all means for me."

"Sam, as the American expression goes, 'you're all right.' But don't be in such a hurry to leave. Whatever happens after you meet Gaby, stay awhile. You've come a long way. Take in this amazing city. At least take one of the many double-decker bus tours," Ari said, smiling sincerely. "Trust me, there's much to see and fall in love with here."

TEN

Sam's second taxi ride was silent. The cab driver did not speak English.

After a few calls, Ari found his cousin. She'd been called in to work. However, he learned Gabriela would likely be available within a half hour or so. Ari wrote down pertinent information on gallery stationery, gave it to Sam, and called him a taxi. When the cab arrived, he walked Sam out and specified the destination to the driver.

"Ari, you've been so kind and helpful. Thank you." Sam extended his hand.

"Don't mention it. Perhaps we'll talk again soon." He shook Sam's hand and gave him a light but earnest clutch of the shoulder.

Once on the road, Sam looked at the embossed logo on the stationery: Galería Alpheratz. He wondered about the name. Ari was the gallery's proprietor. Maybe Alpheratz was the previous owner. *Interesting name*, he thought. Then he read the contact information Ari had written for him: *Dr. Gabriela Martel Cloutier. ABC Medical Center. Transplant Surgery Department, fifth floor.*

The taxi turned onto Reforma Avenue, a grand boulevard running west from the historic city center through the financial district and ending in the towering commercial and residential enclave of Santa Fe. Along the route, he observed snippets of daily life. Sam saw an entourage laboring with cameras, light-softening umbrellas, and colorful backdrops at a fashion photo shoot in a circular park in Glorieta de La Palma. He looked up at arrays of modern skyscrapers and saw various monuments along the long boulevard's center. Couples held hands on the sidewalks or on the many benches along the wide avenue. A responsible young woman picked up after her happy-looking dog. Children ran around and played ball along the outskirts of Chapultepec Park. Vendors offered their wares—from balloons to a myriad of food. The cab turned left and headed south. It passed through a working-class neighborhood filled with people coming and going, enjoying the bright and temperate weekend day.

The taxi then coursed through a long two-way street with green parklands on either side. The previous visual distractions now behind him, Sam looked at the paper again and decided he'd try to look up Gabriela on his phone. He knew in some Latin countries, people used both paternal and maternal last names. Yet initially he just entered her first and last name. The search showed many pages of results, which made it difficult to determine if the information applied to this particular person. He also got a warning indicating he was out of network and data roaming charges would apply. Sam thought he'd adjust his search and enter her name exactly as Ari had written it on the paper. A handful of results appeared. Some seemed to be scientific papers. One hit was from a magazine article written in Spanish and English. Her full name and a reference to the ABC Medical Center on the subtitle matched, so he clicked on it. The article described a recent banquet celebrating a milestone of the organ-transplant system in Mexico: the twenty-fifth anniversary of the first liver transplant in the country. It made reference to positive statistics regarding transplants of other organs, praised several individuals, and specifically honored Dr. Gabriela Martel Cloutier for her new and promising research. A small photo accompanied the article, showing Dr. Martel receiving an award from a pretty presenter. Gabriela appeared to be an elegant and graceful woman in her late forties or early fifties. She reminded Sam of a slightly younger version of Lena Sander. The cab stopped across from the main hospital entrance. Sam paid and got out of the car.

The building looked like a medium-sized, typical hospital with three or four different towers. Sam went inside, where he was taken aback by a small yet bright, striking lobby. The sitting area had high-quality furnishings. The art on the walls, colorful flowers, and plants complemented the gleaming floors and attractive, contemporary infrastructure. The lobby seemed more like the reception area of a five-star hotel than a hospital. He was checked in at the main desk by a polished thirtysomething man who spoke English. When the man asked about the nature of his business with Dr. Martel, Sam was briefly at a loss, then said it was a family matter. The clerk politely asked him for identification, and after scanning Sam's license on a small device next to his computer terminal, the man printed him a visitor's pass. The clerk told him to wait in the lobby and said a hospital volunteer would come by shortly to walk him to Dr. Martel's office.

Minutes later, a chipper older woman introduced herself. She told Sam that she'd be glad to show him the way and that it was nice to be able to practice her English.

"You don't look like the usual drug-company representatives we get from the United States," she said in the elevator. "You are younger and much better looking."

"I'm not a drug rep. But thank you, you're very kind."

"Are you a friend from university? Wait, don't answer that. I sound like a nosy interrogator. I'll just show you around on the way to her office."

Sam thought her question was a little strange but brushed it off. The woman pointed out different departments, art, and some glass cases containing prizes or honors the hospital had received at various times. To the left of the doors leading to the surgery department was a large glass frame. She said, "We are not the biggest hospital in our country, but we are one of the best in the world."

Sam had noticed the blown-up reproductions of articles from *Forbes* and the website Masters in Healthcare, respectively ranking the ABC Medical Center in the top twenty and top ten medical centers in the world.

She delivered Sam to Gabriela's office, which was unlocked. "It was a pleasure meeting you. Have a lovely day, Mr. Gleeson."

"The pleasure was mine," he said.

Gabriela's office was a lesson in interior design. It was minimalist and avant-garde. A black desk with two white block bases was before a bank of windows looking onto a park and distant tall buildings. It held a flat computer screen and neatly stacked papers. Two white leather chairs stood in front of the desk. Against the wall was a black leather chaise lounge and sofa with a glass-top coffee table. The floor was dark gray concrete, and the walls were white. The pop of color in the room came from a sizable red-hued Jackson Pollock painting above the sofa. The opposing wall held various frames displaying diplomas and certificates. No books. No bookshelves. No trinkets of any sort. A door on one wall led to what Sam assumed was a private bathroom.

He wasn't sure where to sit, so he opted to remain standing. Curious, he studied the wall of diplomas. Yale, Harvard Medical School, the Massachusetts General Hospital general surgery residency, and the Northwestern University Feinberg School of Medicine abdominal transplant fellowship. Sam was fascinated. For someone in her late forties or early fifties? *Respect!* he thought. He didn't notice the dates on any of the documents.

"Hello. You must be Mr. Samuel Gleeson."

Sam turned and walked toward the distinguished woman. He recognized her from the internet photograph. "It's nice to meet you, Dr. Martel. I was just looking at your wall here," he said, extending his hand.

She returned the handshake and said, "Yes, very impressive, isn't it? Those aren't mine, though. I am Dr. Castro. Monica Castro. I'm the director of this hospital."

He was surprised. "Oh, I'm sorry. I just assumed. I don't actually know Dr. Martel."

"I see. I'm usually notified when foreign visitors, other than patients, come into the hospital. There was no company or institution next to your name, so I thought I'd come up to check." She sat on the black chair behind the desk and invited Sam to sit as well. "Dr. Martel is important to us. Within the walls of this institution, I feel compelled to look after our staff. May I ask about the nature of your visit?"

"Yes, of course," Sam said, setting down his backpack. "Mr. Ari Martel referred me here. I understand he's Dr. Martel's cousin."

"He is," Monica affirmed with a gentle nod, then briefly glanced behind Sam.

"Well, it's a bit of a long story." Sam was thinking about what to say to her. "I'm from Worcester, Massachusetts. I essentially just got here and—"

"Woostah, huh?"

Sam turned and stood.

"Hi, I'm Gabriela Martel, but please call me Gaby." She shook Sam's hand. "Moni, thank you for looking after me, but I just talked to Ari. I'll be fine. It seems Sam and I have much to talk about."

"In that case, Mr. Gleeson, Gaby is all yours," Monica said, coming around the desk. She gave Gabriela half a hug and a kiss on the cheek and told her, "I'll see you next Saturday at the wedding. Have a relaxing week off." Monica then lightly touched Sam's forearm and gave him a cordial smile before leaving.

"Here, let me slide these around." Gabriela turned a chair. Sam caught on and turned the other chair so the two faced each other. Gabriela slipped off her surgery clogs, gracefully plopped herself on the seat, and crossed her legs yoga-style. Sam also sat down. "So, Worcester. You know, I lived in Boston for nine years, and I never went there. All I know is they have two excellent hospitals—UMass and Saint Vincent's—and that some people say, 'Woostah!'"

"I'm glad you know the area. About Worcester, well, people would say it's a simple town and that you didn't miss much. Although I think its simplicity is what makes it special. I don't know. For me, it's home; it feels perfect," Sam replied, doing his best to mask his awe.

He'd gotten the internet photo wrong. The person he'd assumed was a pretty presenter was, in fact, Gaby. She'd been receiving an award from Dr. Monica Castro. What he'd now pieced together about Gabriela, from a professional perspective, was shockingly admirable.

She wore red scrubs and whimsical socks with alternating red and black horizontal lines. Her light brown hair, shimmering with ashen streaks, was back in a ponytail. Her captivating gray-green eyes filled Sam with an odd sensation. This bright, lively, and exceptionally beautiful woman made him feel unsettled yet comfortable. He'd never before experienced that emotional paradox.

"I'm sure Worcester is lovely," she said. "I'm glad you like living there. I think places are like people—no matter what they look like, what they are like, they always have someone's heart to claim."

"Yes, every place and every person is beautiful in someone's eyes," he replied. *And there are some places and people beautiful in everyone's eyes.* Sam nearly blushed at his own train of thought. At a loss for what to say next, he quickly added, "If you're ever in the Boston area, I'd be glad to give you a tour of my hometown."

"I'll take you up on that. I go to the American East Coast frequently, actually," she said enthusiastically. "I was finishing up an operation earlier when I got a text from Ari. When the OR nurse read it aloud to me, it sounded weird. So I called him as soon as I was done. He told me a little bit about your visit with him. Among other things, he said I should ask you about your kitty." Gabriela set one foot on the floor and crossed her opposite leg. She leaned forward. "But before I do that, where's my jewelry and where's my money?" She said this in a playfully demanding tone. She squinted and puckered her lips in an attempt to look gruff but only managed to look even more charming.

"Yes, right away," he replied and reached for his backpack. Smiling, he produced the jewelry case. "And don't forget about your lovely house by the river in San Antonio."

"Oh, really? Well, that too," Gaby added with a graceful smile. She opened the box and looked dazzled. "These are absolutely gorgeous. Wow." After a pause, she waved the jewelry box in front of her. "All right, before you hand me everything else, tell me all about these things."

For nearly an hour, Sam recounted most of what he'd told Ari.

When he discussed the contents of the safe-deposit box and her grandfather's journal, Gaby got a bit teary. She told Sam it wasn't a family secret her grandfather had fallen in love with someone while away at war. In fact, her grandfather had often told her about it when she was a teenager. She and her cousins enjoyed listening to their grandfather tell stories about his time in Texas and in the Pacific. Gaby had loved her grandfather immensely and told Sam that as she got older, she always felt pain knowing he hadn't remained with the woman he'd loved so much—even if she and some of her cousins wouldn't exist. Her grandparents had always seemed happy, but she would have wanted her grandfather to have lived a life with the person he'd referred to as his "first true love."

At her urging, Sam told her the basics of his life, including a few facts about Tony and Lilly. Also, as previously requested, he told her about his cat. Just as her cousin did earlier in the day, Gaby shed a few tears when hearing about Vin's life in Afghanistan, about the feline's journey into grown men's hearts at the base, and his eventual trek to Worcester, where he currently lived a zestful life with his canine buddy, Nic, and their two human companions.

"They have funny names. Why Vin and Nic? Let me guess, from *The Godfather* movies?" she asked.

Sam smiled. "No. Although you're right, they sound like wise guys. Vin was named by committee. Several of the guys on the base were from New England. Naturally, we decided the cat should be named after one of the Patriots' greatest. After a heated discussion during a poker game one day, where Vin literally slept on the table with all of us sitting around yelling and drinking beer, the votes came in. He was named after Adam 'the Clutch' Vinatieri. This player scored a forty-eight-yard field goal that won the Patriots their first Super Bowl title in 2002. He played in five Super Bowls and is one of the greatest kickers in the NFL. And Nic was a local rescue. I named him just to continue the theme of naming my pets after sports greats. My dog is named after Steve Nicol. In my opinion, he was the best soccer coach the New England Revolution ever had. He led the team to eight consecutive playoff berths in his ten-year tenure."

"A sports junkie, I see. You'd get along perfectly with some of my nephews—my cousins' kids. They play every sport imaginable, especially American football. That sport is big here. Do you still play? You look athletic."

Sam smiled. He wasn't sure if that had been a compliment or a rote observation. "If you count Xbox, then yes. Otherwise, no. Tony and I coach a local soccer team for kids. That's the extent of my team-sport involvement at the moment."

"That's great. Is that what you do?"

"Coaching? No. That's something we do on our own time. Tony and I own a barbershop. That's what I do currently."

"Do you cut women's hair?"

"We mostly do guys. But some women have walked in and left pretty happy. As my friend Tony would say, 'We are freaky good providing services to all the girls.'"

"I'm confident you meant that in an entirely professional way," she said with a laugh.

"I'm not at liberty to say. What happens in the barbershop stays in the barbershop," he countered.

"Not a peep out of me," Gaby said with a lip-sealing gesture. "What do you think about my hair?" She snapped her ponytail band off and let her hair loose. It came to rest in a perfect bob just above her shoulders.

"That's definitely a high-end cut. Not quite barber territory. Although the next time you need a haircut, I can give it a shot and see what happens," he said, an affable smirk on his face.

"Ha, ha. Very funny."

"Your hair color is really nice too. Natural?" he asked sincerely.

"Hmm. I don't know about you, Sam. Maybe you're not as good as you say. Seasoned hair professionals should know that no woman my age even knows her natural hair color. We've colored it so many different ways and so many times…"

"Can I use the barber-rather-than-stylist excuse for not knowing that?" He smiled. "Good to know, though. Learn something new every day." Sam rubbed his chin. "On the subject of bad questions, may I inappropriately ask how old you are? I was looking at your wall there, and it seems like all those accomplishments should belong to someone much older. Oh, and I mean that as a compliment. Believe me."

"Barbers are not the only ones with hush-hush codes. What happens in hospital offices stays in hospital offices, okay? All those diplomas are photoshopped. And I'm not a real doctor. I just play one on TV," Gaby said with another quick laugh.

"Your secret is safe with me," he said.

"I'm thirty-four, Sam. I skipped the first grade and finished high school a year early. That's probably why I seem a little younger than I should be to have this job and this office."

"I'm sure you get this a lot. It probably won't mean much coming from me, but I'm absolutely impressed. Oh, and you look more like twenty-five."

"It does mean a lot to me, thank you. With regard to my accomplishments, well, I'm grateful for all the opportunities and privileges I've had. I've always wanted to do what I do. Plus, I've had an excess of support—more than most people ever get." She looked at Sam with a feigned evil grin. "As Humphrey Bogart said to Captain Renault in my favorite movie of all time: 'This is the beginning of a beautiful friendship,' Sam. So, since our friendship has graduated to asking inappropriate questions in a very short time, where are you staying? And is anybody accompanying you?"

"I got a room at the Hampton Inn in the city center. I haven't checked in, though. I went directly to Ari's gallery. And I came alone."

"Can you hold on a minute?" Gabriela grabbed her phone from her desktop. She nimbly tapped on the screen as if she were texting. Then she put the phone to her ear and began talking in Spanish. The only thing Sam caught was his name. "Okay, Sam. Your reservation is canceled. You're sleeping with me." Almost immediately, she blushed. "I meant *staying* with me. In my guest room, of course. It's really nice and has a private bathroom."

Sam was surprised but honored. He also noticed her trace of mortification and wanted to make her feel at ease. Wittily, he said, "I don't know. Do you have an en suite coffee maker with Starbucks coffee?"

Gaby shook her head and smiled. "No. But I have an espresso machine, Illy coffee beans, and guest bedsheets with an astronomical thread count."

"You got doughnuts or other continental fare for breakfast?"

"I got a phone, and I'm on a first-name basis with the chef of a nearby restaurant who can deliver the best eggs benedict with Nova Scotia smoked salmon you've ever tasted."

"Twist my arm no more. I accept your kind hospitality." Sam leaned back. "Okay, joking aside. Are you sure? How do you know I'm not a psychopath? You've only known me for an hour."

"Are you a psychopath?" she asked, raising her eyebrow.

"No, nothing that interesting."

"Are you kidding, Sam? It's because you're interesting why I want to know you better. I'm certain you are not a psycho because here you are: an ex-soldier who served in the Middle East and who went to great lengths to rescue a cat. You volunteer to coach children in sports. You grew up in the foster care system and love your friend Tony like a brother. You're just a barber from Worcester, who, out of nowhere, inherits millions. And you have the decency to come all the way down here to try to give that away?" Gaby suddenly looked concerned. "Shit! I'm so sorry. I didn't mean to sound condescending when I said you were 'just a barber.' I meant that in a purely factual way."

He smiled when she swore. He thought it adorable and re-freshing. "Don't worry. I didn't even notice, and like you said, it's just the facts. It actually sounded more like a compliment—a compliment for just being me, which is nice. So thank you."

"See? There you go. You're just a nice guy." She set her phone back on her desk. "It seems we've gone off on a tangent. Besides getting to know you better, I also want us to learn more about our grandparents. I'm sure there are things in my grandfather's journal I'll love learning—especially about your grandmother. She must have been special. And there are things I'd like to show you. But before we go any further, you know I was kidding earlier. Whatever you inherited from my grandfather, it's yours. If that's what he wanted, that's the way it should be. I'm grateful you de-cided to come and offer to share it.

"Ari said you were eager to go back home. I don't know what your commitments are like, and I don't want you to feel obligat-ed. But will you stay a little longer in Mexico City? Stay a week. Starting right now, I have the rest of the week off. There are some things I'd like you to see and one person I want you to meet—he knows everything about my grandfather's air force unit.

"Finally, if no one in Worcester would mind, I'd love for you to be my date to Ari's wedding next Saturday. Don't worry, strictly platonic. It'd just be nice to have someone pleasant to talk to and not have everyone I know trying to set me up."

"So you'd like to use me as a buffer? A stunt date?" he exclaimed sarcastically.

"Shit! Did that sound rude again?" she asked, concerned but playful.

"Not at all. I just couldn't help myself, you kind of left the door wide open for that one. Anyway, there's nobody back home who would mind. Plus, I'm certain Tony and the pets can survive on their own for a few more days. The only problem is I literally only brought these jeans, a couple of T-shirts, and a pair of skivvies." Sam mused for a second. "Come to think about it, since you and Ari have passed on the very thing I came here for, it seems I can now afford something suitable to be your date. I'm game!"

"Sam, you make me smile. I promise you'll have a wonderful time. Also, I'm sure we can find something great for you to wear. We have every store on Madison Avenue or Rodeo Drive here. Shopping will be fun."

"Is that where one goes for skivvies?"

"Of course," she said, grinning. "Comfortable, good-quality underwear is important!"

"I'll take your word for it."

"Since I get to be a regular citizen for a week, let's start with a nice dinner and a night out. Maybe we'll join Ari and some friends. They're going to be at the terrace of the Hotel Habita. They have a fabulous outdoor bar with nice city views."

"Gaby, that sounds great," he said. "I never thought the trip would turn out like this. I'm really glad I came."

ELEVEN

"Dude, what do you mean you can't tell me right now? What am I supposed to tell Lilly when me and Nic show up without you tomorrow?" Tony asked.

"Hey, man, it's a little complicated. Can you just trust that I'm okay? I'm more than okay, actually. I'll give you the lowdown as soon as I get a chance," Sam told Tony as he stood by the club's terrace pool. It was a crisp and clear summer night. He could see endless lit windows in high-rise buildings. He felt a breeze as he slowly turned to see the small group—four women and three men, including Gaby and Ari—sitting under trendy aqua-blue lighting near a sparkling fireplace. Subdued house music was audible throughout the terrace. He watched Gaby, who cheerfully gestured and talked to her friends. Before leaving her office, she'd changed into a white tank top, fitted jeans, a black blazer, and black Converse All Star sneakers. She also wore a red leather cross-body Longchamp bag.

How can anyone look that good in something so simple? he thought. She was radiant, the epitome of casual elegance.

"All right, Sam. Since you won't tell me what's going on, I'll just make something up. I'll tell Lilly you're on a sex bender with some chick from Cranston."

"Cranston? Really?"

"You're not classy enough for girls from Boston or Providence. It's gotta sound realistic, my friend."

"You're an asshole, buddy. You know that, right? Anyway, thanks for covering. I don't want Lilly to freak out that I'm here. By the way, go easy on the pizza with Nic. Too much is gonna give him diarrhea. I'll talk to you soon." Sam clicked off and rejoined the friendly group.

"How are Tony and the pets?" Ari asked.

"They're just fine. We were trying to come up with something to tell my sister so she wouldn't worry."

"What did you guys come up with?" Gaby asked.

Sam smiled thoughtfully. "We didn't decide. We'll come up with something tomorrow. Anyway, sorry I had to take his call."

"No problem. We were discussing your earlier question regarding my gallery's name. Eduardo, Gaby, and I were surprised only Paola knew the answer." A perky brunette in a stylish cocktail dress and heels raised her fist as if she'd won something. She invoked a toast to her superior knowledge. Drink in hand, Ari continued. "Alpheratz is the brightest star in the Andromeda constellation. In Greek mythology, Andromeda married Perseus after he rescued her from certain death. She eventually became this important matriarch of a large family. Upon her death, the goddess Athena honored her and turned her into a constellation.

"My grandfather had this thing where he constantly referred to my grandmother as Andromeda. Maybe he was her Perseus, I don't know. Now, it's no secret Gaby was my grandpa's favorite grandchild—*his brightest star*, he'd say. So Alpheratz is what he used to call Gaby."

Gaby raised her hand. "Guilty!"

Ari exclaimed, "Grandpa's pet!" But he blew her a kiss. "I think it started when you told him you wanted to be a doctor like him, right?"

"I don't know. Probably," she said.

"That being said, I named my gallery Alpheratz in honor of Gaby. Because as everyone here knows, she rescued me from myself," Ari said, then elaborated. "You see, Sam, a few years ago, I was an abysmally unhappy architect. I was good at it, but I was essentially doing it because I thought I had to make my parents proud. My brother—like Gaby, like my father, and like many other family members—is a hotshot doctor. My sister is the youngest magnate in one of the family's businesses. Although my passion has always been art, I didn't want to be a disappointment and continued grinding it out as an architect. There was this one period, though, when I was really in the dumps. I told Gaby, and she flew here from Boston. For a week she knocked sense into me and helped me realize what I really wanted and needed to do. After that, I put down my T square and started my gallery." Ari reached for his drink. He looked at Gaby affectionately. "So, to my beautiful cousin, Alpheratz. I owe you my professional happiness. You're truly my brightest star. I love you." Ari raised his glass, and everyone followed suit.

Jokingly, Eduardo said to Ari, "I love Gaby too, but I thought *I* was your brightest star."

"You are my universe. That's why I can't wait to marry you. Just a few more days," Ari replied.

Everybody started chanting, "*Beso, beso,* kiss, kiss…" Ari was on the sofa, kitty-corner from Eduardo. They both stood up half-way, reached for each other, and kissed.

As the evening went on, they all continued to have amusing conversations. Everyone openly embraced Sam and made him feel welcome.

Just past midnight, Gaby announced she wanted to start Sam's tour early the next morning and suggested it'd be a good time to go home. Everybody got up to hug them goodbye. The three other women added a friendly kiss on the cheek when they hugged Sam.

"I could totally get used to this Latin kissing from beautiful women," Sam told them. "Do people get seconds?" he joked.

Paola hugged and kissed him again and said, "Sam, whenever you need a hug and a kiss, you call me, okay?" They all laughed.

Gaby and Sam left the terrace, went downstairs, and caught a cab.

"They'll stay there until dawn," she told Sam in the taxi.

"Really? That's awesome. You guys have a nice set of friends."

"Ari and Eduardo have so many friends. I actually don't know most of them. But the ones I do know are very nice. They're going to talk and drink until six or seven in the morning, then walk down the street to this place called Vips. It's like a Denny's. They'll have breakfast, then finally go home to catch some sleep."

"Wow. Hard-core," Sam said. He pulled slightly on the seat belt and turned more comfortably toward Gaby. "Talking to your friends reminded me of something I wanted to mention earlier, but forgot: I think it's great most people I've met speak English. It's made it a lot easier for me to get along. Even my taxi driver from the airport spoke it quite well."

"Yes, pretty much anyone who has gone to private school here knows English and, often, French. A few private schools have Japanese or German academic systems, so those tend to be the third languages their students learn. The first year of elementary school in most private schools is entirely dedicated to learning English. That was one of the years I was able to shave off my own education. Since I knew English by the time I'd finished kindergarten, I was able to skip that first year. Another of the many perks of privilege. My cousins and I had a bunch of nannies who were essentially teachers. They taught us everything—from English to math—every day after school.

"Unfortunately, the public school system in Mexico is not quite that comprehensive. Only public schools in the more affluent communities have resources to teach other languages. But even people who don't have the chance to learn English early tend to learn it at the university level. They understand it's essential not only from a professional perspective but also a personal one. If nothing else, people want to fully appreciate undubbed American TV shows and movies." She grinned and raised her brows, indicating this may have seemed laughable but was factual. "I'm not surprised your taxi driver spoke English. This city has a gigantic tourism industry. Even people who don't have a formal education—if they want to be in the tourism business—have to learn some English."

"That's really cool."

"It's just the way the economy developed. Most Americans don't need to know another language. But this country is so entwined socially and economically with the United States that people here need and want to know English."

"It must be nice to be bilingual or multilingual. Maybe by the time I leave I can learn at least a few words in Spanish."

"I'll make sure of it, Sam."

"I appreciate that," he replied. "On a different topic, I didn't want to sound stupid, so I didn't ask. Ari and Eduardo seem to love each other. They make a nice couple. But how does gay marriage work here?"

"Same-sex marriage is legal in Mexico. Well, it's legal in Mexico City and several other states. But the whole country legally recognizes marriages in those states, which is great."

"I'm glad that's the way it is."

"In terms of the ceremony, neither Ari nor Eduardo is religious, so everything is going to take place at this hotel called Live Aqua. It's a grand hotel with a boutique feel."

"Speaking of the wedding, are you sure it's okay for me to crash it? I assume the RSVP deadline is long past."

Gaby smiled. "Don't worry. My mom took care of my RSVP a long time ago. In her typical hopeful fashion, she put me down as a plus one. Besides, guest lists at Mexican weddings are never set in stone. There's always room, food, and plenty of booze for more."

The taxi stopped. Gaby dug into her purse, but Sam beat her to the fare and paid.

"Thank you, Sam."

"It's my pleasure." He got out, turned, and offered Gaby his hand. Unlike their previous cab ride, when she was first to step out, Sam felt her delicate fingers on his steady palm for the first time. He experienced an alien sensation: instantaneous but without end. It was similar to the moment you realize everything is okay after being startled by a sudden noise. Or like the moment when fear becomes excitement as you plunge from a roller coaster's high peak. Or like seeing a good grade on an exam you weren't sure you'd even passed. It was shock followed by exhilaration and bliss. His strange feelings aside, he didn't miss a beat after helping her exit the cab. "It looks like we are back at Ari's gallery."

Gaby, too, grappled with a similar sensation the moment their hands touched. Yet seemingly unperturbed, she said, "We are. I live in the residence above."

TWELVE

S am walked through Gabriela's expansive loft the next morning. From its three-story, old-European-style façade, he never would've guessed it had such a slick, contemporary interior. The guest room was on one end. The kitchen, where she was sitting by its island reading a newspaper, was on the opposite end. Noticing him, she gleefully waved hello. He waved back. Her bedroom, above the kitchen, had wall-to-wall glass windows covered by screens. Last night, the window screens weren't there and one could see into her bedroom. This morning Sam had made a point not to come out of the guest suite until he was sure Gabriela was up and about. He now felt more at ease knowing he could be in the living area and not worry about her privacy.

Gabriela stood up from her stool. She wore black athletic leggings with colorful accents. A matching tunic completed her sporty outfit. Her shapely figure was graceful and striking. "Good morning, Sam. I hope my guest room proved more restful than the Hampton Inn."

"Definitely. That foamy mattress is awesome. I've never slept on a bed that comfortable. Your towels and bath products are just as nice. For sure a five-star experience."

"It's a Tempur-Pedic mattress with an extra layer of memory foam. The bath products are Malin+Goetz, which are my current favorite. I'm glad you had a good night's sleep. Please make yourself comfortable. I have juice, and as promised, I'm making you a latte." She went to her espresso machine. "I have skim or almond milk. Which would you prefer?"

"I'll take it the same way you take yours," he said.

"Almond milk it is. I've ordered breakfast. It will be here momentarily."

"Thank you. By the way, your place is huge. I didn't fully appreciate the space last night. I almost needed a bike to get from the guest room to the kitchen."

"I know. Maybe a little too big for me, but it's really nice. It was Ari's. He asked me if I wanted it when he moved in with Eduardo. Of course, I didn't hesitate to take it. The location is super convenient—makes it easy getting to the various hospitals I work at."

"I thought you only worked at the ABC Medical Center."

"My office is in the ABC; I'm in the hepatobiliary surgery department there. But like most academic transplant surgeons, I actually work for the transplant system itself. The organization encompasses several hospitals in the city and many others around the country. Most major transplants, though, are done at the National Medical Center and at the Salvador Zubirán Institute for Medical Specialties. Since I have privileges at these various centers, it doesn't matter where my office happens to be."

The bell rang. Gabriela handed Sam his latte and excused herself.

She returned carrying two boxes. "Okay, Sam, close your eyes," Gaby told him. She placed one of the boxes in front of him, opened the lid, and uncovered some containers. "Voilà!"

Sam opened his eyes. "This looks and smells amazing."

"As I promised: eggs benedict with Nova Scotia smoked salmon." Pointing at the various other contents, she said, "Those are a combination of oven-baked potatoes and hash browns. They're so tasty you won't need any ketchup or other condiment. A fresh fruit cocktail. And a little container of extra hollandaise sauce."

"Gaby, you didn't have to do this."

"Hey, I yanked you out of your hotel, so this is the least I can do," she said. "Besides, I'll be honest. It's what I would've had myself anyway," she added as she opened her identical breakfast box.

They enjoyed a pleasant conversation over the tasty food, also recalling some of the livelier moments from the previous night. The topic of her bedroom being plainly visible from the living room came up. She apologized for not realizing he might've been uncomfortable, as he hadn't known that with the touch of a button, her room could be completely screened off. Both laughed about it, especially when Sam told her he'd put an ear to the wall at various times to make sure she was downstairs. Gabriela thanked him for being so mindful of her privacy.

When they were nearly finished eating, Gabriela told Sam her plan for the day. "I initially thought we'd go shopping for you. But since you still have an extra change of clothes, I figured this would be the best time to have my friend Mario Gomez meet us to have a fun history day. Mario and I grew up together. We went to the same school from the fourth grade on, until I left for college. He's an economics professor, but he might as well be a historian. Mario knows everything, from local to world history. We'll rendezvous with him at Chapultepec Park. There we'll take a tour of a special landmark. Then we can all go have a light lunch. And after lunch, we'll head over to my house. My parents' home, that is. My dad is on a business trip to China, but my mom is home. She'll invariably want to stuff us with food for dinner, hence the need for a light lunch.

"In our library, we have all the memorabilia from my grandpa's time during the war. Years ago, my dad and Ari's dad flipped a coin to see who'd get to keep it. My dad won. I'm sure you'll find some of the items interesting. And it will be nice for me to reminisce about some of the things too. I haven't thought about any of this for years. How does that sound?"

"It sounds great." Sam helped her clean up and drank the last bit of his latte. "I'm still in disbelief I'm here meeting all of you, learning things about your family and your country. All because a lifetime ago your grandpa fell in love with my grandmother—someone I didn't even know about. Pretty wild, actually."

"That's Mario over there. He must've had a hard time finding a parking spot," Gabriela told Sam. They rose from their bench at the edge of Chapultepec Lake and went to meet her friend. She hugged and kissed him on the cheek and then introduced Sam. Mario looked like the quintessential intellectual: round-rim glasses, corduroy pants, textured dress shirt, and a blazer with elbow patches. The only thing missing to complete the stereotype was a bow tie. He was of medium build, just on the verge of chubby. Despite his slightly disheveled hair, he gave off a respectable, modest, and pleasant aura. Sam liked him instantly.

"All right, let's head over," Mario said after thanking Sam for letting him borrow Gustavo's journal. He promised to return it in a couple of days. Gabriela locked elbows with him as they walked. "When was the last time we were here?" Mario asked her. He also looked at Sam to include him in the conversation.

"Ten years, at least. He was still alive," Gabriela replied.

"Time flies, doesn't it?" Then turning to Sam, he said, "I don't know if Gaby has told you anything about where we're going. It's a hidden treasure. A lot of people don't even know about it, probably because it's deep within the park, away from the more common attractions. Or maybe because the current generation overlooks all our great monuments. They'd rather fixate on Facebook and Twitter instead of learning about their own history."

Gabriela said, "No, I didn't mention it. I thought I'd let you tell Sam about it. Besides, I'd love to hear you discuss it."

"In that case, I'll get started. Sam, the monument we're going to show you honors the three hundred men, including

Gaby's grandfather, who made up the 201st Squadron of the Mexican Expeditionary Air Force. They're the only military unit in this country that has fought outside our borders. The monument pays homage, in particular, to the five pilots who died in action and the three others who died in training. In fact, it's partly a mausoleum, as the remains of two of those fallen men are buried there."

They walked along pathways that became progressively more secluded and beautiful. Forested sections of the enormous park, which people referred to as "the lung of Mexico City," became evident. The fresh, almost sweet scent of pine trees enveloped them.

Mario continued telling them about these exceptional men who contributed to a common cause at a pivotal time. A few minutes later, they turned a corner.

"We're here," Gabriela said.

"I give you the Monument to the Fallen Eagles," Mario added, gesturing.

"Wow!" Sam said. He marveled at the white stone, Roman-style monument. It resembled an amphitheater. Steps throughout it led to stagelike surfaces where one could stand to read bronze placards about the aviators killed in action. The structure's center had a large inscription with a dedication and all the names of the 201st Squadron.

Gabriela softly traced the name of her grandfather with her fingers. She sighed and smiled. Before moving on to another placard, she kissed her index finger and touched it to Gustavo's name.

The three eventually sat on the monument's steps. Gabriela and Sam continued listening to Mario expand on the history of that special military unit.

"As you know, the Second World War was a global conflict. Every country, whether they participated directly or not, was affected. Mexico—a traditionally neutral nation but tied into the United States' socioeconomic fate—eventually had no choice either.

"The attack on Pearl Harbor, of course, was the event that caused the United States to join the war in the winter of 1941.

"The two immense oceans flanking North America provided—and still provide—the people from Alaska to Yucatán a false sense of security. Yet by the spring of 1942, the coasts of Canada, the United States, and Mexico were infested with German U-boats in the Atlantic and Japanese subs in the Pacific.

"Mexico was the United States' primary oil supplier at the time—an activity that intensified immediately after the American Congress declared war on Germany, Japan, and Italy. In May of 1942, German U-boats torpedoed and sank two Mexican oil tankers, the *Potrero del Llano* and the *Faja de Oro*. Those were the events that forced Mexico to formally declare war on the Axis powers. The tentacles of the war could no longer be avoided. Unbeknownst to most people on either side of the border nowadays, the people of Mexico were drawn into the war effort.

"Not long after, just as in the United States, farms and factories accelerated production to help supply the Allied nations' military needs. Following numerous diplomatic meetings and negotiations between our two countries, Mexico agreed to have a quarter of a million people head to the US to work in their fields and factories to temporarily replace the American men who'd been called into action. Mexico also allowed the US use of its major seaports—particularly that of Veracruz—from which American troops and supplies came and went freely.

"The two countries mutually decided that Mexico should begin contributing to the war with military units. While these were to participate under the canopy and overall strategies of the American generals heading each major war front, their immediate command and structure would remain under the Mexican military.

"For numerous strategic reasons, it was determined an air force unit would provide the greatest possible impact in any of the war theaters. Mexico had two sizable air bases, one here and the other in Guadalajara. To the surprise of American commanders, these bases had many experienced pilots, many of whom had received training in the United States. That's how the 201st Squadron was born. It was to be the first of many units slated to deploy to the various fronts. Thankfully, the war ended not too long after. And thus, this squadron became the only group to see action.

"What makes this unit special is the men who composed it: they were all volunteers—and the best of the best.

"The Mexican government wanted to make sure the first group it sent abroad represented the country well. They wanted the 201st to set an example for similar units they thought would shortly follow them into combat. So the Mexican military sent out invitations to its installations around the country to compete for the various required services, including pilots, artillery specialists, mechanics, and other positions. For some of the more advanced support roles, like medical and engineering, the solicitations also went out to some civilian outfits.

"Out of thousands of men, after many rounds of testing, only the most physically and intellectually able remained. Many had university-level education. But they came from a variety of socioeconomic backgrounds. Some had underprivileged roots, a few hailed from the middle class, and others came from the country's most important families. Their apparent differences notwithstanding, they became brothers—instantly bound by mutual respect. They all understood the significance of the worldwide conflict that had brought them together. Every one of them wanted to help preserve freedom and self-determination.

"Speaking of that sense of duty, I should mention that—in addition to more than half a million Mexican Americans—about thirty thousand Mexican nationals, from the entire socioeconomic spectrum but imbued with the same desire to make a

difference, had already been going north to join the armed forces of the US and Canada. They're seldom recognized because
officially they figured as either American or Canadian soldiers.
As you can imagine, some joined against the wishes of their loved
ones. But it was a time when idealism triumphed and they did it
anyway. Some came back. Many didn't."

After a moment of reflection, Gabriela said, "I've always thought
that was so amazing. I remember my father telling me that my grandfather initially submitted his application in secret. Eventually, he had
to tell my great-grandparents, which didn't go well. But he'd made
up his mind. He actually threatened to go to the US on his own and
enlist as a soldier. My great-grandfather eventually decided his son
would be safer as one of the two physicians of the 201st rather than
as a frontline private in the US Army. An experienced academic
surgeon himself, he decided to help my grandfather prepare for the
competitive examinations to be selected for the squadron. My grandpa came in first on the written and oral rounds. The practical portion
of the test took place over a week at the Central Military Hospital. The
hospital was so new then its construction wasn't even finished. Little
did my grandfather know that after he returned from the war, he'd
become an important faculty member there. The other medical officer was a general practitioner. Along with two nonphysician medics,
they became the squadron's medical contingent."

"I had no idea," Sam said. "This is fascinating. The way
this unit was formed, including Gustavo's part in it, is really
admirable."

"Men and women of that era were incredible," Gabriela said.
"No matter their country, they had a strong sense of purpose and
duty. Truly the Greatest Generation. I'm so proud to know my
grandfather was part of it." She stood. "On that note, why don't
we put history on hold for now. I want this to be a well-rounded
outing for you, Sam. Let's go join some Japanese and German
tourists, walk around the historic center, and have lunch. We can
pick this up at home later," she said with a smile.

THIRTEEN

They walked around the Zócalo—the city's main plaza—where they saw the imposing colonial-era Metropolitan Cathedral and the National Palace. They were able to go inside the latter and admire Diego Rivera's awe-inspiring murals. These portrayed Mexican history and culture from its ancient Indian civilizations to the revolution of the early 1900s. The murals had been painted on corridor and stairway walls between 1929 and 1951.

After that, they walked west on Juárez Avenue and reached the beautiful Palace of Fine Arts, an Art Nouveau building designed by the famous architect Adamo Boari and completed in the 1930s. Inside, Sam saw works by another great muralist, David Alfaro Siqueiros.

Mario acted as a tour guide. He provided relevant and interesting information about the various buildings and about the art as well, which made everything Sam was experiencing that much richer.

The trio then headed to lunch at the House of Tiles, an impeccably preserved building dating back to the eighteenth century and now the flagship restaurant of the Sanborns retail chain.

As they drove to her parents' home, Gabriela sat in the back seat of Mario's beloved Volkswagen Beetle. Mario had won a lottery that allowed him to buy the car from the last-ever-produced batch. It rolled out of the Puebla factory in July 2003. He used it only on weekends or special occasions.

"I always wanted a *vocho*. That's what these VW Bugs are affectionately called here," Gaby told Sam. To Mario, she said, "Thank you for bringing this car. You know how much I love it."

"My pleasure. Although I'm sure your dad would have a cow if he saw you right now," Mario replied.

"No, I think he's finally given up trying to protect me at every turn."

"Remember when we were in high school and you told him you wanted one?"

"Oh yes. Even *you* got to sit in on that grueling and exhaustive lecture." Addressing Sam, she said, "My dad literally sat us down and gave us a laundry list of reasons as to why it was dangerous to drive a small car. He also explained why I didn't need to—and should not—drive at all."

"But, Gaby, you must admit that being driven anywhere you wanted, whenever you wanted, was pretty cool," Mario said. "I loved it when I got to hang out with you or Ari. To this day, I'm sure your dad would be glad to assign you a chauffeur."

"I still would've loved to have had my own bright red *vocho*. I could have even learned how to drive. I'm a surgeon, with diplomas coming out of my ears, yet I don't have a driver's license. There's something wrong with that."

"You really don't know how to drive?" Sam asked her.

"Nope. After I left for college, I never had the need or the chance to learn. I didn't have to drive at all while living in New Haven. During my time in Boston and Chicago, I was always within walking distance of campus. Now that I've come back, the transplant system provides its surgeons with twenty-four/seven transportation for emergencies or other work-related functions. Plus, with regard to transplants, from the instant a donor is available to the moment their organ actually arrives at the transplant center, there is always plenty of time to get to the hospital. And in this city, public transportation is faster and more efficient than driving."

"Well, if you ever come to Worcester, I'd be glad to teach you how to drive. Although, we'd have to do it in Tony's old Ford Maverick, since I don't have a car either. I sold my previous one, and we used those proceeds as part of the capital to start the barbershop."

"The old Maverick it is. I'd love that, Sam," Gabriela said.

Gabriela leaned forward between the front seats and pointed at various landmarks she thought might be of interest to Sam along the way. Throughout the ride, Sam wasn't sure if he was more enthralled by the sights whizzing by or the inexplicable sensation of her proximity.

With the peculiar rumble of its engine, the feisty VW Beetle left behind a vibrant business district and entered Lomas de Chapultepec and, minutes later, Bosques de Las Lomas.

Sam noticed the dramatic change of scenery. They were now in a residential zone—one unlike Sam had ever seen. Every home, regardless of style—from ultramodern to traditional—was large and stately. Most were enclosed within tall walls and concealing gates. Only their upper portions were visible. Many of these homes had small booths with guards on duty. Sam also noticed the luxury makes of most of the automobiles passing them by or parked on the streets. The sheer number of mansions in this neighborhood was staggering. They seemed to go on forever, visible above and below rolling hills. The closest comparisons Sam could make to such unmitigated affluence were Scarsdale, New York, and Greenwich, Connecticut, both towns he'd briefly passed through.

After what he'd seen and learned the last few days, Sam wasn't surprised Gustavo's family would hail from a place like this. He couldn't help but comment, "We're not in Kansas anymore. This is a really nice area. Is this the city's 'better side of the tracks'?"

Mario and Gaby smiled almost in unison. Mario said, "Not that Gaby wouldn't have the right perspective, but since I'm not technically from this side of the tracks, I'll tackle your question. You're asking if this is the rich-folk part of town." He teasingly pointed to Gabriela with his thumb. "The answer is yes and no. Yes, because as you can see, this area is as upscale as can be. I couldn't possibly afford it, even on my tenured professor salary. Come to think about it, even Gaby—one of the country's top surgeons—probably couldn't afford to live here on her compensation alone, right?" Gabriela nodded in agreement. "It's very exclusive. I don't think anybody can buy a house in this area for less than a couple of million US dollars. And that would probably be slumming it around here. On the other hand, no. It isn't *the* rich part of town per se, because it's not the only one. There are other similar neighborhoods in different parts of the city.

"Mexico City is enormous and has a diverse socioeconomic spectrum. Naturally, there are many underprivileged neighborhoods and painfully poor people, as in most big cities. But what many people here and abroad don't know is that Mexico City is one of the wealthiest cities in the world. So, it's not surprising that there are a number of extremely affluent zones like this one.

"Fortunately, there are many other areas and municipalities that offer beautiful and comfortable living for the likes of me—people smack in the center of the middle class."

"That's interesting," Sam said. "Aside from my time in Afghanistan, a short stint in Iraq, and Baumholder, Germany, I've never been outside the US. Well, unless you count Toronto. I often forget Canada is another country. Tony and I won a trip to see the New England Revolution play a soccer game there. Anyway, I've rarely given much thought to places outside the United States. I guess most of us get caught up in our daily activities and don't give a second thought to how folks live in other places. It's nice to know many people here live pleasant lives."

"Yeah. I think most of the gazillion of us in this town are pretty lucky. Even those who are considered poor seldom go without basic stuff. And in relative terms, even they enjoy occasional luxuries in their lives," Gabriela added.

"Gaby is right," Mario said. "The entire country usually ranks among the happiest places in the world. This may not be evident to Americans, since most people's experiences with Mexicans in the US is limited to stereotypes in movies about drug smuggling, shantytowns, or mariachi bands in dusty Wild West settings. Or they see our compatriots seeking and working jobs in the fields, restaurants, and other manual labor—jobs not often associated with happiness.

"That, however, comes down to geography and economics. We're so close to the US that when the economy in various parts of the country has been lacking, some people in the lowest rungs of skill and education find it appealing to take a bus north and risk trying to cross the border to see if they can do a little better. But this isn't much different than people from poor towns in Alabama or Mississippi, for example, moving to seek better fortunes in richer states like California, Texas, or those in the Pacific Northwest.

"Don't get me wrong, I don't mean to sound condescending or arrogant. I very much admire individuals who have the guts to leave their hometowns to seek better fortunes in the US. But save for a few, most of the people who emigrate north go because they're the least skilled and the least educated in their communities. Consequently, these folks essentially become the face and image of Mexico in American minds, particularly in the minds of those who've never ventured south of the border. Thankfully, our economy has been good enough, for over two decades, to discourage people from seeking their fortunes elsewhere. Contrary to popular belief, most Mexicans would never think of leaving the country."

Mario paused for a moment. They'd turned onto a street named Bosque de Balsas. Mario was trying to be more vigilant as he steered up the particularly winding road. Soon, he slowed. The car approached a black metal gate. It stood at the center of a tan wall made of fine masonry and the number 1825 in relief above the gate. Massive limestone rock formations flanked the fortresslike wall. Only trees were visible beyond the gate. Greenery and colorful flowers draped over the wall. The number above the gate was not contiguous with those of the homes they'd just passed. No other homes were visible on either side of this massive property.

"We're here," Mario said as he pulled into the driveway.

Gabriela leaned forward through the front seats and waved at the gate. Sam gathered there must have been a camera ahead because the gate slid open within seconds.

They drove onto a cobblestone plaza-like lot. A second gate stood across the lot. This gate was made of wrought iron with a striking silver crest in the middle. Within the coat of arms on the crest, Sam could see the number 1825 again. Rows of covered garages were on each side of the cobblestone lot. Two GL-Class Mercedes SUVs were on one side and three Chevrolet Suburbans on the other.

A sixtyish man in a white Lacoste shirt and khaki pants walked toward their car. As soon as Mario stopped and rolled down the window, he came up and leaned in. They shook hands and knowingly greeted each other in Spanish. The man and Gabriela shared pleasant greetings. She also waved to a few other similarly dressed fellows who stood by a corner office attached to a garage. They smiled and waved back. Gabriela introduced Sam to Don Lauro, who extended his hand and, in English, welcomed Sam to the property. The wrought iron gate had opened. After sharing a few more pleasantries with Don Lauro, they drove on.

"What is this place?" Sam inquired.

"This is home," Gabriela answered.

Mario looked over at Sam and nodded.

"I take it those guys are guards," Sam said.

"Some are guards, some are on-call drivers, and Don Lauro is the gatekeeper," Gabriela said.

"They seem friendly and courteous."

"They are. It's funny, though. Many years ago, their predecessors wore these stark fatigues. The place looked like a drug lord's compound," she said.

"Don't let the casual wear fool you. They do have guns in that office," Mario said, smiling.

"Luckily they've never used them. Not that I know of, anyway," Gabriela said. "Sam, that aside, this is a private, gated community. There are nine homes on the premises that belong to various members of my family. There's room for more, but most of the younger generation, myself included, prefer to live elsewhere. That, over there, is where Ari's parents live." Gabriela pointed to a palatial house that looked like a Mediterranean villa surrounded by abundant green lawns and a tree-lined road connected to the one they were on. Farther ahead, they passed by a smaller but still impressive French provincial house with fawn-colored brick and steep gray roofs. It was enveloped within a beautiful stone balustrade. Gabriela pointed to it. "That's where my grandfather lived. One of my older cousins lives there now. It's the oldest house on the property."

"It's where I essentially grew up," Mario said.

Sam turned to Mario. "You grew up here?"

"I did, but I'll explain more later," Mario replied, now turning onto a side road. "Amazing memories of that place, huh, Gaby?"

"Definitely. I spent tons of time at my grandparents' when I was young. The whole family would gather there almost every Sunday or on special occasions," Gabriela said, then pointed to a contemporary white mansion with sharp architectural lines, wall-wide windows, and multiple cube-shaped components. "And that spaceship up ahead is my house."

"That's an awesome house. Straight out of *Architectural Digest*," Sam commented.

"Actually, it has been in a number of design magazines over the years. I generally like contemporary homes, but I think mine looks more like the headquarters of some tech firm than a house. It's impractical. It has ten bedrooms and a large guest suite."

"I don't think it's a suite, Gaby. It's more like a large wing," Mario added.

"I guess. At least it gets used a lot. My parents constantly have guests. Other than that, the house is superfluous for three people. Well, three when I was still home."

"I think your mom sees things differently," Mario said. "She keeps adding spaces to it."

"Yeah, I know. She loves the house. Speaking of my mom, she's great. But, um, she can be a little, ah, over the top," Gabriela said.

Mario let out a short laugh. "Sam, what Gaby really means to say is that once her mom gets to know you a little, she'll invariably start insinuating that you and Gaby should be, you know, *together*. And, yes, she'll do this despite being fully aware you've only just met." Mario parked and turned off the car.

Gabriela shrugged. "Yeah, pretty much. She's far from traditional. Except in the last couple of years, for whatever reason, she's developed a nearly pathological desire to see me married off. For this, I apologize in advance."

"That's funny. Don't worry, I'll do my best to roll with the punches," Sam said with a smile.

"Sam, you're awesome. Okay, let's head in. She's waiting," Gabriela said.

They got out of the car and walked toward the house.

FOURTEEN

As soon as Olivia Martel opened the door, she quickly
hugged Mario and Gabriela. Then she turned to Sam
and led him into her museum-like foyer. "Sam, I'm Olivia.
Welcome to this, your humble home." Sam later learned this
was a traditional expression most Mexicans used whether they
were rich or poor.

"Thank you, Mrs. Martel, I'm pleased to make your
acquaintance."

"No, no, no, Sam. Just Olivia, please," she told him. "Gaby, go
to the kitchen and see if Jimena finished the sangria. Have her
help you bring everybody a glass. In the meantime, I'll give these
two handsome men a tour of the house."

"Mom, you know I'm all grown up—and a surgeon, right?"
Gaby said jokingly as she walked away.

"I know you're on your way to becoming the National
Transplant System's director. But, honey, in this house, you're
not that important. Under this roof, you do what I say—mun-
dane or otherwise. So chop-chop, my dear, we're thirsty," Olivia
replied, grinning. Then she turned to Sam. "That's just one of
our little jokes, Sam. Growing up, she made her own bed and
often helped our staff with their chores—including working in
the garden, cleaning the bathrooms, and everything in between.
She has never been a spoiled brat."

Sam had already sensed that about Gabriela from the moment he met her. It was just another of her fascinating attributes.

How can people this rich and educated be so nice and normal? he wondered.

"I gathered that much," Sam said to Olivia. "Gaby is one of the nicest people I've ever met."

"You know she's beautiful and smart and painfully single, right?" Olivia added with a mischievous expression while squeezing Sam's arm.

He smiled, as did Mario. "I'm not surprised Gaby has turned out the way she has. The apple sure doesn't fall far from the tree," Sam told Olivia.

"Oh, Sam. You're lovely. Do stay with us forever." After hugging him again, she pointed to the first thing she wanted to showcase in the foyer. "Mario is familiar with most of the art here. Mayra, his wife, has curated most of our spaces. This is a little Picasso sketch. It is one of my and my husband's favorites because it hung, at one time, in Gertrude Stein's studio at 27 Rue de Fleurus in Paris."

Olivia continued to show Sam the numerous details she loved about her impressive house. Amused, Mario followed along and occasionally provided pertinent comments. With sangria in hand, Gabriela eventually joined them.

The tour ended at the library.

"Mario and Gaby will take it from here," Olivia said. "I hope you enjoy learning about my husband's family. There are appetizers for you over there: ahi tuna ceviche, serrano ham, and assorted cheeses. When you're done here, I'll have dinner ready. I'm looking forward to hearing more about you, Sam."

The library matched the house's contemporary feel. The modern leather furniture was all white. A frosted-glass-top table with four rolling chairs stood to one side. A tray with Olivia's hors d'oeuvres was on the table. Cerulean throw pillows on the sofas and blown-glass sculptures on display stands added decorative accents. Lining every wall, built-in shelves held books, art, and picture frames. Gabriela directed Sam to a section of shelves with glass panels, sliding them apart.

"These are the decorations my grandfather received after the war," she said.

Sam saw many medals and framed certificates. Most were in Spanish, and many included the caduceus symbol. Gabriela told him Gustavo had received some as a result of his contributions to the medical military school and hospital over the years following the war.

"These, though, you may actually recognize," Mario said. He pointed to the adjacent shelves.

Sam glanced at a double-paneled picture frame. One side contained a medal. This had a five-arm red and white cross. The cross's center was navy blue and contained thirteen gold stars. A green and gold laurel circled the cross. The adjacent frame held a certificate.

THE UNITED STATES OF AMERICA

TO ALL WHO SHALL SEE THESE PRESENTS, GREETINGS: THIS IS TO CERTIFY THE PRESIDENT OF THE UNITED STATES OF AMERICA AUTHORIZED BY ACT OF CONGRESS 20 JULY 1942 HAS AWARDED

THE LEGION OF MERIT

TO: LIEUTENANT GUSTAVO ENRIQUE MARTEL LAVOIGNET

For exceptionally meritorious conduct and service in positions of great responsibility while a medical officer during the period 27 March 1945 to 29 August 1945. These culminated in treatment and amelioration of severe illness and injury of military units and civilians under onerous circumstances of combat.

BY ORDER OF THE SECRETARY
OF THE ARMY DEPARTMENT
THIS 15TH DAY OF JUNE 1950

"I know about this particular medal but have never seen one in person. I don't think they give out too many of these. It's amazing," Sam said.

Mario added, "I read some of the documents that led to awarding this Legion of Merit medal. General George C. Kenney, who commanded the Fifth Air Force in Douglas MacArthur's Southwest Pacific area, directly recommended it. The recognition had to do with Gustavo's actions when they set up camp at Porac air base on the Philippine island of Luzon. He and his colleague were among the highest-ranking and most knowledgeable medical officers there. Along with a few of their American counterparts, they were responsible for the medical care of the 201st, as well as of the entire Fifty-Eighth Fighter Group. They also cared for Filipino civilians and even some Japanese prisoners at nearby detention camps. They were fastidious about preventive care and education to help people minimize their risks of contracting dysentery, malaria, and jungle rot, among others. Additionally, Gustavo performed many operations that would've otherwise required evacuations.

"He coordinated, personally supervised, and flew numerous missions to transport sick patients from the surgical hospital at the nearby Clark Field to either Darwin or Brisbane, Australia. He kept those patients alive during transport and stocked up on medical supplies for the return trips.

"Getting this medal was special. He was the only other member of the group, along with some pilots, who got the award. By the way, some of the pilots also got the US Air Medal, which was rare, since the award criteria was very high for the Pacific Theater.

"Those two decorations were the highest military honors given to members of the 201st Squadron."

Sam acknowledged Mario's comments and continued to explore the items on the shelves. These included the American Campaign, the Asia-Pacific Campaign, and the World War II Victory Medals, all issued by the United States. Other awards included the Philippine Legion of Honor, which Mario told him was given at a special ceremony in Manila in 2004. Gustavo had recently passed, but some family members accepted the honor, Sam was told. The Mexican government bestowed the Medalla Servicio en el Lejano Oriente, or Medal for Service in the Far East, to the squadron in 1945.

"It's so nice to know their efforts were recognized," Gabriela said. She pointed to a drawer below the shelves. "Mario, pull out some of the old photo albums. These have pictures and clippings of my grandfather's experience during the war, from the time he departed to his return home."

After enjoying some appetizers, they took the photo albums to a long couch. Mario and Sam became enthralled by an album containing pictures from the air base in the Philippines. In these photos, men smiled and posed before aircraft. The two had a spirited discussion, trying to determine the types of airplanes. The photos included some shots of a Republic P-47 Thunderbolt, the fighter-bomber craft the 201st Squadron used. Sam noted the custom decals on the nose and sides of some planes—one was Panchito Pistoles, the vivacious sombrero-wearing and gun-toting rooster from the Disney film *The Three Caballeros*. That comical cartoon character had become the squadron's emblem.

Other planes included a Bell P-39 Airacobra, a Vought F4U Corsair, and a Boeing C-108 Flying Fortress.

Mario turned a page, and Gabriela exclaimed, "My grandfather is in that photo!" She pointed to Gustavo, a stethoscope around his neck, on the steps of a Douglas C-47 Skytrain. Three other men and a young Filipino woman were also present. They all wore khaki uniforms and Red Cross armbands. "That must've been after one of their long-range medical transport missions," she concluded.

"You're right," Mario said. "I remember him telling me about it. A cool thing about the photo is that the ace pilot of the 201st, Captain Radamés Gaxiola Andrade, took it. It was shot with your grandpa's—ironically German—Leica IIIc camera."

They continued looking at various photographs, newspaper articles, and other scrapbook memorabilia. Gabriela picked up another old photo binder with a handwritten label that read *Texas*.

Thus far, Sam had felt at ease and welcomed—satisfied to have made the trip. Yet a subtle, nagging sense that he did not belong, that this was all a case of mistaken identity, had remained in the back of his mind. He would occasionally ask himself how an average orphan from Worcester could possibly be part of these people's lives and history. But this changed when Gabriela opened this photo album.

"Holy shit!" Sam exclaimed, looking at the only photograph on the first page. Mario and Gabriela stared at him curiously. "Gaby, may I?" Sam asked. Gabriela handed him the album. "I've seen this picture before. This is unbelievable."

"What do you mean?" she asked.

Sam explained his feelings, his continuing uncertainty about whether he was the true beneficiary of Gustavo's bequest.

"What does this photo have to do with that?" Mario inquired.

"I don't know how to explain it exactly. But if this is the same picture I remember seeing many years ago, then I can be sure I'm actually the descendant of this person Gustavo knew and loved. That this exceptional woman really was my grandmother. That it's okay for me to have met and to be here with you two." Sam turned to look at each of them. "Sorry, I'm babbling. Would you please give me a minute? I want to call my sister." Sam tapped Lilly's number on his cell phone. He went to sit on a rolling chair, elbows on his knees, and stared at the floor. Gabriela and Mario watched him and listened expectantly.

After convincing his sister that he was okay, that he'd explain his absence soon, and to please let him talk, he said, "Lills, listen. I need a favor. Do you remember the music box that was with Aunt Paula's stuff when she died?"

"Of course, it's the only thing in there that was nice," Lilly said.

"Do you still have it?"

"Yeah, I have it in my closet."

"Would you go get it? You know the picture that's in the bottom drawer of the music box? Take a photo of it and text it back to me."

"You want me to do that right now? Sam, what's this about?"

"Lilly, trust me. I'll explain later."

Gabriela got Sam's attention, went up next to him, and said, "Ask your sister to also send a photo of the music box." Sam nodded and asked Lilly to do that too.

A few minutes later, Lilly sent the photos. He looked at the screen and shook his head, feeling a mixture of disbelief and satisfaction.

"Lilly, thank you. I have something amazing to tell you later. Say hi to Leonard and the girls." He clicked off and handed Gabriela his phone, queued on one of the two photos.

Gaby looked and smiled. Then they walked back to the couch and showed Mario. She set Sam's phone next to the photograph in the album. It wasn't the same picture, but it had been taken at the same time. The people in both photos were in slightly different positions. There were three men in suits and two women in simple, elegant dresses typical of the 1940s. It appeared to be a fun outing among friends. They stood before a box office and behind a sidewalk sign for the movie *To Have and Have Not*. The small marquee above the poster read "The Majestic Theatre presents Humphrey Bogart and Lauren Bacall in…"

"The picture was taken in San Antonio before they shipped off to war," Mario said.

"How do you know?" Gaby asked.

"The date on the marquee. Look, these photos were taken in 1944. They didn't leave for the Philippines until 1945," he said.

"Ah, good catch," Gabriela said. "Sam, my grandfather is to the right of the movie sign. And despite having that other guy's arm around her, your grandmother is the beautiful woman on the opposite side." She tapped Sam's phone, zooming in on the photo and focusing on the woman's face.

"Wow, really?"

"I'm absolutely sure," Gabriela said, now bringing up the photo of the music box on his phone. "I have a photograph my grandfather gave me just months before he died. It's a close-up of the same lovely woman on a balcony, with a river in the background. In it she's holding this music box. My grandfather told me he took the photo on her birthday. The music box was his gift to her. He told me to keep the photo private so nobody in my family would doubt the love he had for my own grandmother. But the woman in the photo had been, and would forever be, the love of his life. The back of the photo says in Spanish, 'The love of my life. San Antonio River. 1945.' I'll show it to you when we go back to my loft.

"Two other cool things about that photo. One, it was the only picture he took with him to the Philippines. He kept it with him at all times. And, two, have you ever listened to the melody in the music box?"

"I have, but I don't remember it. I was sixteen when I listened to it. The only other time I heard it was when I helped Lilly and her husband move to their new house. I was twenty-two," Sam said.

"The melody is 'Clair de lune.' It was his favorite, and he selected it specially for your grandmother. He knew that the composer, Debussy, was inspired by a poem Paul Verlaine wrote in the latter part of the nineteenth century. 'Clair de lune' began as a love poem, and it became a love song. It meant a lot to him. And it means a lot to me, actually. That's why I know all this.

RAFAEL SILVA

"Along with everything he shared with me about the music box, about how much he'd loved your grandmother, my grandpa told me the day I thought of someone when listening to my favorite song or reading my favorite poem would be the day I knew I was in love." She sighed thoughtfully.

"That's truly amazing, Gaby," Sam said. "I'm still in disbelief. But this means a lot to me. I now have this odd, although good sense of belonging. I feel like I finally have a story, a history behind my life—my happy but very ordinary life. Thank you both for showing me and telling me all this." He pointed at the albums.

"I'm so glad, Sam. It's great that after all these years—even if the circumstances were serendipitous and a little weird for you—we were able to connect. You being here, us thinking about these historical events, pays homage to our grandparents and the love they shared. It's what my grandfather would've wanted. I'm sure."

Mario said, "I actually think this is a case of cause and effect. Gustavo was smart enough to do what he did in orchestrating Sam's bequest. He may have consciously steered and increased the probability that your two families would eventually meet."

"You might be right," Gabriela concurred.

They continued to look through the photo albums. Now feeling completely certain about his grandmother and about his past, Sam particularly enjoyed seeing photographs in which she appeared. He took pictures of the photos so he could show Tony and Lilly when he returned home.

Later that evening, they had a congenial dinner with Gaby's mother.

FIFTEEN

S am had never experienced shopping quite like he did the following morning.

He picked up underwear and socks at El Palacio de Hierro, on the corner of Horacio and Moliere Avenues. There they were offered complimentary espressos and fresh-squeezed grapefruit juice. A few blocks away, he bought shirts and casual pants at the John Varvatos boutique. At this store, in between Sam trying on clothes and Gabriela having a laugh at his poor modeling skills, they enjoyed brunch bowls of frozen acai berries, yogurt, apple cider, and granola also on the house. Then they headed next door to Hugo Boss, where they politely declined any more food but did enjoy Bellinis. There, Sam got a suit and a pair of Adolfo Domínguez shoes he planned to wear for Ari's wedding.

"It looks great on you, Sam," Gabriela said while a tailor pinned the bottom of his pants.

Sam looked at her in the mirror and smiled. She sat behind him on a maroon velvet couch. "I think a suit like this would look good on anyone," he said, briefly holding up the price tag of the Arly/Hattin dark gray suit. He wore the jacket over a black wool long-sleeve shirt. "I've only bought one suit before this—while looking for a job after I finished my military service. It was on sale at the Men's Wearhouse. I paid a hundred and forty-nine dollars for it." He shook his head affably. "The dress code for the job I got was casual, so I never thought I'd ever buy a suit again—definitely not one that's ten times the price of my first one." Sam looked at himself in the mirror. "This does feel nice, though."

"You still don't have to buy one. This one is my treat," she said.

"I can't let you do that, Gaby. I'm really happy to get it myself, especially now that I can totally afford it. I only made those comments because...well, I never thought I'd buy clothes like these. It's kind of strange but cool."

"I knew you would say that. But it's a done deal, Sam. I already gave Gema my card."

"Really? I came here to try to give stuff away to you guys," he said, smiling. "Yet somehow, I keep getting more and more from you and your family—most of which can't be given a price tag."

"Please, Sam. Don't worry. It makes me so happy to do this."

"Apparently, you've left me no choice. So, thank you."

The friendly man doing the tailoring indicated he was finished and invited Sam back into the dressing room.

"Thanks," Sam said to the tailor. Then to Gabriela, he playfully said, "Let me change back into my no-name rags. I'll be right back."

She shook her head and gave him a big smile.

"The suit will be ready tomorrow. We can deliver it anytime between noon and five," Gema, an elegantly dressed woman behind the register, told them as she returned Gabriela's American Express Centurion Card.

While signing the electronic pad, Gaby said, "You can drop it off at the gallery downstairs anytime."

"Great, I'll make a note of that. Thank you both. I hope you continue to have a fun shopping day." She looked at Sam. "I'm sure you'll have a fabulous time wearing this suit at your event."

Gabriela stopped briefly at the Uterqüe store, where she bought two casual tops for herself. Then, before they crossed the street, Sam registered the name of the business on the corner.

"Gaby, wait." He pointed toward the wall flanking the entrance door. A chrome sign read *Berger Joyeros*. "This name sounds familiar—from your grandfather's journal. I'm pretty sure it's the store where he bought the jewelry in 1945."

"Really? This is one of the best jewelry stores in Mexico; I've just never bought anything here. I rarely wear jewelry. Do you want to go in? Maybe we can ask someone if it's the same business from back then."

"That would be awesome. Let's do it," Sam said eagerly.

Inside the luxurious establishment, Gabriela asked a stylish sales representative if he knew anything about the store's history. The cheerful, knowledgeable fellow didn't speak English but invited them toward a far counter, where he began to relay what he knew about his employers. He told them the founder, Alex Elías Berger, had emigrated with his family from Belgium to Mexico in 1943. The sales representative pulled a hardback book from a shelf behind the counter and showed them some pages of photographs that traced the business's history back to 1918 Holland. Gabriela translated to Sam what the sales rep was saying, as well as the photo captions. Then she told the man the reason for their interest.

The young man responded to Gaby in Spanish, and then she translated for Sam. "He says the company's manager is here today, that he is very close to the owners, and would probably love to hear about all this. He's just finished up with a client over there. And he speaks English."

After the friendly introductions to Mr. Ulises Vidal, Sam told the refined and sociable man about Gustavo's jewels. As soon as Sam mentioned Van Cleef & Arpels and 1945, Mr. Vidal's face froze. Wide-eyed, he asked, "Was it a diamond necklace, a pair of matching earrings, and a fabulous engagement ring?"

Sam and Gaby looked at each other incredulously. They nodded.

"My God. I'm astonished. Please, you have to come see something." Ulises Vidal invited them through a door at the showroom's far end. They went up a beautiful marble staircase and into an elegant office. He slid open the cherry wood door of a closet. A small array of filing cabinets came into view. Ulises opened a cabinet drawer and thumbed through some files. He pulled out an old accordion file folder, from which he gently retrieved a small document in a plastic cover. "Do you know a Gustavo E. Martel Lavoignet or Maribel Martel Vega?"

Gabriela put a hand to her mouth. Sam was also taken aback. She said, "They were my grandfather and my first cousin twice removed."

"Here, take a look. This is the store copy of the original receipt." Gabriela and Sam examined the old paper. Ulises then consulted another document in the folder. "It looks like Miss Maribel Martel had been a preferred customer and referred Mr. Gustavo Martel to the store. Because of that, she was to receive a fifteen percent discount on her next purchase." He flipped to a page with a photograph and technical information. "I've worked for the family a long time. They've showed me this before, but I've not seen it for years." Mr. Vidal then offered them the old photograph, which showed the jewelry. They confirmed it was the same set in Sam's possession. He invited them to sit before he continued.

"That jewelry is very special to the owners and everyone who works for this company," Ulises Vidal said. "We all know the story. It was one of ten extremely valuable items the founder, Mr. Alex Elías Berger, along with his wife and grown children, brought with them from Europe in 1943. The other nine included three Chopard necklaces, two Bulgari bracelet and earrings sets, two Cartier diamond rings, and two wristwatches—one a Vacheron Constantin and the other an A. Lange & Söhne.

"When they arrived in Mexico, their plan was to establish the business in New York. But from the moment they set foot here, they fell in love with the city and its people. Alex Berger just wasn't sure how successful they could be. He felt that Mexico was just beginning its transition into modernity and didn't know what demand there would be for high-end jewelry in the city. So he told his family that if, in addition to the jewelry they manufactured themselves, they could also sell the ten special items by the end of 1945, then that would indicate the population could support their business. Your jewelry set was purchased in December of 1945. It was the last of the ten items sold—just in time to meet Alex Berger's self-imposed deadline.

"The sale of these ten special pieces helped provide the capital to establish the original flagship store on Madero Street. The rest, of course, is history. The Bergers now have six locations within the greater metropolitan area. And aside from the family's own label, we carry the most exclusive brands of jewelry and timepieces. Berger Joyeros is among the most successful family-owned jewelers in the world. In a sense, the Berger family fortune was due, in part, to your jewelry."

"I'm in awe," Gabriela said.

"Really fascinating," Sam added.

"Let me amaze you even more. I suspect you're not aware of the jewelry's current value. Based on the specifications I have here, you have just over nine carats of diamonds of the highest quality. Those are all set in twenty-one-karat white gold. I estimate the current value at about one hundred twenty-five thousand US dollars. However, that simply reflects their physical value. They're an authentic Van Cleef & Arpels product. Plus, the set is over seventy years old—vintage and rare. If they're in good condition, at auction, I wouldn't be surprised if they sold at five times that."

"Holy crap!" Sam exclaimed.

"*Holy crap* is right," Mr. Vidal agreed. "I'm so pleased to know they still exist. They reflect my employers' history—and yours as well, I'm sure." To Gabriela, he said, "I'm ecstatic to know they ended up with you. Jewelry this unique was made to shine and dazzle, and to be worn by someone of your exceptional beauty."

"You're too kind. But they're not mine. Although they were intended for someone wonderful and beautiful," Gabriela said with a smile.

They briefly told their grandparents' story to Mr. Vidal. He was enthralled and thankful they shared that with him. He asked if they would bring the jewelry by at some point so he, his staff, and members of the Berger family could take a commemorative photograph with it. Sam and Gaby were happy to oblige and agreed they'd do so later in the week.

Following that pleasant encounter, they headed around the corner to Maque, an international-fare restaurant, for lunch.

Gabriela and Sam were enjoying lunch, still in disbelief over their surprising encounter with Ulises Vidal. About forty-five minutes into their lunch, her phone rang.

Sam didn't understand what she was saying, but she sounded serious. As soon as she finished the call, Gabriela asked him to excuse her for a few minutes. She had to make a few more calls.

He told her to take care of whatever she needed. He was happy to sit back and give her space.

As she continued to talk on the phone, Gabriela seemed articulate and assertive. There was a problem, but she appeared unfazed, and her demeanor suggested a logical thought process.

They were essentially done with lunch. But Sam began to pick at a few unfinished items on his plate. A moment just before, he'd been relaxed and happy to watch Gaby converse on the phone. But suddenly he got a strange chill. He took a sip of water.

Sam felt attracted to her.

Yet it was a strange attraction. There was something more—something he couldn't quite pinpoint. Sam told himself it was probably the same thing anybody would feel in the presence of a woman of such allure and substance.

Fortunately, Gabriela soon finished with her calls. He quickly snapped out of his unexpected introspection.

"I'm sorry, Sam. One of my cousins called to see if I could put him in touch with someone regarding a computer network malfunction at the family's clinics. The entire system went down, and they can't access patients' charts or imaging studies. I've been trying to contact a couple of the IT guys I know from the hospitals I work at. They are familiar with our particular network, but they aren't available at the moment. We're in the process of restructuring our digital systems. So our three senior computer guys who could fix the problem are in Germany. They're getting special training on the new equipment. And the company that installed the old system went out of business a couple of years ago. It's a bit of a disaster.

"I told my cousin our only choice is to bring back one of our guys. The earliest he can be here is tomorrow afternoon, though. In the meantime, we're going to have to shut down some services at the clinics."

"That sounds bad," Sam said. "But I'm pretty sure I can help. Gaby, call your cousin back and tell him to hold on for a bit. Don't yank your guy out of his training course in Germany or close down the clinics just yet."

"Are you sure?"

"Absolutely! That's what I studied in college. As luck would have it, the situation at your clinics is my area of expertise. My job in the military was to set up and maintain computer and communication systems. My first job after the army involved managing the digital radiology systems at Worcester Medical Center," he said. He didn't mention it then, but she later learned that Sam had graduated magna cum laude in computer engineering from Worcester Polytechnic Institute, one of the oldest and best science and engineering universities in the US.

"Sam, you continue to amaze me," she said.

"Don't be too amazed yet. Let me actually fix the problem first," he said lightheartedly.

"Let's hurry over there," she said, signaling the waiter for the bill. She called her cousin back to let him know. Minutes later, they caught a cab to the clinic that housed their main computer servers.

SIXTEEN

Gabriela and her cousin Alberto stood behind Sam as he examined a string of code on a workstation monitor and typed on the keyboard.

"Several problems. The DICOM headers have conflicts, and metadata is missing. AE titles on lab and imaging studies are not parallel. Wavelet compression schemes are not supported. Also, it looks like you use a UNIX backend that hasn't been rebooted."

"That vaguely sounds like English, Sam, but I'm not sure," Gabriela said.

"Oh, I'm sorry. I was mostly talking to myself. You got a psych ward here?" He smiled and swiveled to face them. "It looks like you have systems from three different vendors, and the programs that bind them together got frazzled, so the whole unit went down. But there is hope. I'm just going to reload some patches and reboot the whole thing. This will probably take about thirty minutes. Bear with me for just a bit longer."

"Sam, we'll step away for a bit so we're not breathing down your neck. We'll be in the break room across the hall," Alberto said.

"Sure, I'll let you guys know when this is done," he said.

Gabriela and Alberto left the break room door open so Sam would feel free to come in once he was done. They sat at a table, and reverting to their native Spanish, she told her cousin a little bit about Sam.

"Really? That's nice of him to come all the way here to do that. I kind of like this guy," Alberto said. "And if he can get our computers working again, I'm going to like him even more. How about you? Do you like him? He sure is nicer, better looking, and younger than that prick you're dating."

"I'm not dating Carlos anymore. I never really dated him. We only went out a few times."

"That's not the gossip I heard—something about a weekend at the Hacienda. You can't tell me you went down there with him and didn't have sex. That's dating."

"I hope that's not a question, because I'm not telling you about my sex life," she said, half smiling, half in disbelief.

"That means you did. Gaby, that's gross. He must be at least twenty years older than you."

"Alberto, it's none of your business. Besides, he's not a prick. He is smart and sophisticated."

"Good, at least you didn't say you loved him. We wish Carlos would just disappear," Alberto joked.

"Very funny! By the way, who is *we*?" Gabriela asked.

"*We* is the whole family. Even Aunt Olivia. Nobody likes the guy. He walks around like he owns everything and everyone." Alberto nodded in Sam's direction. "I think you should look at Sam a little closer. I've only known him a few minutes, but I have a good feeling about him."

"All right, all right. Just shut up. I don't want Sam to hear your idiotic comments," she told him.

"I thought Sam didn't understand Spanish."

"He doesn't. But we're talking behind his back. I don't like that," she said.

"Gaby, I'm not talking about Sam as much as I'm talking about your abysmal taste in men. I don't get it. *We* think that *you* think men are intimidated by you, and that's why you get involved with these high-profile assholes. But there are plenty of men who'd love a smart and independent woman. I mean, look at you—you can have anyone you want. Can't you see that?"

"Beto, this is neither the time nor the place. Besides, what if I don't want a relationship, much less to be married? Lately everybody has an opinion about who I should or should not be seeing. What if I want to be independent and free and have meaningless sex for the rest of my life? What's wrong with that?"

"Fine, fine. I know. It's just that I hardly get to see you anymore, and, well, I love you. We all love you. We want you to be happy," he said.

"I'm plenty happy. I have everything anyone could possibly want. Please don't worry about me," she said, a hint of uncertainty in her mind.

Gabriela tacitly considered that her cousin might have a point. Maybe she didn't have everything. Maybe something was missing. Perhaps she'd dated people she knew would only be temporary. Perhaps love was impractical in her life. Or perhaps she just didn't know what love truly was. How could she ever know?

As she pondered these uncertainties, she found solace in her grandfather's assertion: maybe she'd know she was in love when she found herself thinking about someone in particular while listening to her favorite song or reading her favorite poem.

Slightly flustered, she stood. "We should go see how Sam is doing."

"Sorry, Gaby. I didn't mean to be an ass. I still think of you as the baby of our generation. I often forget you're all grown up," Alberto said, coming around and giving her a hug. "I'll leave the unsolicited advice to Uncle David and Aunt Olivia. As far as I'm concerned, you can be a spinster if you wish."

She playfully punched him in the arm. "I love you too. I know you mean well." She kissed him on the cheek. "Surprisingly, Dad doesn't say much anymore. He just lets me be. Mom, of course, continues to speak her mind. She spews loving criticism at every turn."

They decided to rejoin Sam in the server room just as he was finishing up with the job.

Then the three of them walked around the clinic to test the network at various computer stations. Gabriela, Alberto, and other staff members were overjoyed to learn the system was up and functional. Some thought it appeared to be even faster than before it had gone down. They went into a small, high-tech conference room and telecommunicated with people at other clinics to verify the computers were back up and operational there. Indeed, the problem had been solved system-wide.

Sam learned the Martel family owned these clinics, which essentially were small hospitals. Four were located within Greater Mexico City. One was in Xalapa, Veracruz, and a sixth was in Monterrey, in the northern state of Nuevo León. Alberto explained that their clinics were born out of a generations-old family tradition of providing care to people in their communities. He told Sam that initially, the clinics had been dependent on other arms of the family's business. But now they were self-sufficient and profitable. Over time, the clinics had become well known for their high standards of care—to the point where the most affluent coveted their services. They'd figured out a way to harness that demand and allocate capital so they could expand their services to people of lesser means.

"So you overcharge the rich to help provide services to the poor?" Sam asked, boiling down the concept.

Alberto laughed and said, "Well, not quite overcharge. Rather, I'd say, fully charge. But, yes, something like that."

"It seems like a win-win for all involved," Sam said.

They spent three hours at the clinic. Before leaving, Alberto told Sam he felt offering him payment for his expertise and timely help would be crass. Instead, he wanted to invite him to meet his family and enjoy dinner with them that evening. Sam and Gaby gladly accepted the invitation. She told Sam that Alberto was not only a fine gastroenterologist but, when teamed up with his wife, a serious culinary force.

Alberto drove Gaby and Sam to his house. While in the south-side district of Coyoacán, they stopped at the Green Corner, a well-stocked market offering organic products. The three of them had a fun time gathering several items for the dinner Alberto and his wife had planned.

At Alberto's home, Sam met his wife and their two children. He got a tour of yet another posh and spacious residence. Sam had thought to help prepare the meal. However, Alberto's ten-year-old son had determined he would be a worthy opponent and challenged him to a *Madden NFL* bout on Xbox. Nearly an hour later, Gabriela and Alberto peeked in on the game and told them dinner was ready, thereby rescuing Sam from a virtual shellacking.

Tony also frequently beat Sam at *Madden*. However, he'd never considered himself all that bad at the game. Clearly, though, his skills were no match for Alberto's son.

"Did you let him win?" Gabriela asked Sam as they went to the dining room.

"I wish! This kid is a phenom," he said with a smile.

Over a beet and cucumber salad, the boy excitedly told everyone that, like him, Sam had also played linebacker and wide receiver in school. He invited Sam to his football game that coming Sunday afternoon but was disappointed to learn Sam would be flying home that day. Sam did, however, agree to throw a football around after dinner.

Dinner was fabulous. They had sautéed monkfish topped with a mushroom gravy, parsnip puree, and roasted carrots.

Alberto leaned over to top off Sam's wineglass. "Sam, I'm so thankful you saved the day for us. But I was wondering, how is it you're currently a barber while you have a computer engineering degree? You're obviously good at the computer bit."

"Thank you," Sam said, acknowledging both the fine chenin blanc and Alberto's compliment. "It's a bit of a long story."

Taking a sip of her wine, Gabriela said, "We're all ears."

"It was a combination of factors. All started in high school," Sam began. "I wanted to go to college but didn't have money to pay for it. Luckily, I did well academically and was fortunate a really amazing teacher helped me. Not just me, actually; she also helped other students. She had contacts at three colleges in Worcester and knew about available scholarships. So we brainstormed paths that would allow me to go to school while avoiding the painful route of getting a job, going part-time to community college, and hoping to eventually transfer to a bachelor's degree program.

"There was a tech company offering specific scholarships at Worcester Polytechnic Institute. I fit all their requisites. All I had to do was get into the school; choose a major in computer, electrical, or robotics engineering; and maintain a high GPA. I got accepted to WPI and got that scholarship. But it only covered about half of what I needed for tuition, room and board, and books. My only other option was to join the military, which, contrary to popular belief, does not entirely pay for college. I signed up for a program that allowed me to pay for the remainder of my college expenses in exchange for four years of service after.

"As Gaby knows, I grew up with my friend Tony. For all practical purposes, he's my brother. He's all heart and very smart in many ways. But a formal education wasn't quite for him. When I went to college, he got a job at a towing company and also got gigs plowing snow in winter. Our plan was for him to do that while I was in school. Once I finished, he'd also sign up for the military.

"I knew that with my degree I'd be a shoo-in for the army's Communications-Electronics Command. In this department, officers often got to choose their posts, especially if these were in active conflict areas—where Tony would surely be sent. Nothing was definite, but we hoped we'd end up deployed to the same places or at least close to each other.

"A few weeks after my college graduation, Tony had signed up for the army. When he went in for his physical, they reviewed his medical records and rejected him. Tony had had one of his kidneys removed as a child. Neither of us knew at the time, but that made him ineligible for the military."

"Why did he have the nephrectomy?" Alberto asked.

"At the time, we didn't know. Despite the scar on his side, Tony hadn't known he was missing a kidney. Neither his caseworker nor his initial foster parents passed that information on to our foster parents when he joined us. Several foster parents and caseworkers later, any pertinent information became further diluted.

"We asked the foster care system office and eventually looked into his medical records. By the way, Tony is okay with me sharing his story with friends. He does it all the time," Sam assured them. "When he was three, his mother had been in and out of a drug camp near Springfield. This is where junkies go to shoot up and live. According to some documents, his mom had left him there one day 'in the care of' other addicts. A few days later, he got sick. Luckily, those junkies had the forethought to call an ambulance, and after an initial evaluation at a local hospital, he ended up transferred to UMass Children's Hospital. The police and social services investigated and got statements from these junkies and others at the drug camp. Other than that, we have no record or any information about Tony's parents. His mother never turned up.

"At UMass, they discovered he had a tumor in his kidney. Apparently, it had bled, which had made him sick."

"Probably a Wilms' tumor," Gabriela said.

"Yes, that's what it was," Sam said. "I'm sure you know it was a cancer. They had to remove his kidney, and apparently he got some chemotherapy. Fortunately, it never spread. Whether it was the surgery or the chemo or both, he got cured. But the tumor came back to haunt him after all—it kept him out of the military. This hampered our plan. And worse, it destroyed his dream.

"I then went away to fulfill my service. As much as I tried to keep in touch with him and as much as my sister tried to be there for him, Tony fell into a horrible depression. He got involved with the wrong crowd and even got arrested for petty things a couple of times. Basically, he had it bad for a while.

"After the military, I thought the best way to help Tony would be to get a decent job and get settled. I started managing the radiology computer system at Saint Vincent Hospital. I rented a nice apartment and bought a car. Tony came to live with me, and we began to work on a variety of things to get him going in a better direction. But he continued to have problems coping. He just couldn't hold down a job. After a couple of years of ups and downs, he decided to go to barber school. As much as he tried, though, Tony just couldn't concentrate enough to do it on his own.

"I realized that learning a trade was probably the best thing for him. The money was decent, and he wouldn't have to deal with too much work politics. But I also realized I'd have to be by his side to get him through it.

"So, I quit my job. We moved to a less expensive apartment, and we both enrolled in barber school. I sold my car, and with that money—along with some of my savings—we paid for school and also had enough to start the business about ten months later. It has worked out great. Tony has been completely stable since. I do some IT jobs on the side, and we've made do pretty comfortably. That's how I became a barber and added to my skill set," Sam told them with a forthright smile.

"Just like that? You gave up your apartment, your car, your job, and possibly a career for your friend?" Alberto's wife asked.

"Yes. I did what I thought was best and what Tony would've done for me if our roles had been reversed," Sam replied.

"That's real friendship. It's amazing," Alberto said.

"That's love," Gabriela added, looking warmly at Sam.

"Yes, and definitely mutual. Like I said, Tony is all heart. If my or Lilly's well-being depended on him giving up everything he owned, he'd do it—no questions asked."

"I'm glad you guys have that kind of relationship," Gaby said.

Later on, Sam played with Alberto's son in their large and lush backyard. For a few minutes, Gabriela joined them. Sam taught her how to throw a football. A couple of times, he gently sandwiched her hand between his and the ball's leather surface. They interlocked fingers as he demonstrated how the laces would allow her to spin the ball. She eventually threw a few short passes, which the agile boy easily caught. With Alberto, his wife, and their daughter watching, they all had plenty of laughs.

Gabriela and Sam, once again, each perceived but consciously overlooked that peculiar yet comfortable feeling their mutual touch evoked.

Back in Gabriela's apartment that night, they thanked each other for a wonderful day and bid each other good night. Sam walked toward the guest suite. She headed toward the stairs to her bedroom but then swiftly turned around.

"Sam?"

He turned at the sound of her voice.

"Few people surprise me," Gabriela told him, her eyes shimmering in the subdued lighting. "Again, good night," she added with a gentle wave.

He thought about returning the compliment but found himself unable to get any words out. It all happened so quickly. He simply smiled and barely managed to wave back.

With nothing more said, both headed to their respective bedrooms and turned in for the night.

SEVENTEEN

Sam had truly enjoyed his trip. It came to what seemed an abrupt end on Sunday afternoon. He wished he could've stayed longer. But there was no plausible reason. As he sat on the jetliner heading back to San Antonio, many instances from the last few days flashed through his mind.

He thought of the day Mario invited him to attend a soccer game at Azteca Stadium. Mario had only had one spare ticket, and the game was sold out. Gabriela had been happy to stay behind so Sam could have that experience. During the soccer game, her family's affluence had come up. Mario told Sam that despite their immense wealth, and except for the inevitable handful of oddball relatives, her family was modest, generous, and exceptionally hardworking. Mario shared that he'd been one of their countless beneficiaries. His mother had been a cook and maid at Gustavo's house. But all the children of those who worked personally for the family had been offered the opportunity to attend the same schools the Martel children attended—at no cost. To this day, he'd been treated like family. In fact, he told Sam, the current CEO of the main corporation heading the Martel family's diverse enterprises wasn't even a family member. It was Don Lauro's daughter. She'd had an aptitude for mathematics and business, which Gabriela's father had noticed and nurtured. Following her college degree from Mexico's ITAM and a Stanford MBA, this girl of modest roots, her father a gatekeeper, became the head of a family's billion-dollar conglomerate.

Three other key moments, in particular, also stood out in Sam's mind.

If only he could have taken a photograph. Instead, he'd have to rely on his memory to remember each seconds-long episode: First, when he initially saw Gabriela in her hospital office. Second, when he was stunned by her walking down from her bedroom in a cocktail dress and heels—wearing Gustavo's dazzling diamond necklace and earrings. Sam had insisted she wear the jewelry to Ari's wedding. And third, when he took one last glance at Gabriela in the airport waving goodbye through the crowd on the other side of the security scanners.

He'd shelve these memories along with all the good ones in his mind, he told himself, hoping to rationalize his feelings. *I guess that's that,* he thought as the wheels touched down in the Alamo City.

After dinner that evening, Sam sat on his hotel room's balcony, which faced the beautifully lit River Walk. He dialed Tony and told him every detail of his trip.

As Sam talked, Tony quickly sensed the magnitude of the brief adventure. He abstained from his standard brassy comments and chintzy jokes. Sam's account fascinated him.

"So do you know the whole story of Gustavo and your grandma?"

"I do now. Gaby and I spent last Thursday and Friday evening reading the rest of his journal. I'd love to tell you about it now, but it's getting late. I have to get up early to go see Lena Sander. Besides, I want Lilly to hear it too. I'll tell you guys the details next time we go to her house."

"No problem, Sammy. I'll pick you up tomorrow. Delta, right?"

"Yes. Eight o'clock," Sam said.

"Got it," Tony replied. A few silent seconds followed. "Hey, Sam, can I ask you a question?"

"Sure."

"Did you have sex with Gabrielle?"

Tony's question disconcerted Sam. Not so much the content, but the way he phrased it. He would've expected Tony to say something more along the lines of *Did you bang the chick?* Sam didn't know what to make of it, so he simply answered, "There it is! A typical Tony comment. By the way, it's not Gabrielle. It's Gabriela. Call her Gaby. And no, I did not sleep with her."

"Uh-huh. Did you want to sleep with her, though?"

"No," he said. "I didn't."

"I see. All right, Sammy. Have a good night and a good flight."

They got off the phone. That last question showed insight on Tony's part. More importantly, Sam's own keen and honest response dawned on him. He'd never seen or interacted with a beautiful woman without feeling, at least briefly, some cursory sexual attraction.

Why didn't he immediately feel that with Gabriela? Sam wondered introspectively. Instead, why did the simple thought of holding her hand make him jittery? Why did the notion of kissing her propel him into a trance of trepidation and delight? Worse, why was he even thinking about holding her hand and kissing her at all?

The trip and Gabriela in the past now, Sam couldn't allow himself to ponder these things. Yet he sensed the fleeting possibility that love—a hitherto abstract thing in his life, at least in the romantic sense—was the underlying meaning of his uncertainties. It was unnerving. It was also practically impossible. For the sake of self-preservation, he had to deflect, or at least try to deflect, further speculation.

Aside from that, Sam told himself, he would remember everything else fondly. He would remember *her*, fondly.

EIGHTEEN

"You knew more about the Martels than you let on, didn't you?" Sam asked Lena the following morning.

With a smile and a cognizant expression, she essentially conceded this.

"I was also going to ask if you sent me there because you knew they were so wealthy they wouldn't have cared about the money," Sam said. "But now that I've come to know them, I'm sure they rejected everything on principle. They all referred to the fact that Gustavo intended the gifts for me, and left it at that."

"Actually, you sent yourself there. I'm glad you did, though, and I'm pleased you got to know them. They are admirable people. Because of that, yes, I did have an inkling about how they might respond."

For a while that morning, they went over all the documents necessary to transfer possession of the house and the trust fund to Sam. Lena matter-of-factly asked him if he'd made any plans for his new assets. He told her that he had thought about a few things that could positively impact his life in the short run, like paying off some minor debt. But that he was probably going to leave it at Frost Bank for a while, leisurely consult a financial adviser, and be certain to make the most of it for himself and for his family in the long run. And about the house, he said he'd probably rent it but expressed his intention to keep it.

"With business out of the way, now the only thing left is to make sure you enjoy some true Mexican food. Nine days in

Mexico City notwithstanding, I suspect you had none there—at least not the kind we're used to."

"I did have enchiladas suizas at one restaurant. But come to think about it, you are right, there were no burritos or nachos in sight. Everything else I ate was so, I don't know, international. All delicious, though."

"They do have restaurants that dole out fabulous traditional Mexican food. However, in my experience, traditional cuisine is as much of a treat to the people there as it is common for us here. So, let's go to this lovely place called Rosario's, a San Antonio institution offering the best Mexican dishes you'll ever have. After that, Ruben can take you to the airport."

Following lunch, Sam had plenty of time before his flight home. He asked Ruben to drive him to the house by the river. He took several photographs of the interior, as well as of the exterior surroundings. He wanted to show the folks back in Worcester. Sam also tried to capture the site where his grandmother had held the music box, with the river in the background.

Returning to the car, he asked Ruben if he could sit up front, since he felt odd sitting in the back. Ruben said of course, and Sam settled in the Suburban's front seat. After closing the car door, he took one last glance at the house.

Sam finally accepted that this once bizarre affair was real. And that the beautiful home getting smaller in his side view mirror, along with its special history, now legitimately belonged to him.

NINETEEN

"What are you all doing here?" Sam asked, stooping to hug his two nieces. Lilly; her husband, Leonard; and Tony were at the Providence airport waiting for him.

"Just showing you some family love, man," Tony said. "Plus, Lilly had to see for herself. She didn't trust that I was picking you up. She also doesn't believe I don't know much about your trip, aside from you visiting a friend in Texas. She thought I was coming to bail you out of jail." Tony winked at Lilly.

"What am I supposed to think? Last week Tony told me you were on a you-know-what kind of bender with some woman in Cranston. Then I get this strange call from you, telling me you're in Mexico. And now, something about a friend in Texas? I've just been worried sick about you, Sam. Tony wouldn't tell me anything else."

"I told you, I don't know anything!" Tony exclaimed with a crooked grin.

"Yeah, right! I know how you two characters operate," Lilly said.

"I guess you got some esplainin' to do, bro." Leonard gave Sam a welcoming hug.

"There's much to explain. When I'm all done, you guys probably won't believe it. For now, let's get out of here, shall we?"

"Uncle Sammy, can I ride on your shoulders?" Lilly's six-year-old daughter asked.

"Of course, come here." He lifted her with a quick swoop. "I'm sure your dad or uncle Tony can grab my bag."

They strolled toward the exit. The four-year-old sibling wasn't going to be outdone by her sister. She motioned to Tony, who lifted her onto his shoulders. Leonard grabbed Sam's carry-on roller.

"What's with the fancy Bottega Veneta suitcase? The spelling seems right. It don't look like a knockoff," Leonard said.

Perhaps trying to entice Sam to start recounting the details of his adventure, Tony added, "That's right. What's up with that? You left here with a backpack."

As the three walked side by side behind Lilly, Sam said, "Definitely not a knockoff. I wasn't expecting to stay as long as I did, so I had to buy some clothes. At the last minute, when it was time to come back, I realized I didn't have anything to pack them in. So, I borrowed the suitcase—at least I think I borrowed it. It was just offered to me. It may have been a gift."

"A gift from your friend in Texas?" Leonard asked.

"No, from my friend in Mexico," Sam said.

"Huh? I'm confused."

"I'll tell you guys about it later."

They negotiated their way out of the crowds. The two girls towered above, giggling and ecstatic to be looking down at everyone.

Once they left the airport, Lilly weighed in on the matter of the suitcase. "A Bottega Veneta handbag is at least a couple of grand. A suitcase like that? Probably twice as much. So, if that roller isn't a knockoff, it sure ain't a gift. Nobody gives away things like that."

As they approached the parking lot, Sam said, "Ten days ago, I probably would've agreed with you, Lills. Now, I know there are exceptions. Whether the roller is a loan or a gift, it comes from one of those exceptions."

"I guess if you're super rich, you could give stuff like that away. But it's all relative. Maybe the people who end up with the things we donate to Goodwill or at the shelters think the same about us," Lilly said.

Standing near the van and watching Lilly and Leonard strap the girls into their respective car seats, Sam responded, "You're right. Someone recently told me about the value of big gifts and small gifts." He was remembering the anecdote about Landon Taylor. "When we take food or new socks to the shelter, we give them sincerely and wholeheartedly. I'm pretty sure my friend offered me the suitcase with the same honest intention. So, the 'value' of those socks from Walmart and this designer luggage is the same. It makes sense to me now. I just wouldn't have given it a second thought before."

"Before what, Sam?" Lilly asked. "Something tells me it's not about the suitcase, which, by the way, I'm still betting is a knock-off. You sure don't have friends who can spend a month's salary on luggage. Come on, where exactly did you go, and what have you been doing for a week?"

"Uh-oh. You better spill, Sam. Or else face the wrath of Lilly," Leonard said.

"Yeah, dude. Lenny speaks from experience. You know he lives in constant fear of that," Tony said in jest.

"Zip it, Tony! You're still in the doghouse for keeping me in the dark," Lilly said, looking back from the passenger seat, pointing an accusatory finger at him, and sporting a mock frown.

"Since our dogs don't actually live in doghouses, I guess I'm all right," Tony retorted.

Everyone laughed.

"I definitely want to tell you guys everything," Sam said. "It's an amazing story, but kind of long. So I wanted to wait until next weekend. Maybe Saturday evening. And if we happen to stay up late talking about it, we'll still have Sunday to rest and take in what it means to all of us."

"Well, *that* sounds mysterious! It seems to me you just want time to make up a good story. Why can't you tell us now? At least some of it," Lilly said.

"Trust me, I'm not making anything up. I just don't want to piecemeal it to you guys; it's so special to me, I honestly think it would be best to tell you everything in one sitting. And, Lills, I promise this will be very special to you too. I want to do justice to what I've learned and to the people I've met in the last few days."

"Fine, fine. Just answer me two things. Are you in any kind of trouble?"

"Apparently I'm in trouble with you." Sam smiled broadly at Lilly. "No, I'm not in any trouble. In fact, the opposite."

"Good. I'm glad. Okay, two: Has Tony known about this all along?"

Sam and Tony looked as if they'd been caught with their hands in the cookie jar. Then Leonard, in the highest pitch he could manage, said, *"Michael, is it true?"* He transitioned into a firm, lower voice. *"Don't ask me about my business, Kay."*

Tony immediately caught on, and in a half scream, said, *"Enough!"*

Sam laughed and said, *"All right. This one time…this one time, I'll let you ask me about my affairs."*

"Is it true? Is it?" Leonard said again in the same feminine voice.

Tony whispered to the girls. Then, in unison, the girls, Tony, and Sam, yelled, *"Nooooooo!"*

Lilly couldn't help but laugh. "I don't want to know," she said, shaking her head.

"Honey, really? Nothing?" Leonard said. "It's the scene from *The Godfather* when Kay asks Michael if he had Fredo, his own brother, killed. Even though he did, he firmly says no. It's the manly thing—and only thing—to say to your innocent wife."

"I can't believe you three. You're all punks," Lilly said. She looked at Sam and said, "So, Mr. Godfather, is *that* gonna be your answer?"

"Say no, Michael Corleone, say no!" Tony implored.

Sam turned to Tony, a defeated look in his eyes. "We are busted, man."

"Dude! You are a disgrace to Michael Corleone and Vito Andolini. I don't know you."

"I knew it!" Lilly told them with satisfaction.

"He told me not to say anything," Tony said, then turned to Sam. "Man, aren't you going to defend me?"

"You're the one who put me up to this," Sam replied, grinning.

"Ouch! That's cold. And by that, I mean the industrial-sized knife deep between my shoulder blades. We'll see who helps you out next time you need to put a body in the trunk," Tony said, flinging one of the girls' sippy cups at Sam.

"All right, you two," Lilly said. "Funny business aside, we ain't waiting five days for you to tell us about this covert trip. If your little affair is special to me too, and somehow has to do with all of us, it must be worth staying up for."

"It would take a while, and it's already late. Don't you guys have stuff to do tomorrow?"

"I have tomorrow off, actually," Leonard replied.

"How complicated can it be? Besides, it's summer vacation for the girls, so I'm good," Lilly said. "It looks like you two are spending the night."

"Fine with me too. Lisa was going to open the shop in the morning anyway. I'll join her in the afternoon," Tony said.

"All right, if you people are okay with it. Lenny, let's stop by the apartment to pick up Vin and Nic, though," Sam said. "You still have litter for Vin at your house, right?"

"Yes, plenty of it," Lilly answered.

During the remainder of their ride back to Worcester, Sam began his account. But Tony excitedly interrupted and took over the initial part of the story. He told Leonard and Lilly about the law firm's letter. At one point, Lilly exclaimed, "Oh my God, Sam. Please tell me you weren't dumb enough to go there because of that letter."

"That sounds like an African prince scam only old people fall for," Leonard said, his eyes on the road.

"Relax, you two. Just let Tony finish. I'll warn you: you're both going to have tons of similar questions as we tell you all this. So don't fret, just go with it and listen."

Tony told them he'd made sure everything was legitimate before sending Sam on this quest. He was particularly proud of having salvaged the letter and of impersonating Sam when first contacting Lena Sander. Finally, Tony told them how he'd managed to get Sam to go.

Then it was Sam's turn. He shared his experience at the airport's USO lounge, described his hotel in San Antonio, and told them about his encounter with Lena Sander.

"A key?" Lilly and Leonard asked simultaneously.

Before reaching their apartment, Sam discussed the events and interactions at Frost Bank, just getting to the part about the off-site vault. Lilly and Leonard were enthralled.

"Hurry up and get the pets. This is getting good," Leonard told them. Their girls were still happily lost in the world of cartoon games on their bargain-priced tablets.

Sam and Tony went up to their place. Sam took the suitcase up with him but retrieved his backpack from within. They put a placid Vin in his carrier, harnessed an excitable Nic, and quickly grabbed what they needed to spend the night at Lilly's.

TWENTY

eonard and Tony brewed a large pot of coffee and prepared sandwiches. Sam took care of the pets and then set out chips and cookies. Once the girls had gone to bed, they sat comfortably in Lilly's living room.

"So you went to this vault. Whatcha find in there? A treasure beyond your wildest imagination?" Leonard asked facetiously yet eagerly.

Sam smiled. "Actually, yes. Pretty much."

"Really? Are you going to tell us you found gold bars or something?" Lilly said lightheartedly, although she looked doubtful.

"I've been thinking about how best to tell you guys this," Sam said, grabbing his backpack. "There is a 'gold bar' element to what I found in the safe-deposit box. But the real treasure is in the story—in the history and the people behind it." He pulled out the jewelry and the old Fendi leather-bound journal. "Initially, I thought I'd just tell you the story before showing you this. But without some tangible context, I might lose you. This is the first thing I saw in the vault. Here." Sam handed the Van Cleef & Arpels case to Leonard.

"Holy crap, Sam. Are these for real?" Leonard exclaimed, examining the diamond jewelry.

"Hand that over!" Lilly demanded.

"Impatient much?" Tony said, extending his hand toward Leonard. "You gotta wait your turn, Lills. I'm next." He took a look at them. "Sam, did you find out how much these are worth?"

Sam smiled. "Does it really matter, Tony?"

Knowing the rest of the bequest, Tony replied, "Yeah, you're right. It doesn't."

"How come it doesn't matter?" Leonard asked, incredulous. "Are they fake?"

Tony passed the set to Lilly.

As soon as she saw the lustrous jewels, Lilly gasped, her right hand instinctively nestled on her chest. "These are gorgeous—and real. Aren't they?" She looked at Sam.

"They are," Sam answered.

"Really? Sam, I know you want to tell us a story and all, but I'm really curious to know how much they're worth," Leonard said and looked at Tony, hoping he would agree.

Tony turned to Sam, indicating it was up to him. Sam just patiently looked at Lilly.

She was contemplating the jewels again, absorbed. "These must be related to the music box. They have to be." She lightly touched her lips. Pensive, she continued, "You said the key to the bank box was from 1945? These could not belong to our parents. The timing doesn't make sense. And as far as we know, they were pretty poor. But I don't know. I feel some kind of connection. It's weird. Sam, did these belong to some relative?"

"Yes! Well, more specifically, they were meant to belong to our grandmother on our mother's side." He leaned back on the couch. "It's amazing. You know, it just occurred to me our grandmother never wore those. If she had, Lilly and I probably wouldn't exist."

"What?" Leonard exclaimed.

"Wow. That's right," Tony concurred. "That's wild."

Lilly looked at Tony and Sam quizzically.

"All right, I think this is a good time to tell you guys how much the jewels are worth. But after I do, hold your comments until I finish the whole story. I'm sure in the end you'll understand where the real treasure lies."

The three were stunned, speechless. Observing their deer-in-headlights expressions, Sam felt better telling them about Gustavo and his grandmother's story before revealing the remainder of the bequest. Judging from his family's response to the jewels, he surmised the shock of knowing about the house and the trust fund would most likely impair—at least temporarily—their ability to assimilate the subjective value of everything else he wanted them to know. As he'd previously done himself, Sam knew they would immediately envision ways the funds could be used. He was fine with that, as he'd already thought to share and utilize the assets for everyone's benefit. But there would be plenty of time for that later.

Picking the story back up, Sam undid the brass snap on the leather flap and opened the journal. He grabbed Gustavo's letter with one hand.

"Look. These are the other two things I found in the safe-deposit box. These tell an extraordinary tale—one that has already changed my perspective on life. I hope it has a similar effect on you three." He thumbed through the notebook, opened it to one of the sections he'd previously marked with sticky notes, and then set it on his lap. He lightly waved the old envelope in front of him. "This letter summarizes things. After I read it, I thought this was a case of mistaken identity. But after everything that happened later, and after fully reading this journal, I came to terms with the fact that *we* are truly part of this account. And that by keeping the people and events on these pages in our minds, we'll keep this story going."

"That sounds poetic," Leonard said.

"Hon, shut up. Go on, Sam," Lilly said.

"Definitely poetic, Lenny. This journal belonged to a remarkable individual—a young doctor. He was a medical officer in a little-known, unique air force unit that fought in the Pacific during World War II. His original entries are in Spanish. They span from the summer of 1944 to the winter of 1945. Before leaving this for me, before locking it up for about seventy years, he translated his entries and arranged them in narrative form so I'd understand them."

"I know I almost slapped Lenny for interrupting. But why are you saying he wrote to *you?* That doesn't make sense," Lilly said.

"Believe it or not, he did leave these for me—specifically. Everything will make sense in the end, trust me," he assured his sister. "Rather than paraphrasing what's in these pages, I'm going to read a number of excerpts exactly the way he wrote them. I think the passages I've chosen will sufficiently convey the story. After that, I'll read you this letter. And finally, I'll tell you about where I've been and who I've met in the last few days."

He tucked the old envelope in the notebook. "So, without further ado, hear these words and help me keep this story... these people...alive."

Sam began to read.

TWENTY-ONE

24 July 1944

We parked ten blocks from the train station. My father was too practical to have done it any other way. He thought attempting to get any closer would prove too chaotic. At least that was his argument.

He'd insisted my mother and siblings bid me goodbye at home. I knew this was my father's way of spending a few minutes alone with me. Once he turned off the motor, he glanced at me and pointed to the glove compartment. Then he looked emptily ahead. I opened the glove compartment and retrieved a small box. A parting gift.

I smiled broadly when I saw the contents and adjusted the Omega Marine watch on my wrist. My father told me about the instrument's new water-resistant technology. Then, with hand extended, he declared his intention to keep my old timepiece safe until my return. As I handed him my old wristwatch, he gripped my palm and fingers for a brief moment. It was his silent, unemotional way of telling me what I already knew, what I've always known: he wished me the best, he would miss me, he was proud, and he loved me. We acknowledged this with a mutual glance and a nod.

As I got onto the sidewalk, he pulled my packs from the back seat. With the large duffel by his feet, he motioned so I'd turn around. My father helped me strap my smaller rucksack on my back.

No hello or goodbye from my father ever came without instruction or sermon. When I turned to face him once again, in a resolute voice, he offered me simple advice. He reminded me I was not only an officer but a surgeon. Above all, my job was to save the lives and preserve the function of those under my care—whether it be the brave soldiers wearing identical patches as those sewn on my shoulders or anyone else, friend or foe, in need. That for them, from this moment forward, I needed to be strong and focused.

With his words echoing in my ears, I lifted my large duffel and walked away without turning back. Knowing my father, I'm sure that's what he wanted.

I headed north on Insurgentes Avenue. My father had been right. About five blocks from the Buenavista Station, traffic was at a standstill. A gradually increasing number of people walked on the streets and sidewalks, all going in the same direction. A few minutes later, I saw the station about a block ahead. But the mass of people obstructed the way. I excused myself as I tried to weave through the crowd. A small group noticed me. Pointing at my uniform, they asked if I was a member of the 201st. As soon as I answered affirmatively, they began to shout at the crowd, imploring others to clear a path. And so, people did. The multitude in front of me parted.

Some people in close proximity shouted cheers and praise. I waved, smiled, and thanked them in return. As I passed by, I occasionally felt tugs on my rucksack. I realized folks were tying small bags of food, candy, cigarettes, and even flowers to my straps. Once I reached the train station, the guards looked at my rucksack and smiled. It was barely visible beneath all the small gifts attached to it. These items were tokens of love and respect from my fellow citizens—the men, women, and children of all ages and walks of life who'd come to see the 201st off to war.

I later discovered at least a dozen other squadron members had passed through similar masses of humanity trying to reach the station's gates. They'd also experienced the same warm outpouring of sentiment and gift-giving from the crowd.

Only a few family members, some pertinent dignitaries, and a few civilian passengers were allowed at the official ceremony that took place just prior to boarding the Laredo-bound train. We all took our places in our official military formation. The aviators and commanding officers stood in the forward rows. I stood at the rear along with the other nonoperational officers. The remainder of the squadron filled the ranks in between.

Several politicians gave speeches from a podium in front. It was another example of Mexico's pride over knowing the 201st would officially enter the war. We felt it. The whole country felt it.

I momentarily disconnected from the voices coming out of the loudspeakers and looked in front of me. My squadron was filled with young, intelligent, fearless men eager to help bring down the Nazis. Just a month prior, the massive D-Day landing had taken place at Normandy. The Americans and British had led that incredible offensive. But we all knew about the ten other countries—from Australia and New Zealand to Canada and Poland—who had provided large units in the massive operation. We knew that soon our small contingent would have the privilege to take part in similar operations.

My fellow soldiers' uniforms displayed various insignias. We were emblazoned with the tricolor of our flag on one shoulder, our squadron's patch on the opposite shoulder, brass depictions of the eagle and serpent on our belt buckles and our hats, and the American military's white stars-and-stripes emblem on our forearms.

We all felt honored to wear those identifying articles and to be part of this unit. Perhaps we would help in the struggle to liberate Paris, Brussels, or Amsterdam—in the same way Rome had been liberated from the Fascists. Perhaps we would get to assist in the surely difficult undertaking of invading Berlin. Perhaps in doing so—in doing anything required of us after these speeches were done and our pilots began to fly—we would help prevent the horrors of war from reaching any more innocent people around the world. And, ultimately, keep such horrors away from Mexico.

I looked at the dark green train cars emblazoned with *Ferrocarriles Nacionales de México*—the National Railways of Mexico. These train cars provided the backdrop to the stage and podium before us. Yet they also stood ready to take us away—on the first leg of our voyage into territories unknown.

Turning again to my fellow soldiers' faces in profile, I briefly quivered. I was suddenly overcome by the reality of our circumstances. My father's words returned to me. I became cognizant that once we reached whatever battleground we were meant for, the lives and physical well-being of these men, and perhaps those from other allied units, would be my responsibility.

It has now been over four hours since we left the capital. Earlier, through the train windows, Mexico City's dwellers flanked the tracks for many kilometers to wave goodbye to us. But the previous euphoria has mostly subsided. A lot of the kindly received food and sweets have been consumed. Cigarette smoke permeates our cabin. Most of the men now rest quietly. Some are engrossed in card games. The setting sun's crimson light shines on a few faces. A few read newspapers or comic books. And now tired, I write the last few lines of my first journal entry.

My brother packed me four books: *Los de abajo* by Mariano Azuela González, *The Promise* by Pearl S. Buck, *Belle de jour* by Joseph Kessel, and Arthur Conan Doyle's *Complete Sherlock Holmes Short Stories*. I thought I'd start with Sherlock Holmes to clear my mind and perhaps soon welcome sleep. We have nearly twenty more hours before we reach the border. Rest is surely in order.

TWENTY-TWO

29 July 1944

've not been able to write another entry until late this Saturday evening. On the war front, there continues to be substantial Allied progress.

On the Texas front, the last few days have been a whirlwind for us all. But things are finally settling down, at least for us four in the medical contingent. Besides myself, this includes Manrico, a general practitioner, as well as José and Alfonso, our two medics.

We arrived in Nuevo Laredo late Tuesday afternoon, after a surprisingly comfortable twenty-seven-hour train ride. After a warm and spirited reception from many of the townsfolk, we boarded American charter buses. And thus, we set course north. Within twenty minutes, we were passing over the Río Bravo.

The moment we crossed the bridge's midpoint, the demarcation between the United States and Mexico, was chilling. We had just left our homeland behind. I quietly considered the genuine possibility some of us might not return to it again.

I've been to Texas before. I spent almost a year at the University of Texas Medical Department in Galveston. I was a surgical apprentice with Robert Shelby, one of my father's good friends. Galveston and Houston seemed modern, busy, and vibrant. My time there was satisfying and constructive. I traveled there by ship, from Veracruz. Unlike that maritime experience, the scenery flanking the road from Laredo to San Antonio was surprisingly rural and desolate. Of the few vehicles I saw during the three-and-a-half-hour ride, only a few were sedans. Almost all were flatbed, styleside, or flareside work trucks.

Once we entered the San Antonio city limits, civilization became apparent again. The buses eventually passed through the gates of Randolph Field. We all stood to straighten our uniforms and remained standing until the coach stopped in front of Building 100. Everyone stooped and looked through the windows, eager to see the landmark we all knew from *West Point of the Air*, starring Wallace Beery. Seeing this building from our favorite war movie was a big deal. It was like standing before the Empire State Building for the first time after seeing *King Kong*.

West Point of the Air had been filmed on location at the base. Randolph Field is one of the most important aeronautical training centers in America. Most aviators currently in a war theater have likely set foot on its grounds.

The whole squadron has seen the motion picture, probably multiple times. It has been the subject of conversation during our trip here. While maintaining our composure, we all silently admired the famous building as we stepped off the buses. Its domed central tower rose above an inviting set of arches. Its simple but exotic accents reminded me of some regal fortress. I could envision it in Morocco or Tunisia. But I could also see traces of palatial Indian architecture and understood why the building was affectionately referred to as the Taj Mahal.

Our amusing encounter with a snippet of Hollywood was short-lived. We were immediately assigned to small groups. We were then ordered to gather our gear from the coaches' undercarriage bins and proceed to a nearby tent for medical examinations. These were expeditious and efficient. During this process, we discussed among ourselves and pointed out the staff's excellent organization and courteousness. Naturally, we also whispered about the charm and appeal of the female nurses who tended to us, and of the lovely aides who ushered us around the base.

The medical testing ended in the early evening. We were directed to an area a good distance from the Taj Mahal. It was essentially a tent town. A few structures were made of wood and even fewer were made of corrugated metal. An American aide told me most of the metal barracks had been taken down so the raw material could be used to build ships and airplanes.

Many uniformed men and women came and went on foot, or they drove Jeeps or rode in the backs of large COE military trucks. Everything and everyone seemed to have a purpose. We were amazed at the large military installation's orderly atmosphere. We marched toward and then threw our belongings into our assigned tents. The whole unit then proceeded toward the mess hall. This was an actual brick-and-mortar building equipped with cool climate units. It was a welcome respite from the sweltering summer heat. We dined on plentiful servings of beef stew, potato mash, and steamed green beans with carrots. This food did not look appetizing, but to everyone's surprise, it was tasty. Also, it paired well with the automated pop fountains dispensing abundant Coca-Cola, 7UP, and—a dynamite hit among many of us—A&W Root Beer, a drink none of us had ever tasted.

Most American soldiers have been civil to us, even friendly. During dinner, some passed by and watched us with what seemed like simple curiosity. A few others glanced at us with speculative, almost suspicious looks. Perhaps because, as a group, we probably seemed incongruous to them. As in any Mexican community, the soldiers in our squadron ranged from white to brown. Also, we spoke in Spanish and interacted casually among ourselves. This was unlike our American counterparts in the mess hall, who seemed divided. They were segregated. Some tables were solely occupied by white men. American Indian and colored soldiers sat on separate tables. Even among white men, those of Italian or Irish descent also sat by themselves. Women were relegated to a far corner.

We were only allotted an hour for dinner. Afterward, the testing resumed. The unit was divided into its groups: aviators, mechanics, artillery and munitions, private-level support, and my group—officer-level support. They tested our proficiency in English. They also gave us a psychological evaluation and a peculiar examination that tested our knowledge of the war: current landmark events, geography, and our ability to recognize Allied and Axis Coalition uniforms or insignias.

We finally returned to our respective barracks just past ten. In our tent, the nine other men and I gathered around a table for a few minutes before lights-out. We decided we all deserved to take a load off. Everyone enjoyed a smoke and drank root beer from our previously filled canteens. By eleven, exhaustion sent us all to bed.

Wednesday morning began with a hearty breakfast and our first commendation as a unit. A Sgt. Finney requested permission from our commanding officer to congratulate the squadron, as we had all received a grade of good or excellent on the written examinations. We were then led to the Taj Mahal, where we took care of a number of administrative endeavors. These included fingerprinting, having photographs taken, and receiving our American military dog tags. We strung them along our Mexican ones. At nine, we returned to our tents and changed into physical training uniforms. Fitness testing began at nine thirty. There was a break for lunch followed by a quick base tour. Two locations were particularly useful: the general store and, next to it, the after-hours snack post—affectionally called the Fridge. Here, one could get free soda pop, sandwiches, and other light fare from 11 p.m. to 5 a.m. Unbeknownst to us then, only a few squadron members would get to enjoy these establishments.

After the base tour, fitness testing continued for the rest of the day. I didn't need to wait for the examination results. I knew every private and officer in our ranks was in superior physical condition. This was corroborated the following morning as the men were told they had passed with high marks. Of course, this generated some muscle flexing, boxing stances, and Popeye impersonations.

Save for one-hour meals and two hours of physical training drills, Thursday and Friday were spent in classroom-style lectures. These covered a variety of tactical, survival, and practical combat issues. These sessions went late into the evenings and were followed by more testing on the subjects we'd just covered.

Late yesterday, at the end of one lecture, we received news the unit would be split up for specialty training. We each received our specialized assignments. The pilots would go to Pocatello, Idaho. Some of the mechanics would be sent to the Republic Aviation Corporation training facility in Long Island, New York. Artillery and munitions men would be split between military installations located in Illinois and Florida. A few officers and privates in support roles would remain at Randolph Field. And the four of us in the medical contingent would be moved to the nearby Fort Sam Houston—home of Brooke General Hospital.

This morning, we all wished one another good luck as we went to our separate training assignments. Most boarded buses en route to the train station. We four in the medical team waited a few minutes after the buses departed. Then a slinky fellow from the Military Police Corps drove up in a Willys to fetch us. Manrico beat us to the passenger seat. José, Alfonso, and I squeezed in the back, where we hung on for dear life. As soon as we left Randolph Field, the MP blazed at high speed through busy city roads and shook us like cowboys on a bucking bull for the entire thirty-minute trip. Finally, we arrived at Fort Sam Houston. We felt lucky to have made it in one piece. The MP dropped us off in front of the imposing Brooke General Hospital. More impressive than the building were the medical tents proliferating in every direction around the main hospital. We later learned how the tents were organized: triage units, which were busy with incoming sick or injured soldiers from every war front in the world; medical and surgical convalescing sections; and physical rehabilitation units, which were the most plentiful. There was also an interesting sector to the base's far-east perimeter, which was cordoned off by chain-link fences and barbed wire. This section housed sick Nazi soldiers who'd been captured primarily on African war fronts. Only very sick or immediately post-op patients were housed within the hospital.

Upon arrival, we met our two liaisons. Col. Townsend was the chief of surgical services, and Capt. Sackrin was the chief of medical services. They were both career military doctors. Their formal officer uniforms, emblazoned with multiple ribbon bars and medals, made them initially appear intimidating. But we quickly discovered that Drs. Townsend and Sackrin were as laid-back as could be. We met them while waiting in the hallway outside the personnel office. When they walked over, we immediately stood up and saluted them. As the secretary tending to us made the introductions, Col. Townsend smiled and blithely told us to drop the act and to save the soldiering for "shitholes across our oceans." We all shook hands. Then, over a side table in the hallway, they handed each of us a manila folder with papers containing the details of our assignments. The men took some time to explain what these would entail.

After their explanation, Dr. Sackrin smiled at Manrico and me. With some candor, he added that getting to do everything they'd just mentioned would depend on us demonstrating, within a month, the medical proficiency expected of faculty-level physicians, which they had been assured we already possessed. Before they left us in the secretary's care, they shook our hands again. Good-humoredly, Dr. Townsend added, "We're both from the East Coast. We haven't seen many of your kind wearing white coats and stethoscopes. So let's see if you're any good. We'll see you at our rounds tomorrow morning. In the meantime, enjoy the rest of the day. I'm afraid you'll soon find that free time is overwhelmingly scarce."

The Women's Army Corps secretary showed us to our assigned sleeping quarters. These were located within the main hospital, on the top floor of the staff wing. We were surprised and frankly ecstatic with this arrangement. Our windows overlooked the impressive esplanade of tents, people, vehicles, brick buildings, and lawns. The quarters had two pairs of bunk beds with a small table and chairs in between. Four ample storage chests provided adequate closet space for our belongings. Above a small sink, a shelving unit was replete with towels and laundered white coats. And to our delight, the room came with its own toilet and shower. We couldn't have hoped for better lodging.

The young, attentive WAC girl then led us on a tour of the various departments within the hospital and on its grounds. She pointed out the general store and the mess hall, where we stopped briefly to have lunch. During the detailed orientation, she told us how to catch free transport buses to the various other military fields, as well as to downtown San Antonio.

We saw the medical and surgical wards, the operating theaters, the laboratory, the X-ray department, the pharmacy, and units where we could find day-to-day medical equipment. These would be important going forward, so we wrote down important facts about each. Our tour ended under the canopy of twilight. She guided us back to the mess hall and politely said goodbye. We thanked her for her guidance and recommendations.

Not knowing anyone yet, we sat by ourselves at dinner. We discussed our good fortune with regard to the accommodations and the program in store for us. We only saw two downsides. One, no root beer was available in the mess hall. And two, toward the end of our orientation, the pretty WAC secretary mentioned her fiancé was stationed in London. José had been dismayed. Earlier at lunch, he'd assured us that by next weekend, he'd be dancing with her at the nearest USO club. He'd been planning to use his best Casanova move at the conclusion of today's tour. But sadly for José, this was not to be. Nothing was as off-limits, as respected, and even protected as a fellow soldier's beloved.

We gave José a rotten time about this and his other failed conquests. After the laughs and carrying-on, we used his temporarily broken heart as an excuse to find some distraction. So we planned to attend the newsreel and movie that had been advertised on bulletin boards throughout the base.

In the end, I decided reading our informational documents was a better idea. I told the guys to go ahead to the movie. I assured them I'd let them know about anything important before morning.

The documents say, as expected, that Manrico and I have been assigned to a medical and a surgical team, respectively. José will be Manrico's assistant, and Alfonso will be mine. However, for the first week, we are to shadow, observe, and undoubtedly get examined at every turn. Only if our ward commanders deem it appropriate will we be allowed to fully participate in team activities and involved in direct patient care. Once we become completely integrated, we will occasionally break for an hour or two to attend a number of biweekly lectures. These will range from general military procedures to specific field-medicine training. All in due time, I suppose.

This is enough writing for now. I'm going relax and read until the guys return from the movie.

TWENTY-THREE

18 August 1944

've recently gone overboard with my daily writing. The urge to log all our favorable experiences these past twenty days has been too much to resist. Perhaps the detail, along with the sporadic photographs I've snapped, will interest my friends and family if we have the fortune to return home. Perhaps in the future I'll read my own words and see our participation in this great war with different eyes—ideally with more insight. Today, however, everything I've previously written seems inconsequential.

This is my shortest entry yet. I simply don't know what else to write. This is frazzling. It's my hope that in the near future I can dedicate more than these few words to someone I met today.

She seems special.

And, I'm smitten.

TWENTY-FOUR

9 September 1944

On the last page, I wrote I was smitten. What an absurd understatement. I hadn't known my life would never be the same again.

It has been some time since that last journal entry. I didn't want to put ink to paper again until I could write something meaningful about Alessandra. I wanted her at the forefront of my next account. Fortunately, I now feel the inspiration to jot down what has transpired, and I'm certain I can do justice to the dearest subject of the words below.

Alessandra Blake is a flight instructor with the Women Airforce Service Pilots. They mostly operate at Randolph Field. One of her jobs is to ensure the WASP core is ready for frontline service if the American government decides to approve their militarization. Additionally, she and her crew are also responsible for training male pilots—something our squadron found surprising. But this is another reality of the war. Male pilots and instructors are scarce. As with every other aspect of the war effort, women have stepped up. Through the WASP core, female aviators are employed as flight instructors or to transport airplanes—whether it be cargo, bomber, or fighter craft—anywhere they're needed.

Alessandra joined this group in 1942. She did this soon after being informed her husband had perished during the Allied invasion of North Africa. Despite her grief, or perhaps in order to deal with it, she answered a newspaper ad and moved from Massachusetts to Houston for initial training. After excelling in every category and logging countless hours in the air, she was promoted to instructor and sent here. She has only been in San Antonio for about a month.

Before I continue, I should summarize something important. While they thought the process would take a month, Drs. Townsend and Sackrin deemed us apt for clinical service after our first week at Brooke General. They were highly satisfied and apparently surprised with our medical acumen. In particular, Dr. Townsend couldn't believe I was only twenty-six years old and possessed what he deemed "uncanny surgical talent." I explained to him that in Mexico, medical school begins after high school and lasts five years, as opposed to four here in America. I was only seventeen when I formally began studying medicine. I also told him that since I was fifteen, I'd been shadowing my father and other family members who were physicians. And that for the last three years, I'd been a surgical apprentice at home and at the University of Texas Medical Department in Galveston. Manrico is older, and his knowledge and expertise are less surprising. At any rate, we've been allowed to function as senior members of the medical staff alongside our American counterparts.

That being said, three weeks ago, a female pilot under Alessandra's command fell ill. On that fateful day, I was lending a hand in the general surgery admissions tent. We were in the triage section, managing wounded soldiers.

Hours earlier, Alessandra had been advocating for her sick pilot through the channels available to women. They were being rejected at her own base's various infirmaries. "Simple indigestion," they were told without a formal examination. Instinct told Alessandra her trainee was suffering from something more severe. In a Willys MB, she drove her ill pilot nearly twenty miles to Brooke General Hospital. Even here, almost every department dismissed them. Eventually, they were referred to our service. At our massive tent's entrance, a nurse initially rejected them—told them to take a place at the back of the line.

After everything they'd gone through, Alessandra was not about to accept that. Her companion was now barely able to stand. Supporting her trainee, Alessandra pushed past the nurse's desk, behind the curtained-off boundary, and into the examination area. With the front-desk nurse protesting just behind her, Alessandra eased her pilot onto a bed. She then told the nurse to shut her trap and summon a doctor. When the nurse refused, Alessandra called to my group as we were reviewing an X-ray nearby. In a stern voice, she said, "I need a goddamn doctor. Now! Unless all of you want a dead aviator on your conscience."

I'd never heard a woman take that tone in public. I doubt anyone else in the tent had either, judging from the sudden silence throughout the expansive quarters. We all turned around. That's when I first saw her.

My superior gestured to me, indicating I should see what the commotion was about. As I walked toward the two women, the previous activity in the tent resumed and the silence dissipated.

Alessandra's determination saved her friend's life. After my examination, I diagnosed the pilot with appendicitis. I initially only assisted in her operation. But after the senior surgeon ascertained my ability to finish up on my own, he let me take over. This obligated me to follow up with Alessandra after the surgery, to inform her all had gone well and her trainee would fully recover. She was in the waiting room, wearing the WASP uniform—a Santiago-blue Eisenhower jacket and matching slacks. She stood as I approached. Toward the end of our conversation, this intelligent, spirited, and knockout of a woman invited me for a drink the following day. By the end of the weekend, we were in love.

As she has a Jeep at her disposal, Alessandra and I have spent most evenings and nearly every weekend at each other's sides the last three weeks. Despite the circumstances of war and the horrors the dailies make us privy to, we've found comfort and hope in our mutual, tender affection. We have learned about each other's pasts. She has learned about my family, and I've learned she essentially has none. I've been amazed by her up-bringing, which explains her warm character and her resilient, forward spirit. Not to mention her soft features and captivating aura. Alfonso refers to her as a raven-haired Vivien Leigh—as she looked in the picture *Waterloo Bridge*. I'm only too happy and proud of such a comment. Although I feel that when you love someone this much, no parallels can do her justice.

She was born Alessandra Conti to Italian immigrants in Boston. When she was five, her parents were forced to return to Italy, and she was left behind under a distant relative's care. She never saw her parents again. With only marginal care and tute-lage, she found a way to educate herself through high school. She has not shared more details, but I can only imagine the hard-ships in her life. Her kind and honest character, in conjunction with her raw determination, have culminated in the brilliant per-son she is today. Hailing from my established family and having never lacked for anything, I only admire and adore her more. With Alessandra, my fate is sealed.

Tomorrow we'll be going to the city center to visit the San Antonio River. We're told it's the most relaxing and romantic spot in town. I look forward to it.

TWENTY-FIVE

22 October 1944

Most of the unit reunited a few days ago and is now beginning to train together in Pocatello, Idaho. Our intelligence officers and radar men remain at Randolph Field. We four have also stayed put at Fort Sam.

Luckily, our continued stay in San Antonio has allowed me to spend more time with Alessandra.

She and I understand what brought us together. Our commitment to our jobs remains at the forefront of our minds. Defeating the Axis powers is of utmost importance. This worldwide conflict is always palpable, especially during our daily activities on base. Yet every moment Alessandra and I share together, no matter how short, we somehow momentarily forget the world is at war. Although there are many different things at stake for people around the world, our time together also reminds us that we fight for the freedom that would allow every individual to have what Alessandra and I have. We fight for the opportunity to be in love, to hope for love, and to steer such love in the directions we choose. When this war is over, perhaps we'll have a world where love, not dictators, shapes our lives.

Today was a particularly pleasant Sunday. Landon and Lucy, his fiancée, invited us to brunch at an establishment called Earl Abel's. The diner's exterior looked like a flying saucer. Its interior was also amusing. Placards with funny and creative messages hung on the wall, were painted on the tables, and were even inscribed on the dishes and glasses. I remember a couple of the jokes from our table: "Eat here and diet home" and "It was a brave man who ate the first oyster." Also on the wall were framed photographs showing the owner alongside stars like Bing Crosby, Charlie Chaplin, and others. Earl Abel produced music for motion pictures and knew many Hollywood personalities. But when work dried up after the stock market crashed, he started the restaurant to support his family.

The food was a wonderful all-American fare. We had biscuits, pancakes, omelets, roasted potatoes, bacon, and sausages. And it was economical, which is why I didn't argue when Landon insisted on settling the check. I knew he was struggling to make ends meet, but I also realized he very much wanted to treat us—a gift of sorts to commemorate Alessandra's birthday.

We had a lively time. I had taken my camera along, so I took various photographs of us inside and outside the restaurant, which we left by early afternoon. Landon had a commitment at his family's farm and, having just recently resumed his law studies, needed to make time for reading. We all jumped into his father's 1936 Plymouth sedan, and he drove us to the city center. He left us on the corner of Main and Commerce Street. This was a convenient spot to carry out my plan. We waved Landon and Lucy goodbye.

As we'd now done a few times before, we rejoiced in being out of uniform. Arm in arm, Alessandra and I walked down the busy avenue. We took pleasure in being able to blend in with the locals who similarly browsed and patronized the stores and eateries along the way. The weather was crisp. But the sun broke through the mantle of clouds. Our wool coats kept us warm. Our tightly held hands made us happy. This could not have been a more delightful autumn day.

A substantial fund transfer from my family's holdings at New York's Merrill Lynch & Co. had recently been deposited into my

San Antonio bank account. So my instinct was to purchase anything and everything that made her smile as we browsed.

Alessandra sensed my desire to shower her with gifts. She
told me she didn't need anything. Everything she wanted, she
already had: my company and my love. With a playful wink, she
also reminded me of the impracticality of having anything but
the essentials in her cramped quarters on base.

Farther down Commerce Street, we ended up at the beautiful and colossal Joske's Department Store. It reminded me of El
Palacio de Hierro, a similar establishment in Mexico City. Both
stores were modeled after the iconic Harrods of London and
Le Bon Marché of Paris. Joske's offered a variety of fine products, from clothes and personal accessories to kitchenware and
furniture. More importantly, it housed an ice cream shop and
soda fountain. We'd been there about a month prior. Despite the
cold, we'd been anticipating returning so we could once again
indulge in a root beer float for me and a sundae for her. We were
amazed and pleased the soda jerk remembered us. The nice
fellow was generous with the delectable ice cream he served us.

Afterward, we walked and browsed the store. I was hoping Alessandra would allow me to buy her a piece of jewelry.
Something of her choosing. Something that would symbolize my
love and also complement the rest of the surprise gift I was planning to give her. But she didn't seem particularly fond of jewels.
Luckily, she took kindly to a silver Tiffany pin shaped like a flower. I purchased it, and she wore it proudly on her coat's lapel.

Weeks earlier, along with Manrico and our fellow medics,
we met Alessandra and her friends for a late-evening snack at
the Fridge in Randolph Field. We had a few bites, drinks, and
a most congenial gathering. During the conversation, we spoke
of what was dear to us, and she mentioned a music box that had
belonged to her mother. As a child, she'd frequently played the
melody at bedtime. It soothed her and helped her sleep. For
years, it also made her hopeful she'd one day be reunited with

her parents. Unfortunately, during one of her relatives' many moves, the music box got lost. The loss saddened her, but she still fondly remembered the keepsake.

After that night, I decided to scour the city for businesses where I might find her a replacement music box. I wanted to surprise her with it. A hospital aide told me of a master clock-maker who'd recently immigrated from Switzerland. He made cuckoo clocks, as well as exquisite music boxes. Once at his shop, I settled on a beautiful box that was also a jewelry case. It was made with elm and had a high-gloss finish. The lid was inlaid with two intertwining hearts in red and gold. It had an addition-al drawer at its base that could fit a few necklaces. I imagined Alessandra enjoying the soothing melody and slowly filling the box with meaningful jewelry for years to come. He unfortunately didn't have the mechanism for "Clair de lune." This was my most beloved song and the one I wanted her to hear whenever she opened the box. He would have to order it from his purveyor in Houston. As luck would have it, the process would be expedi-tious. He was able to install the musical component, and the box was ready to be picked up today.

I hailed a taxi in front of Joske's and directed the driver to the clockmaker's shop. The gift was everything I'd hoped it would be. Upon opening the lid and hearing the music, she cried and smiled. She assured me her tears were ones of remembrance, hope, and love.

We made small talk with the shop owner. He proudly explained to Alessandra the process of creating her gift. Then he told us about his life, his family, and how he had ended up in South Texas. Reciprocally, we shared a little about ourselves. We expressed our admiration for his skillful artwork and bid him goodbye.

The small shop was not far from the San Antonio River, and we walked happily in that direction. We turned east on Guilbeau Street and then north on West River Bank. We continued our stroll, parallel to the river, until we came upon a trio of beautiful

Victorian homes. The house overlooking the river had a walkway along its side that led down toward the water. So we set out on the small trail. Closer to the house, I noticed a For Rent sign and a telephone number. Alessandra then pointed to a deck behind the house. It offered a sublime view of the river and the city.

I thought resting on the deck would be nice. I grabbed her hand and—trespassing—led her to the deck's stairs. She was happy to be my accomplice and followed along, smiling. Once on the wooden deck, we peeked through the rear windows. The house appeared unoccupied. It was sparsely furnished, but despite that, it seemed generally cozy. Alessandra's face lit up as she commented on various aspects of the home's interior. She sighed and said, "Wouldn't it be lovely to live in a place like this?" Her tone was wishful, a desire for something out of reach. I wanted to assure her that if the war was won, we could live in an even more beautiful, larger place. Although, I must confess, this particular home and its surroundings seemed special. I had a fleeting vision of us living happily here. But I didn't want to create false hopes—everyone's future at that moment was uncertain. I simply agreed with her comment.

We then leaned on the railing to survey the riverscape. I still had unused film in my camera, so I snapped a few shots, including one of my darling Alessandra with her new music box in hand.

I excused myself for a moment. I left the deck and went around front to write down the telephone number on the For Rent sign. I suddenly thought it might prove useful. Eventually, we headed down to the riverbank and walked to the city center. Once there, we explored downtown San Antonio some more, found a homey restaurant for dinner, and then took a taxi back to our respective bases.

TWENTY-SIX

. . . .

16 December 1944

As we do every Saturday, we spent part of the day at Randolph Field going through physical training drills. Due to inclement weather in Idaho, the main group has been at Majors Army Airfield in Greenville, Texas, since the end of November. Today, our commanding officer informed us he received a telegram saying Capt. Paul B. Miller, commander of the Second Air Force, has proclaimed all the Mexican pilots' judgment and skills to be within a range of excellent to superior. With this official announcement, the 201st Squadron was now ready for deployment.

18 December 1944

Today was bittersweet. Our unit was declared apt for combat two days ago. We all thought the squadron would be sent to provide support in what has been called the Battle of the Bulge—Hitler's recent attempt to reconquer Belgium. But late this afternoon, we were informed the high command has determined the Asia-Pacific campaign has become more pressing. It has become apparent the Japanese will stop at nothing to maintain control of their empire. Significant portions of Allied resources, including the 201st, will now be destined for the South Pacific. It's still uncertain whether we'll provide support for the British and Australians in New Guinea or participate in the Philippines' liberation. This new assignment requires additional training. Since we were initially intended for combat in Europe, the pilots and mechanics have been training on the P-51 Mustang. Now that we'll be serving in the Pacific Theater, our aviators and mechanics need to gain expertise in flying and maintaining the fighter-bomber used almost exclusively in the Pacific campaign: the Republic P-47 Thunderbolt.

Because of this necessary delay, our active participation in this war is still on hold.

TWENTY-SEVEN

25 December 1944

Almost everyone has gone home or to their respective base. Our bunkmates are staying the night so we can go out to breakfast tomorrow morning. We're lucky to have been allowed the Tuesday after Christmas off. Alessandra and Betsy will share one bedroom. Manrico laid claim to his own bedroom on Saturday, when he came to help us decorate the house for the Christmas party. Alfonso and José were so inebriated we could've left them on the living room rug. But we put them in the third bedroom. They definitely needed the comfort of a real bed.

So here I am on the living room couch, reminiscing about our genial holiday celebration. Everyone seemed to enjoy themselves. My Alessandra was ecstatic, and I shared her excitement. It felt as if we'd invited our friends to our own home, as if we'd settled here long ago. I'm so glad I thought of renting this house on the river for her—for us. I'll try to work out a lease for a while longer so we can welcome in the new year before leaving for Asia. In the interim, Alessandra and I, and our friends, can enjoy the comfort of this place—away from the cramped, damp, and cold barracks.

Alessandra didn't have to say anything before she went up to bed. I saw her love in her glistening eyes. I felt it in our good-night kiss. Inexplicably, the San Antonio River has become the sanctuary of our love. Why would we ever want to be away from here? I can be a physician anywhere. And if we win this war, she can continue to do what she loves—whether in the US Army Air Forces or in civilian aviation. It's so clear to me. Our future together is in this city and in this house.

TWENTY-EIGHT

18 February 1945

Final training for our pilots took place at Brownsville Army Airfield. It ended on Friday the 16th. They arrived in San Antonio late this afternoon. The four of us trekked over to Randolph to welcome them back and have an official dinner together. To our delight, American members of other units had organized this gathering. It was a surprise to congratulate us on finishing our training. A graduation party of sorts. At any moment we could leave for battle. The dinner was a farewell tradition among our American counterparts, our fellow soldiers.

News spreads like wildfire on a military base. Information about our unit was no exception. Details of how we became the 201st, as well as reports of our squadron's exceptionally high marks in all categories, have spread everywhere. Even some civilians know about us. People seem to have a positive impression of our unit. The atmosphere today was notably different from the day we first arrived. Our squadron did not sit alone in the mess hall tonight. Instead, our American friends sat with us.

The 201st Squadron is finally together again. And after tonight, we know we're not alone. Our friends and allies have our backs, and we surely have theirs. Our fates in this great war and in the future are inexorably intertwined.

22 February 1945

We now know why we had the farewell dinner as soon as our pilots arrived four days ago. Thirty-six hours after that, we were on buses to Majors Army Airfield, near Dallas. The pilots have been to this base recently, but it's new to the rest of us.

Today there was a ceremony on a training runway. A dozen fighter planes were before us. A small band played, and after a few speeches, we officially received the Mexican flag from our commanding officer and the American flag from the base's ranking US officer. We're to raise the flags at any camp we get stationed at. They are to fly high at all times unless every last man in our squadron gets either killed or captured. We are no longer trainees. We are now battle-ready soldiers, ready for deployment.

There was little time between when we received our orders to leave San Antonio and when we left for Dallas. I didn't have much time to say goodbye to my beloved Alessandra. But we both knew the day would come when duty might suddenly separate us. Fortunately, we did get to spend a few moments together the night before the unit left San Antonio. There wasn't much to say. Outside her barrack we just remained in each other's arms for as long as we could.

I carry her photograph in the breast pocket over my heart. Along with all the memories, it will help me get through whatever is next. I will take strength from our recent past and from my hope for our future.

We don't know how long our unit will be here in Dallas before deploying to the war front. Until then, our squadron will continue to run drills. The men, the brothers around me, are ready. I *am* ready.

TWENTY-NINE

31 March 1945

O nly the pervasive smell of cigarette smoke relieves the funk of body odor and bad breath. We're sardines in a can. We've felt like this for four days now, since we boarded the SS *Fairisle* last Tuesday evening. Many of us stood on deck as we left port. We all pointed to the gradually dwindling crimson Golden Gate Bridge. We sailed away from the San Francisco Bay and, literally, into the sunset.

This vessel, one of about two thousand similar Liberty ships built since 1941, is as bare bones as it gets. It creaks with every passing wave and thumps loudly, constantly, at every turn. We pray we avoid becoming the target of a Japanese torpedo but also hope this rusty canister made of reclaimed pots and pans—surely collected at some scrap-metal drive—doesn't break apart in the middle of the Pacific. It has to hold together—and hold us—for thirty more days. During our mission briefing, we were told a trip like this would ordinarily take about two weeks. But due to the Pacific conflict's nature, this will be a perilous voyage that will take twice that long. The course will be erratic in order to avoid enemy submarines and will follow elaborate Allied-protected maritime routes.

Two of the giant cargo holds have been converted into living quarters. Both hold giant scaffolds containing 550 bunks spread out in rows and stacked in tiers. We also have a galley, a mess hall, and a barely sanitary washroom. Over a thousand of us—from various units—float slowly toward the Philippines. The other cargo compartments of our "ugly duckling," as President Roosevelt has christened these workhorse steamships, are packed to the brim with Jeeps, light tanks, ammunition, ambulances, giant crates of meal rations, and other assorted war supplies.

In the ship's bowels the air is damp and stifling. Manrico, José, Alfonso, and I, along with an armored division's medical unit from Oregon sharing the living space with us, have just finished a plan to have our men spend several hours a day on deck to get fresh air. When not involved in drills—fire or attack simulations headed by ship staff—we'll rotate in groups. We've also made sure that every man in our cargo hold avoids sharing canteens or cigarettes, immediately reports coughing or illness, and constantly washes his hands. We hope this will maintain some basic level of hygiene and prevent any communicable disease from spreading. No matter how mild, a simple illness would prove chaotic in such a cramped enclosure. In the next few days, we'll also create a mandatory schedule of card games, charades, and bingo. We're sure to get resistance from many of the manly men in our two units. But the isolation, the environmental conditions, and the underlying apprehension over possibly being blown out of the water at any second can take a psychological toll. These games-turned-tasks should engage everyone and provide temporary distraction.

This is the last leg before we go to war. Unlike that summer day nearly a year ago, when we left the Buenavista Station in Mexico City, the fanfare, the flowers, the sweets, and our hometown's crisp air are nowhere near. But our will, spirit, and determination remain unchanged.

THIRTY

10 May 1945

The heat and humidity are constant. The air is as thick and oppressive as the jungle around us. The mud is restrictive. The stench of makeshift latrines, burnt diesel, boiling food from the mess, and DDT relentlessly permeates our clothes and adheres to our flesh. At Porac Airfield, the circumstances are miserable.

So we focus on the silver linings. Ten days ago, when we arrived in Manila, we found out Adolf Hitler had committed suicide. Earlier this evening, we celebrated what dailies around the world are calling V-E Day—Victory in Europe. Germany signed an unconditional surrender three days ago. It seems fate is squarely in the Allies' favor. We will continue to forge ahead, despite all conditions here, until we drive the Japanese from Luzon and inch closer to Tokyo. We feel the conflict on this side of the world will end favorably too. We look forward to victory over this last Axis power. We hope for a worldwide V-Day. But the job is not done.

Our unit is now fairly settled in. These last few days, Manrico and I have more or less finished putting the fear of God in our men. We've explained what happens if they contract malaria, dengue, cholera, beriberi, hepatitis, leishmaniasis, jungle rot, and syphilis. We've ordered them to put halazone tablets in their canteens before filling them. And to only fill from chlorine-dosed Lister bags. Many of the fellows feel indestructible, but we've stressed that a tiny mosquito could easily have them down for the count. We've implored them to keep nets secured around their tent openings and their cots. We've reiterated the importance of keeping their feet clean and dry and their boots powdered. They understand the importance of coming to us to assess if they need antibiotics for even the slightest trauma or lesion. We've dispensed their daily vitamin packs. And we've reiterated the importance of using rubbers if anyone fraternizes with the apparently abundant WAC and local Filipino girls working at nearby Clark Field. Even the few who have most struggled with English have been made to memorize and practice the witty yet befitting American military slogan "Don't forget: put it on before you put it in." Or else, we've assured them, their penises will look like Mexican corn on the cob with everything on it—before they fall off entirely.

We share this base with the Fifth Air Force's 58th and 310th Fighter Groups, as well as the 375th Troop Carrier Squadron. Just like the Oregon unit, which disembarked at Legaspi, the Americans here have been very congenial. But they have also been frank. They told our commanding officer they expect our pilots to get up to speed quickly—practicing with a handful of spare aircraft. And as soon as our brand-new Republic P-47 Thunderbolts arrived, the 201st would start rotating in on flight missions. Similarly, we four have integrated well into the medical detachment. The two physicians and four medics serving over a thousand men, plus locals and Japanese POWs, were ecstatic to see us. They are a good but ragged bunch working an overloaded medical tent. We're glad to dive right in and lend a hand.

On that note, it's time to get some sleep. Clinic starts early every day. Let's see what the South Pacific sunrise brings to light in the days ahead.

THIRTY-ONE

25 May 1945

The whole lot of us could not help it. We cried today. Tears of pride.

Since May 17, two or three of our pilots at a time have joined squadrons from the 58th Fighter Group on short reconnaissance exercises. Yet Alfonso and I have probably logged more hours in the air on our first med-transport detail to Australia than all our pilots put together. But that will begin to change today. The 201st Squadron has begun independent missions using our recently arrived Thunderbolts.

This afternoon many of the guys lining the runway were shirtless and smeared in black, used-up engine oil—a by-product that works surprisingly well as an insect repellent. Stained, heavily wrinkled khakis barely seemed like a uniform. Everyone on base looks like this—everyone, that is, who maintains not only airplanes but also all the improvised infrastructure in this inclement, carved-out parcel of jungle.

I snapped several photographs—pictures of our men with reddened, tearful eyes. Anyone seeing these in the future, without proper context, might believe the men are a pitiful band of godforsaken souls. But behind the dirt and the exhaustion were exuberant and candid smiles. They would see joy on the faces of a small delegation of servicemen who left their modernizing but fundamentally modest nation and traveled across an ocean to help counteract a global assault on human rights and self-determination.

One by one, we saw twenty-three of the squadron's twenty-five new aircraft go briskly down the runway and, far afield, soar into the clouds. We saluted and waved off all our aviators. We proudly pointed at the Mexican Expeditionary Air Force's insignia affixed alongside that of the United States Army Air Force's on the fuselage flanks. With the sun high above us, the green, white, and red colors of our flag shined distinctively from the tail of each airplane. Some pointed to the emblems they'd painted on the aircrafts' noses. These designs included the eagle and serpent, the Popocatépetl volcano, the caricature of a sombrero-wearing bomb, a colorful Day of the Dead skull, Walt Disney's Panchito Pistoles, and risqué portrayals of our cinema queens Esther Fernández and María Félix.

After the last Thunderbolt lifted off the airstrip and became a dot in the sky, we exchanged pats on the back, handshakes, and even hugs.

The euphoria was short-lived. Slowly we began to break up into groups. Despite the momentous occasion, we didn't have respite from our daily duties. The squadron was now expected to fly one or two daily missions, engaging all thirty pilots. Therefore, the work of maintaining the aircrafts, coordinating missions, and looking after the pilots had just intensified for the ammunition and bomb-arming specialists, the mechanics, the communications technicians, the general aides, the operations officers, and for ourselves. This is what we'd signed up for.

I had three wound-debridement procedures and saw a dozen men in clinic—two of whom need surgery tomorrow. Just like most of the men, I kept busy to avoid thinking of our aviators' fates. Today, their mission was to provide ground support to the US 25th Infantry Division and to troops from the Philippine Commonwealth Army as they engaged fierce Japanese battalions in the Cagayan Valley. Ordinarily, this kind of mission would last no more than three hours, as the older P-47s have a maximum range of eight hundred miles. But our squadron received the aircraft's newer version, which has an eighteen-cylinder radial Pratt & Whitney R-2800-77 Double Wasp engine and larger capacity fuel tanks that can hold an impressive 1,200 gallons. This gives them a range of over 2,300 miles. The planes have speeds ranging from three hundred to four hundred miles per hour, so our men can be up for nearly eight hours. This translates into many more hours of worry for us on the ground.

From now on, in addition to our usual daily activities, we on the ground will keep count of each plane's takeoff. And we all hope that when we tally each landing, the number of takeoffs and landings remains equal.

The math was favorable today. After the squadron's first offensive sortie, all twenty-three aviators returned safely to base.

THIRTY-TWO

9 June 1945

Today's local newspaper made the barely noticeable black ribbons tied around our upper arms feel just a little tighter. The front-page story was about an imperial conference in Tokyo. Although the Japanese accept that their ability to sustain large-scale warfare is critically hampered, their government has decided they will continue to resist until their last bullet is gone. From the report, it's also evident the citizens are behind their emperor and willing to fight to the death.

Our squadron's daily operations began two weeks ago. All our combat missions have been successful. But these successes have come at a cost. Two of our aviators have perished in combat. Despite all hope and prayer, we know this is the reality of war. The newspaper article provides a stark reminder that this war continues. We continue to fight against a hostile and determined opponent.

The future might bring more losses for our unit. But we'll deal with whatever comes our way on a day-by-day basis. All of us continue to do our jobs to the best of our abilities. Along with the Americans, British, Australians, New Zealanders, Filipinos, and the Papuans on these islands, we are just as determined as the Japanese.

THIRTY-THREE

17 June 1945

A pack of good cigarettes can go a long way.

Most surgical procedures we perform at Porac Airfield are minor, and we handle the required sedation or anesthesia ourselves. We send any cases that require more specialized care to Clark Field. Those in need of major surgery or prolonged hospitalization, we ship off to Australia. Yesterday evening we trekked three miles to a detention camp to examine a Japanese prisoner who seemed particularly sick. Indeed, he had an acute abdomen—a condition that requires urgent surgery. Given his abdominal scars, which indicated prior surgeries—in addition to abdominal distention and hyperactive bowel sounds on auscultation—his problem was most likely a bowel obstruction from scarring and adhesions.

Mirna, the young Filipino nurse who came with us, looked at me and James—the American general practitioner—with painful resignation. As usual, she simply awaited our approval to carry on with the most prudent course of action. This was my first such encounter. But I quickly realized what her expression meant: following our order, she'd load the patient up with morphine, ease the pain as much as possible, and—to provide some measure of dignity—stay by the soldier's side until he died.

For a moment we stood silently in that hot tent, which reeked of body odor and stagnant air. It was evident this man needed surgery. But to get him transferred to the hospital at Clark Field in time to save his life—through the official process—was impossible. James looked at the young Japanese soldier drenched in sweat, his lips and eyelids compressed in discernible pain, and bearing his lot in silence. James shook his head, defiance in his face as the gas lamps flickered above us. He declared, "This ain't right. I didn't fight my way out of Richland Parish to see young folks die like this. No matter who they are."

James is a tall redhead in his early thirties. He is a no-nonsense man hailing from a poor town in northern Louisiana. He became a general practitioner after attending Tulane University in New Orleans for both college and medical school. In his peculiar Southern accent, he caught Mirna and me off guard when he asked if I still had any "fancy cigs." I nodded. "Good. I've seen you work that scalpel pretty good. If I get you an anesthesiologist, an instrument nurse, and an operating room, can you fix this fella up?"

I told him I could.

With the help of two MPs from the detention camp, we packed up the dying soldier, put him on a flatbed truck, and headed back to base. Once there, we picked up Alfonso and two packs of Dunhill cigarettes. I'd bought a couple of cartons in San Francisco before our departure. The guards at the gates to Clark Field didn't care about our hidden cargo. After glancing at our ranks and credentials, they simply waved us in.

Due to the unofficial nature of the situation, none of the medical staff on duty would have agreed to leave their posts—possibly jeopardizing care of Allied personnel—to assist a Japanese prisoner without authorization. But James knew the right off-duty people, where to find them, and how to incentivize them to help. We all knew bribery was unnecessary. The Hippocratic oath and the Nightingale Pledge are not taken lightly by anyone, anywhere. Yet James insisted that offering the "currency" of the region always padded favors nicely. Smokes being the prevalent currency among soldiers, the Dunhills would be a nice prize.

And so we commandeered an operating suite and secured a willing anesthesiologist, as well as an instrument nurse. With James's and Alfonso's assistance during the operation, we took care of the ill Japanese soldier. After the intervention, we monitored him for three hours. Then we took him back to our base.

It has been nearly a day since the surgery. The young man will recover nicely—even if his fate is to fight against us once again. Everything that transpired last night came with an added benefit. We've now discovered a way to take care of our own men. Having access to a proper operating suite when necessary is certainly worth all my remaining cigarettes.

After fifty hours awake, I need to sleep. Perhaps in my dreams tonight I can be by the river with Alessandra. I want to tell her about this rugged, sweltering jungle but also about its silver linings—the noble spirits of everyone willing to go out of their way and help save a life.

THIRTY-FOUR

9 July 1945

"Twenty…twenty-one…twenty-two…twenty-three… twenty-four…" We all counted aloud—a minute or two apart—as one by one, our Thunderbolts landed safely on the airstrip. There was one more to go.

We'd held our breaths a bit too long. Everyone on the base had gathered to see our fighters return. This was the fourth long-range bombing sweep of Formosa. Due to our P-47s' capabilities, our unit was the only one from Porac Airfield that participated. Formosa is the last obstacle in the campaign to take the Japanese mainland.

We had yet to lose a pilot during these particularly dangerous missions. So we all scrutinized the crimson sky for several agonizing minutes. I heard the fizz of a Coca-Cola bottle whose cap had just been popped. I knew nobody would've done this unless they'd spotted our last bomber. Without binoculars, it took me a few more seconds to finally see a dot, which got progressively larger. By the time I'd made out the wings, the soda pops and beer had begun to flow. I felt myself decompress. "Twenty-five!" we all shouted happily after Captain Gaxiola touched down.

The small celebration is still happening, but I thought it best to write these lines before I rejoin the group and lose track of time. We'll have a few days of rest before we receive new orders. Our next set of missions may soon put our aviators over Tokyo.

THIRTY-FIVE

A s Sam continued to read, he had to nudge Vin. The cat had settled across his lap and partly over Gustavo Martel's journal. Time had elapsed quickly, into the early morning.

A few more passages detailed additional particulars regarding the life and endeavors of the 201st Squadron.

Sam read the journal entry from August 5, 1945, in which Gustavo described the tragic crash of Lieutenant Mario López Portillo. On July 21, his P-47 had gone down in the Bataan region between Balanea and Mariveles, ten miles from the Porac Airfield. Colonel Antonio Cárdenas had organized an expedition consisting of twenty squadron members and two Filipino guides. Despite the treacherous jungle and the possibility of enemy attack, the group recovered the downed pilot and returned to base safely.

In a solemn ceremony, Lt. López Portillo was buried at the Second American Cemetery in Manila. Sam told them that years later the pilot's remains were exhumed and transferred to Mexico City, where he was laid to rest at the Monument to the Fallen Eagles.

The young doctor's entry from August 10, 1945, was particularly poignant. In it, almost as if writing a letter to Alessandra, he documented how on August 6 and August 9, the United States had dropped atomic bombs on Hiroshima and Nagasaki. Such massive and instantaneous loss of life affected him deeply. Upon hearing the news, Gustavo had described a sobering and frigid emotion that had taken hold of him despite the ambient heat and humidity. He felt the world had irreversibly changed—even as he recognized that the monumental undertaking of World War II had come to an end.

The last journal entry Sam read was dated October 5, 1945. Gustavo had written it from aboard the *Sea Marlin*, as the 201st Squadron sailed from the Philippines toward San Pedro, California. Among other things, Gustavo listed some of his unit's accomplishments.

The 201st Squadron had participated in ninety-six combat missions and 785 offensive sorties. The pilots had logged 1,966 hours in combat and 2,842 flying hours. They had dropped 1,457 bombs and used 166,922 rounds of ammunition. Four of their offensive sorties had involved dive-bombing missions, which demonstrated the highest degree of skill, determination, and fortitude. They had destroyed a large number of Japanese convoys, artillery, and military installations. The 201st Squadron was credited with putting over thirty thousand Japanese soldiers out of action.

Gustavo described how every squadron member had contributed to such commendable statistics. He was thankful most were sailing home. He paid homage to the five pilots who had died in the Philippines: Pablo Luis Rivas Martínez, José Espinoza Fuentes, Héctor Espinoza Galván, Fausto Vega Santander, and Mario López Portillo—the men who, like many others from around the world, had honorably sacrificed their lives so others could live and freedom could prevail.

With pride, Gustavo concluded that journal entry with what he knew about the participation of Col. Antonio Cárdenas Rodríguez and Capt. Radamés Gaxiola Andrade aboard the USS *Missouri* in Tokyo Bay on September 2, 1945. Along with others from each Allied country that participated in the Pacific campaign, they were the representatives of Mexico who'd witnessed the Japanese Empire's surrender.

Sam closed the old notebook. "There are many more enthralling entries. But I think the ones I read tell the essence of the story." A few silent seconds followed.

Then Lilly said, "That's a really beautiful story, Sam. But what does it have to do with us?"

Sam smiled. "It has to do a lot with us because Alessandra Blake, born Alessandra Conti, was our grandmother!"

Lilly and her husband were stupefied. Some of the things Sam had read about, particularly regarding the music box, immediately dawned on Lilly.

Sam grabbed the parchment envelope. "Hold on, let me read the letter I initially found alongside the jewelry box. It will help you make sense of it all." He unfolded the old papers and read for a few more minutes.

Then Tony interrupted, "So, Sammy, how come Gustavo and your grandma didn't end up together?"

"Well, it turns out that days before Gustavo's return to San Antonio, our grandmother received news that our grandfather was, in fact, alive. He was also in the army and had participated in a secret mission in North Africa, which had been unsuccessful. The army believed his entire company had been lost in combat. Somehow, he and a handful of his fellow soldiers survived and had convalesced for months in Morocco. But long before they reached safety, our grandmother and the families of the other men had been told all unit members had died in action. Soon after that, she left Massachusetts and didn't tell anyone about her plans to join the WASP core or her eventual move to Texas. She wanted a fresh start. After our grandfather finally arrived at a hospital in London, the army took a long time to locate our grandmother. Once they did—unfortunately for her and Gustavo—she felt obligated to return to Massachusetts to care for her husband, who'd soon be shipped home."

"Man, that sucks," Lenny said. "But I guess Tony is right. If your grandparents hadn't gotten back together, you two wouldn't exist and we wouldn't be having this conversation. Pretty wild indeed."

"Yeah, it does suck," Sam said. "But despite the way things turned out for them, because of the relationship our grand-mother shared with Gustavo, I ended up in San Antonio. So, now that you know this background, he didn't just leave me—leave us—this amazing story about our grandmother and this Van Cleef & Arpels box. He left us much, much more."

Sam told them about the house by the river and the trust fund.

Lilly and Lenny were in shock. After this subsided, they all gleefully spent a while contemplating ways in which Sam could use these assets. In turn, Sam reiterated the bequest was for all of them. He wanted everyone to benefit, but told them he'd be prudent and get professional advice so the effects of this amaz-ing gift would be long-lasting.

Finally, Sam told them about his experience in Mexico City with Gabriela and her family. He shared every anecdote he could think of, as well as all the photos he'd taken on his phone.

Lilly, too, felt the same sense of belonging and satisfaction from knowing their grandmother's admirable history. She shared a deep respect for Gustavo—the man who, through a bequest rooted in love, had ensured Alessandra's memory and spirit would transcend time.

THIRTY-SIX

The ensuing weeks were difficult for Sam. Gabriela kept in touch.

Her correspondence was friendly, limited to texts or emails. She'd generally write in the evenings or late at night, after work, every day or every other day. Sam initially responded immediately to each message. After a few days, he felt writing back the following morning was more prudent.

At the beginning, their messages were polite exchanges about their family members' well-being or about Sam's pets. While typically short, the exchanges gradually became more casual and, in some cases, overtly silly. Yet their correspondence remained platonic.

"Pet peeve?" she wrote one evening.

"Paper towels in public restrooms. Yours?" Sam responded the next morning.

She wrote back that night. "That's one of mine too. It pains me to see trees and other natural resources wasted. My pet peeve: inevitable cruelty."

Sam texted back the next day. "I initially assumed you meant 'cruelty' in general. But then realized it's not the same thing. I give up. Do explain."

She responded, "Any kind of cruelty bothers me. But theoretically, there's hope for those who commit premeditated or even unintended cruelty. 'Inevitable cruelty' is different. For example, some people who love animals are vegetarian because they can't stand the thought of killing animals. Usually, these people own pets—dogs or cats. Although they may be vegetarian, their pets can't be. So they have to condone the killing of animals so their pets can eat. It's an inevitable, cruel reality. A bit of a paradox. And it bothers me."

"Gee, thanks. I had to spit out my ham sandwich after reading that! Okay, I lied. I ate it—although with a sliver of guilt. Now I get what you meant. It sucks for sure. On the subject of paradoxes, I have another for you. You know I'm an engineer. I believe in science. We live in a fabric of time and space. Therefore, it's theoretically possible to travel in time, to the past or future of our own lives. If this is true, then it follows that the course of our lives is essentially set, no matter what. According to Einstein's theories, our fates are sealed. Most people think discussions of fate should be relegated to the realm of the divine. But fate can theoretically also fall into the scientific realm. I find this paradoxical."

"Wow. Nerdy. But okay. I think I need to watch a few YouTube videos and refresh my knowledge on relativity theory. However, I don't think the physics and math involved here take into account human feelings, memories, and hopes. Even if our fates are sealed, our thoughts and sentiments—at any one time—are not. The not knowing of what time and space will bring makes our lives interesting, potentially wonderful, sometimes extraordinary, possibly just boring, potentially tragic, but—in the end— worth living."

"Damn! Good point, smarty-pants," Sam wrote the next morning.

This kind of interaction continued through summer. But their messages gradually became more sporadic by the time foliage in Worcester began turning orange and burgundy. As the leaves fell and the air turned brisker, their texts and emails became scant.

She is a busy surgeon, Sam told himself—again and again when he checked if he had new texts or emails. He tried to remain objective and levelheaded. Logic and circumstance dictated he should detach himself. But he just couldn't shake his thoughts of her—that inexplicable void.

Gabriela, too, felt a vacuum in her heart. But she similarly realized that the facts of their respective realities called for prudence and practicality.

They both hoped, every time they read each other's messages, for something truly personal—some hint of something less platonic between them. That hope never materialized.

Perhaps when they both realized their correspondence would be limited to friendly banter, they let their texts and emails dwindle.

THIRTY-SEVEN

The season's first flurries blanketed the city. Not a single message from Gaby in that time.

Sam carried on with his daily activities, but he often seemed like a zombie. Tony could sense his friend's affliction but thought giving him some space was best. When Sam popped into his room one Sunday morning and asked if he wanted to go to Bagel Time, Tony declined. "Thanks, but it's too fuckin' early for me, bro. Just bring me whatever," he said, and then promptly went back to sleep.

Sam drove north in the old Maverick through an icy morning fog. A carpet of snow was along Park Avenue.

"Hi, Sam. Haven't seen you in a while. Your usual?" Stephanie asked him once he got to the counter.

"Hey, Steph. No, I think I'll try the lox special on a jalapeño-cheddar. And a twelve-ounce latte for here," he replied.

"Well, that's a curveball order for you. But okay, lox with the works and a latte coming up." Stephanie punched in the details on a stationary iPad. "Where's Tony? I didn't think that umbilical cord between you two could be cut."

"He decided to sleep in today. Can you add an egg and sausage on poppy seed for him?"

"No problem. Just let me know when you want me to fire that one up," she said.

"I'll take it with my order. It's gonna cool off on my way home, anyway. He'll just nuke it when I get back there."

Sam took a small table by the window. Between sips of coffee and bites of his bagel, he gazed at the street and sidewalks. With this kind of weather, most towns would've been deserted. But not Worcester. Thick snow and frigid temperatures didn't prevent cars from driving down the avenue, weekend warriors from jogging past the bagel shop, or kids in puffy jackets from running around. In Worcester, life went on despite the elements.

"Enough," Sam murmured. He felt a sudden clarity of mind. The scene beyond the glass imbued him with an odd but welcome awareness. He'd been sleepwalking through the past few weeks. Whether with certainty, hope, or both, he now accepted that life goes on. He acknowledged that void in his chest, that his fascinating ties to Gustavo and Gabriela Martel were probably over. But he recognized it came from something wonderful and beautiful—as wonderful as his own life and as beautiful as the city he loved.

Moments later, just as Sam stood to bus his plate and coffee mug, his phone rang.

He almost didn't answer, because the call came up as unknown. But he pressed the green icon on the screen and held the phone to his ear. "Hello?"

"Hi, Sam. It's Gaby. I hope I didn't wake you."

He was instantly flustered. Yet within seconds, he felt that inexplicable comfort and joy he'd so often experienced since he'd met her. Sam sat back down. "Hi, Gaby. Not at all. I'm out having breakfast. Actually, I just finished breakfast."

"Great. What did you have?"

"A lox bagel with an industrial-sized schmear of cream cheese. It was great. And a latte."

"Yum. I'm having some boring cereal and fruit. I wish I'd been there with you. By the way, do I get credit for making you a latte convert?"

"As a matter of fact, you do. The lady who took my order knows me and was surprised when I ordered the lox and the latte. Up until now, my standard fare had been egg and sausage on a plain bagel and drip coffee. I'm enjoying the change."

"I'm glad. Hey, I know this seems out of left field, but I wanted to say hi and see how you, Tony, and the pets were doing. I thought it best to call rather than send a text or email. I'm sorry to have gone radio silent. I've just been crazy busy at work."

Gaby had been unsure how to address the recent gaps in their communication. But she just couldn't stand to lose their connection. So she gave Sam the most plausible excuse.

Despite their previous reservations and uncertainties, at that very moment, they both felt happy.

"No need to be sorry. I totally understand," Sam assured her. "Did you get a new phone? The number came up as unknown. I'm glad I answered, though."

"Oh, no. I was too lazy to walk up to my bedroom to get my mobile. I called you from my home phone," she said.

"I'm impressed. You knew my number from memory?"

Sam couldn't feel the sudden flutter of Gaby's heart or see her slightly rattled yet charming whoops-a-daisy expression. He did, however, hear the feeble gasp that escaped her lips.

"I could lie to seem super smart and say I did," Gaby said. "But the truth is, I had your number programmed on speed dial. I know, totally archaic—even more so to still have a landline. But I constantly misplace my mobile phone, so this gives me more options."

"Ah yes. Old-fashioned but convenient," Sam said. He started telling her a few trivial facts about Tony and the pets, thus avoiding further discussion regarding her landline phone. He didn't want her to feel embarrassed. The significance of him being on her speed dial was mutually obvious—it left no doubt he was important to Gabriela. It was a hint that their friendship had the possibility of something more.

Gaby brushed off the speed-dial matter too. In turn, she gave him a brief update about herself and her parents. She also discussed some of the family members Sam had previously met. "I could go on and bore you to death. But Sam, there was another reason for my call. An ulterior motive of sorts. I was invited to a medical symposium in San Antonio. It will take place the week before Christmas. I thought maybe we could rendezvous there. You could show me the lovely house by the river, and we could both check out a few of the sites my grandfather wrote about. I can take care of the lodging. You'd just have to show up."

He looked out the window again, almost emptily this time, as he tried to quickly digest her invitation and find the right words to reply with. During this seconds-long interlude, she added, "I know this is short notice, and it's totally okay if you can't. It's just that...I mean, it suddenly occurred to me, and I thought it would be nice."

Her added comments had given him more than enough time to consider her proposition and respond. He simply said, "That sounds like a great idea."

THIRTY-EIGHT

I t was Friday, late afternoon in mid-December.

In the lobby of Holly Auditorium at the University of Texas Health Science Center, Sam showed his driver's license to a conference facilitator. She cross-checked his name on her notepad, handed Sam a guest badge, and ushered him into the auditorium.

He stood in front of his reserved seat along the rear wall. With both hands in his jeans pockets, Sam contemplated the large lecture hall. Hundreds of physicians were here from all over the world. They'd gathered for the annual International Transplant Congress. At the moment, there was a break between presentations.

Some attendees socialized along the aisles or talked by their seats. Others came and went with snacks or drinks from the large spread in the lobby. A few sat awaiting the next lecture. Then a soft bell sounded throughout the venue. The attendees returned to their seats.

The overhead lights were dimmed, and a slide was projected onto the screen behind the stage. The slide showed an aerial photo of the National Medical Center in Mexico City. The overlaid text read:

Gabriela Martel, MD

Machine Perfusion in Organ Transplantation and New Advances in Mesenchymal Stem Cell Conditioning of Ex-Vivo Liver and Pancreas

Dr. Ian Dodd, the conference organizer and emcee, walked onto the stage. The room went silent.

"All good things must come to an end," Dr. Dodd began. "We've had a fantastic gathering the last few days. Before I introduce our final speaker, I want to thank all of the distinguished presenters who have enlightened us with their lectures. I also want to thank you all for attending this important meeting. By continuing to learn how different communities around the globe work to advance organ transplantation—from social implications and public education to the scientific, surgical, medical, and pharmaceutical advances that make this process possible—we will continue to give those with failing bodies a second chance.

"I hope to see you all at our gala tonight. And I hope to see you all again next year in Vienna.

"Without further ado, I'd like to introduce our next esteemed colleague. She's one of the most genial people you'll ever meet—which, for a surgeon, says a lot. Some of you met her during our small-group seminars yesterday. A few of you have had the pleasure of working with her. And all of you know her from her journal publications.

"She's the section chief of hepatobiliary surgery at the ABC Medical Center and codirector of transplant research at the National Medical Center in Mexico City. She obtained her bachelor's degree at Yale and her medical degree at Harvard. She completed her residency at the Massachusetts General Hospital and her transplant fellowship at Northwestern. She returned to Boston, where she joined the faculty at Harvard for a year, before returning to her native Mexico. She is a full professor of surgery and medicine at the Universidad Nacional Autónoma de México."

Dr. Dodd stooped and produced from behind the podium a diploma-sized frame.

"And, on behalf of the University of Texas system and in light of the close interinstitutional collaborations this center has had

with her research team in Mexico, she is now a clinical professor
of surgery at the University of Texas School of Medicine in San
Antonio. Ladies and gentlemen, Dr. Gabriela Martel."

As Gaby walked toward the podium, Sam noticed some people in the audience look bewildered. She wore a dark blue pant-
suit and a white top. For those who had read her publications
but who'd never seen her in person, her youthful and striking
appearance was surely surprising. Once she took the podium,
she was engaging.

"Dr. Dodd, thank you for that kind introduction," she said,
briefly holding up the certificate. "I also want to thank the UT
School of Medicine for this wonderful honor." She placed the
frame behind the podium. "Now, I want to present one of several
new, promising, and exciting studies we've been working on…"

Forty minutes later, she concluded with a slide featuring a
panorama of the Angel of Independence—a gold-plated statue
of an angel crowning a 118-foot Corinthian column in the middle of Reforma Avenue—the symbol of Mexico City. The words
Thank you were overlaid on the photo.

After ebullient applause, the lights came back on.

Many attendees made their way to the exits. A small crowd
gathered around Gabriela, who had come down from the stage.
Sam observed her from a distance. People took turns asking her
questions, and she was addressing each individual. One by one,
the people around her appeared pleased with her responses,
thanked her, and walked away. The last person was an older man
with a cane who had patiently waited his turn. Sam assumed he
was an academic. He wore a corduroy suit, a bow tie, thick-soled
leather shoes, and glasses that hung from a cord around his
neck. After a few minutes of conversation, Gaby gestured toward
the back of the auditorium and offered the professor her arm.
More as a sign of respect than a need for physical assistance, she
walked arm in arm with him up the wide center aisle. Under the

frame of the exit doors, Gabriela bid the old gentleman goodbye. Then she turned to face Sam, who had begun to walk toward her.

Seeing each other again felt like fireworks. But they curtailed their excitement. When they reached each other, they simply converged into a quick, gentle hug. Gabriela kissed Sam lightly on the cheek. As they had months prior, each felt a puzzling emotion—agitation, almost—at the other's touch. Yet as before, a sense of peace and delight instantly followed.

"So nice of you to help that young fellow," Sam said.

Gaby smiled. "That was Professor Krause. He was one of the original members of the Harvard committee on brain death. They were a group of medical ethicists and physicians from all disciplines who, in 1968, published a paper stating that irreversible loss of brain function should be accepted as death. The document was pivotal because it allowed organ harvesting from people whose bodies could be kept alive but who no longer had brain function. Without that ethical tenet, the practice of transplantation wouldn't exist. It's amazing to meet living pioneers of medicine." She shook her head. "Sorry, I'm still in a lecturing frame of mind. Anyway, it's so nice to see you again, Sam. Come on, let's walk outside."

"It's great seeing you too," he said, walking beside her into the lobby. "I really appreciate the invitation."

"I thought roaming this city together would be fun. I've been here a few times but have never really explored it. I still can't believe you wanted to come hear me lecture. I bet you were bored out of your mind. You want to sit here for a bit?" They sat on a couch in the lobby.

"I wanted to see you in your element. And I wasn't bored at all. On the contrary, I was totally amused. The less I understood your lecture, the more I noticed folks in the audience nod and smile. Like some light bulb had just flashed on in their heads. I loved your occasional funny slides and jokes. You command an audience well."

"My true element is the operating room. And also, as you can see, research. Lectures are an inevitable part of this. So it's nice of you to say that. I do try. No matter how amazing and cutting-edge your material is, you always have to throw in a little humor. Otherwise you put people to sleep," she said.

"Not the case here. They were mesmerized by you. You're like a rock star to these people."

Gaby burst into a quick giggle, playfully smacking him on the wrist as their forearms rested next to each other on the couch's backrest. "You always make me laugh, Sam."

"Oh yeah? You'll like this, then. You know when you were concluding that those meschy-something cells…"

"Mesenchymal," she said.

"Yeah, that. When you said those cells showed so much promise, I swear, some of the older folks in the audience really perked up. They probably got excited because they're hoping your research bears fruit quickly. They may need some *meat* replacement of their own pretty soon. You know, Dr. Frankenstein-style."

"Oh my God, Sam, you are terrible." Laughing, she pretended to hit him on the head with her framed certificate.

Faking a defensive move with his arm, he responded, "Hey, I couldn't help it. It's what popped into my head at the time."

Following their laughter, she said, "Well, the conference is over. I'm freee!" Gaby raised her arms in a victory gesture. "We can now tour the town and try to find the places our grandparents shared. Maybe we can trace their steps. And maybe, maybe I can have a drink!"

"I'm all for it. Wait, did I detect a little too much eagerness for a drink? Doctor? You got a problem we should talk about?" Sam asked jokingly.

"Yes, I've been looking forward to a large, sweet alcoholic beverage."

"When did you last have a drink?" Sam asked.

"Not since Ari's wedding."

"Damn. Really? That was months ago. Why is that?"

"I don't drink at all, unless I have scheduled time off," Gaby responded. "I'm always on call—whether for a surgical procedure, administrative emergency, or media event. I didn't mention this before, but part of the job—the same for all surgeons in the system—is community outreach, to promote organ transplantation."

"Respect! That's some cold, hard discipline. How many days do I have to get some booze into you?" he inquired, grinning.

"Five days. Five carefree days."

"Well, I'll be delighted to be your partner and counselor as you embark on this short intoxication adventure."

She burst out laughing again. "Sam, I just meant a drink or two with dinner. That I rarely drink means I have super low tolerance. Any more than that, and I'd probably end up in the ER with an IV in my arm...or in jail," she said wryly.

"That *is* funny. You in the tank for 'drunk and disorderly,' rubbing elbows with other lady perps."

"Ha, ha," Gaby retorted.

"So, what's the plan? I thought you had a gala to go to."

"Oh no. I don't have to go. Unless you want to," she said.

"Where is it?"

"It's at the hotel I'm staying at. Most of the conference people are lodged there too. It's close to here. They have a shuttle we can take to it right outside."

Sam thought for a moment. "I suppose the advantage to that is free grub and liquor. But the downside is it's free *hotel* grub and liquor. I'd be okay with that, but since quantity isn't what you're after, this might be a low-yield endeavor for us. We might be better off elsewhere with a higher quality factor."

"I'm on board with that. I just have to go around the corner to Dr. Dodd's office to pick up my coat and briefcase. I'll let some folks there know I'm leaving. Then we can be on our way. Do you want to come with me?"

"Yeah, let's do it." Sam helped her up from the couch and pointed across the lobby. "Let me get my jacket from the coat check over there."

After leaving the medical center, they picked up her luggage from the Omni Hotel at the Colonnade and caught an Uber downtown.

Before their trip, Gabriela had offered to get Sam a room at her hotel. But Sam asked if she'd allow him to be their guide while in San Antonio. And that he'd arrange their lodging following the conference. She'd agreed to his request.

THIRTY-NINE

Sam leaned forward from the back seat and surveyed the surroundings ahead. "All right, my friend. We're nearly there. Close your eyes," he cheerfully said.

"Sounds like a dicey proposition. But okay, here we go. Eyes closed," Gaby responded.

"No cheating, okay?"

She smiled and traced a halo over her head.

They were on their way to the house by the river. He thought it would be fun to make her first view of it a surprise.

While not the intended purpose, having Gabriela close her eyes allowed him to freely study her face's graceful and delicate contours, including her Cupid's bow lips—the color of red hibiscus. Her soft hands lay comfortably on her lap. Without motive or agenda, he contemplated her as one might the aurora borealis or any poetic spectacle of nature. Her beauty complemented her intelligence, her sense of humor, her self-confidence, her optimism, and her care for others.

This was the precise moment Sam realized he was inexorably in love with Gabriela.

Sam no longer needed to try to detach himself from what he'd thought were uncertain emotions. He no longer had to doubt the possibility he could love someone.

But the moment was also bittersweet.

He and Gabriela were worlds apart—in terms of physical distance and the particulars of their lives. Logistics and circumstances just didn't add up. Above all, he didn't know if she felt the same way about him. Sam would have to live with that uncertainty, unless—somehow, at some point—Gabriela communicated she loved him back. He'd have to make the best of her company for now. In the near future, electronic correspondence might be his only connection to her. He'd eventually have to ask himself if this could be enough.

For the moment, all Sam could do was be her friend.

"Is this where I get driven blindly to a rusted-out warehouse and made to perform an illicit kidney transplant on some ailing mafia boss—using greasy wrenches from a toolbox?"

"Are you kidding? No. Fat Momo is connected. His crew carjacked one of those mobile animal spay-and-neuter trucks. It's got clean scalpels and latex gloves. Trust me, this will be a classy gig for you. And it's not a kidney. Fat Momo needs a pancreas," Sam said.

Even the Uber driver laughed. The car pulled up to the curve in front of the house.

"Still no peeking, Gabs. Don't make me pull out the black hood. You gotta hang in there while I take your suitcase out of the trunk."

"I'll be right here," Gaby said, now cupping her hands over her eyes.

Sam put her luggage on the sidewalk, then opened Gaby's door. "Give me your hand and I'll help you out." Sam thanked the driver and gently guided Gaby onto the sidewalk. "Are you ready? Shazam! Open your eyes."

"Wow, Sam." She looked at the old, impeccably kept house. "It's so beautiful. Look, you can see the river back there."

"You would've loved the colorful flowers on all those bushes this summer," Sam told her.

"Yes, I'm sure. Can we go in?"

"Of course." He gestured her forward. "I'll grab your roller."

At the front entrance, Sam punched in a code and the door opened.

"High-tech lock for this lovely old house. I like it." Gaby went into the front hallway.

"The lock is new. Lena Sander recommended doing that. It allows me to let maintenance people in when I'm in Worcester. I could've opened it with my phone."

"Very convenient," she added, exploring the living room.

"Take a look at the mantel," he told her.

Gabriela walked up to the fireplace. She stared at the photo in the small picture frame. Then Sam heard a gentle sob. He approached her hesitantly.

"Gaby, I'm so sorry. I had a copy made of the old picture we had in my grandmother's music box. I just wanted to honor your grandfather and my grandmother. I mean, this house is really theirs. I thought you'd like that."

"Oh, Sam. I do. I love it," she said, tears in her eyes. She hugged him. "It's great. I just can't believe my grandfather was here over seventy years ago. I can almost feel his presence."

Sam gave Gabriela a tour, which ended on the back deck. She stood over the place Gustavo had snapped a photo of Alessandra holding the music box, the green river flowing in the background. They admired the many trees along the manicured riverbank. She pointed at the large hotels across the river and wondered what, if anything, had stood in their place more than half a century ago.

Eventually, they went back inside. Sam locked the French doors as Gaby leaned against the kitchen island.

"A bit chilly out there," he said.

"Yes. But it felt so nice. Especially because our grandparents probably stood out there in similar winter weather when they invited their friends for Christmas and New Year's back then," Gaby said. "Have you picked a room? I didn't see your luggage anywhere."

"About that. I initially thought it would be great to stay here. I'd planned to head to Target or Walmart from the airport to pick up everything we'd need to make the house livable. But I realized I wasn't going to have enough time if I wanted to attend your lecture. Then I thought we might be more comfortable at a hotel. As luck would have it, there's a nice little inn next door, so I booked us rooms there. My stuff is already there. I got you the Yellow Rose Penthouse. It has great views, and the room is comfortable and modern but still nods to the Victorian age."

"That sounds great. I agree with you. It'd be better to spend the time exploring San Antonio rather than making the bed or worrying about taking out the trash," she said.

"Cool. Do you want to walk over?"

"Oh yes. I'd love to. I want to get out of these heels."

Sam grabbed her roller on their way out. "By the way, I brought back the suitcase you let me use. I wasn't sure if you wanted it back."

"Oh, Sam. Don't be silly. You can keep it. I hope you didn't bring the empty thing here."

"I didn't. I used it for my own clothes…with plenty of skivvies this time. But I thought I'd just go get another one if you wanted to take it back."

Gabriela shook her head and, with a smile, playfully elbowed his side.

FORTY

"All right, Gabs, here's your key. I'm one floor down, in the Lone Star Suite. Just come-a-knocking when you're done."

"'Gabs,' huh? I thought I heard you say that earlier. Nobody has ever called me that."

"Oh, sorry. I didn't even think about it."

"No, no. Don't be sorry. I like it. Now I have a nickname for my nickname. It's kind of cool. Okay, I'll see you in a bit."

A short while later, they crossed the inn's back lawn to the San Antonio River's west bank. They headed north, toward downtown. On their walk, Sam told her he'd researched the small shop where her grandfather had purchased his grandmother's music box. But unfortunately, it no longer existed.

"I did, however, locate one of our grandparents' favorite hangouts. It still exists, sort of. That's where we are headed. It's right next to the Alamo. So, we'll hit two sites at the same time."

"Which place is it?" she asked.

"You'll just have to wait and see," he replied.

They climbed a set of stairs from the river level to East Commerce Street. They walked a few blocks down to the Losoya Street roundabout. Minding the traffic, Sam took her hand and drew her across the street. Once on the roundabout's island, they walked past *La Antorcha de la Amistad*, or the Torch of Friendship—an abstract sculpture that was a gift from Mexico presented to San Antonio in 2002. Now facing northeast, Sam stopped.

"There it is," he exclaimed, pointing to a large building across the intersection.

"Dave & Buster's and H&M? It looks like the entrance to a mall. What am I missing?"

"You kind of got the forest but you're missing the trees. Think about what our grandparents liked to do while downtown."

"Hmm." She gazed again at the façade. "A big building with molding along the top edge and carvings below each window. A black metal railing along the second floor. It's actually an old building." Then she said excitedly, "It's the department store where they came for ice cream!"

"An old building in disguise, indeed. It's the old Joske's Department Store, though like you said, currently a mall entrance. Let's go to the lobby. They have pictures of what it used to look like in the forties."

They took in the historical display, recalling some of the instances her grandfather had written about. Then they went next door and toured the Alamo—another site that had figured in their grandparents' short but meaningful sojourn in the river city. Gustavo and Alessandra had spent hours in each other's arms sitting on a bench in the old mission building's courtyard.

"Where to now?" Gaby asked eagerly once they exited the Alamo's visitor center.

"Plenty more timeworn steps to trace," Sam said, pointing toward Houston Street and then offering her his arm.

Linked at the elbows, as they'd done a few times before, Gaby and Sam walked along—platonically—in sync. But to the many tourists and locals who saw their palpable chemistry, they seemed like a beautiful couple in love.

A few blocks later, Sam stopped. "Look familiar?"

"The theater from the old photos," she said, gleeful. "Do you still have the pictures on your phone?" she asked, once they both stood under the Majestic Theatre's marquee.

Sam found the photo of their grandparents standing in that location more than half a century ago. "Here," he said, handing his phone to Gaby.

"This is unbelievable! It's the same ticket booth. Perfectly preserved," she said, alternating glances between the phone and the theater's entrance. "All right, Sam. Go over there." She pointed. "I want a photo of you where your grandmother stood." Gaby tapped Sam's phone. "Oops. I think I locked it."

"The code is one, eight, two, five."

"Got it. Okay. Say cheese." She snapped the photo. "My turn. Here," she said, giving his phone back. Just as they were about to trade places, a young woman offered to take a photo of them together.

"Very kind of you," Sam told her. He joined Gaby next to the old ticket booth. They put their arms around each other and smiled for the camera.

They thanked the young woman again and then glanced at their photo. "I like it. Maybe we should frame this one and put it on the mantel next to our grandparents' picture," she said.

"That's a good idea. I'll take care of that."

"I just realized this is the only photo we've taken together," Gaby said. "I'll have to ask Ari if there are others from the wedding. Let's take more pictures from now on, okay? For starters, email me these ones."

Sam tapped quickly on his phone. "Already on the way." As he sent the pictures, he wondered why Gabriela had made that request. Did she want pictures of him—of them—as short-lived mementos of this trip but soon to be forgotten in the confines of her computer hard drive? Or had she missed not having a photo of him—as he'd certainly regretted not having any of her? Did she want these as a way to help soothe that constant void she might feel when they once again parted ways? Sam promptly reassembled his thoughts. "Okay, let's walk a few steps down that way for dinner."

"Great. I'm hungry." As they began to walk, she added, "If I ever remember to keep my phone with me, I'll also send you any photos we take with it. I think it's on the bed, back at the inn. Oh well. Luckily, you're good at keeping yours with you, and since I know your passcode now, I suppose we'll be okay. Hmm, are you sure you want to trust me with that?"

"I have nothing in my phone I wouldn't want you to see… well, save for maybe a few off-color texts and emails from Tony and a few other friends. But something tells me you'd probably get a kick out of those too."

"Oh my God, yes. Can I see them now?" she said jokingly.

"If you're bored, my phone is all yours whenever you want it. In the meantime, we're here." The Houston Street Bistro was just a few steps west of the Majestic Theatre. Sam had made a reservation. Inside they were immediately escorted to their table. They ordered drinks and then studied the menu. Sam lowered his. "By the way, to answer your earlier question, I wouldn't just trust you with my phone. I'd trust you with my life."

"Aww, Sam. That's so sweet of you."

"Who wouldn't? I'm sure all those folks whose innards you've changed or tuned up can vouch for you."

"Innards? Tune-ups? I love that," she exclaimed with a laugh. "Sam, you sure have a funny way with words. Your wisecracks keep my endorphin levels pleasantly high."

"Endorphins? Hmm. *Nerdy, but okay*," he said.

"Hey, that's my line," she said with a playful frown.

"It *is* your line. But it totally applied, so I had to borrow it."

"Fine, fine. I guess I deserved that one," Gabriela conceded. Then she seemed thoughtful, leaned forward, and whispered, "Wait a minute…one, eight, two, five? Your phone passcode is the same as my home address?"

"It is."

"No wonder I memorized it right away. How did you decide on that?" Gaby asked.

"Well, up until recently I'd never had an access code. But since I installed the security system for the house here, and since I now have this pretty wild bank account I can manage on my phone, I thought it was a good idea. I picked your home address as my password for both, my phone and the home's security system, because I thought it should have some connection to your grandfather. And I don't know why, but the number stuck with me when we visited your mom."

"That's very flattering, Sam. I guess I now have access to your phone and your house."

"You sure do. *Mi casa es su casa*," he said lightheartedly.

"Wow. Pretty good accent."

The waiter returned to take their orders. She opted for the Vivaldi, a tomato basil soup with Parmesan and herbed couscous to start. He chose the Tchaikovsky, a crab cake with Cajun tartar sauce. For their main dishes, they each ordered the Cabaret, grilled salmon over lentils, sautéed spinach, and Southwest vegetables.

"That's so creative to name each dish after a famous show or composer," Gabriela said after the waiter retreated.

"I agree. I'm sure it's to do with its proximity to the theater. This is probably the go-to or, I guess, the come-to place before or after a show," he said. "Hey, on the subject of my passcode, I wanted to ask you about the number. I noticed it was not only the address to your family's complex but also on the coat of arms of the wrought iron gate behind the cobblestone courtyard. Does it mean anything?"

Gabriela sighed. A thoughtful expression in her eyes and an amicable smile preceded her comment. "It means everything to my family."

"Oh yeah? How so?"

"Wow. Where do I begin? As kids, my cousins and I always heard stories about our family's history. But I've never actually told it to anyone."

"Start from whatever beginning you remember. I'm all ears," Sam told her.

For the remainder of dinner, Sam learned about the origins of and then fully understood the Martel family's extraordinary nature.

FORTY-ONE

"The year 1825 was when my ancestors set foot in Mexico. And by ancestors, I mean my fourth great-grandfather, Gaspard Martel; his wife, Claudine Vautier; and his cousin Tristan Martel.

"Tristan and Gaspard were similar in age and had been close as children. They'd been born into a Parisian family that for generations had maintained its social status and economic stability by forcing all its men to become professionals in one of five fields: medicine, architecture, engineering, chemistry, or mathematics. Whoever initially made that decision was either very smart or very evil. To this day, we occasionally still debate this in my family.

"Prior to the French Revolution, in the late 1700s, the Martels generally served the monarchy—some did so in Paris and others in Versailles. They were neither royals nor aristocrats, but their professions gave them a place in society as close to the aristocracy as you could get. And because they also served the commoners—whether as physicians or as the designers of public buildings, bridges, and other infrastructure—they also enjoyed a positive standing among them. During the revolution and throughout the Napoleonic era, unlike many royals and aristocrats who were either executed or exiled, the Martels continued to live in much the same way—serving whoever happened to be in power.

"Tristan had always had an affinity for adventure. He was still a teenager when he befriended a family of businessmen, traders, and sailors. Through this connection, he ended up making trips to the South of France, and from there, he went on voyages as far away as Morocco, Algeria, and Tunisia. Exploring new lands and the possibility of making a living through trade fascinated him. Because he'd been exposed to foreign lands and different people, he developed a strong sense of liberalism. He believed all humans were equal, and he despised societal norms involving caste or class.

"When he came of age, around 1820, Tristan announced his intention to forgo his expected professional course. His family did not take the news well, especially because they knew of his newly acquired philosophy. His views aligned with the progressive trends that had led to the revolution. After Napoleon's fall in 1814, the reign of the Bourbons had been restored in France. In light of this, his family felt that Tristan might jeopardize their neutral political and societal position. They gave him an ultimatum: get in line with Martel family expectations or be disowned.

"Of course, Tristan chose his principles and left Paris.

"He left behind his parents, siblings, and sadly, his favorite cousin, Gaspard. True to his spirit and beliefs, he soon established himself in the port city of Toulon. From there, he continued to sail the Mediterranean for the next few years. He made a modest yet happy living from trading goods in ports along the coasts of Spain, France, North Africa, Corsica, and Sardinia.

"Gaspard Martel, on the other hand, had followed his prescribed path and became a physician. Despite this, he was also disowned and disavowed.

"One evening, on his way home from a house call, he was stopped by a young woman wearing a begrimed dress and tattered shoes. But under her shroud of poverty, he saw a dauntless, kind, and beautiful woman. She offered Gaspard a pair of silver cuff links in exchange for his services tending to her chronically ill father. Unable to turn away from someone in need, he followed her to a Paris slum. Once there, Gaspard did his best to care for the sick man. And he also fell in love with this woman.

Luckily for Gaspard and for me, her feelings were mutual. That woman was Claudine Vautier, my fourth great-grandmother.

"As the months went by and their relationship flourished, Gaspard announced to his family his intention to marry Claudine.

"As you can imagine, they refused to endorse the nuptials. They valued the status quo of the family in Parisian society above all else. Also, Claudine's father had been accused of and temporarily jailed for a petty crime, albeit wrongly. The Martel family informed Gaspard they couldn't be associated with a classless commoner, much less the daughter of a criminal. His father demanded that Gaspard cease his relationship or suffer the same fate as his cousin Tristan.

"For Gaspard, there was only one course of action. Love won out.

"Given his family's influence in the community, Gaspard knew being shunned meant he'd have to seek a life away from Paris. He'd anticipated his family's response and planned for such eventuality. For several months he'd been communicating with Tristan about his situation. In turn, Tristan offered Gaspard his humble home in Toulon, which he hardly used. When the time came, Gaspard secretly said goodbye to his mother and younger sibling. He and his bride then traveled south. His plan was to establish himself professionally in Toulon or a nearby coastal town. Once he got his practice going, he'd send for Claudine's parents and siblings so she could have her family close by.

"After arriving in Toulon, Gaspard stayed afloat by making house calls. Once word got out about him, he did even better. He began providing physical exams to the many sailors who lived in or passed through the port city, and he also began delivering babies. In a relatively short time, he amassed enough of a nest egg that they'd soon be able to move into their own home in nearby Le Pradet. As soon as they had settled there, they would extricate Claudine's family from their Paris slum.

"Gaspard could never have predicted what came next.

"On an ordinary evening, Tristan returned from one of his seafaring journeys. He exuberantly hugged them both, gave them presents, and told them an amazing story. Tristan then presented Gaspard and Claudine with an extraordinary proposition.

"He'd just come back from Gibraltar, where he'd met a group of Spanish and French sailors who'd spoken to him about this amazing land in the Americas that had just become independent of Spain. This was a land free of monarchies and with people of warm dispositions. The population was ripe for the establishment of democracy, liberty, and equality. In addition, these people were in need of basic goods—the kind commonly taken for granted in Europe. Mexico, they told him, was a land of peace and opportunity. Given that Spain was imploding economically and also being invaded by France, this group of sailors wanted to organize a voyage across the ocean. Their plan was to fill a galleon with people who wanted to escape the current climate of inequality and oppression. They wanted to escape the never-ending wars and the shame of European colonization and pillaging of African territories. They wanted to start their lives anew.

"What Tristan heard from these sailors had been music to his ears. His progressive ideals had been shelved after the French monarchy was reinstated. If he could make a truly free life for himself while helping make a difference for others, in a faraway land, no less, it would be a dream come true. Tristan was convinced this journey was the right choice for him. But he also had an inkling a new life in Mexico would similarly appeal to his beloved cousin.

"Tristan asked Gaspard, 'Don't you want your future children to grow up in a beautiful, fertile land surrounded by oceans? A society where they'll never have to kneel before a heartless royal or get conscripted to fight some pointless war or invade some poor unsuspecting tribe somewhere?' He added that those

210

unsavory possibilities were plausible, since they no longer enjoyed the favors that came with being part of their family in Paris.

"When Gaspard brought up Claudine's family, Tristan smiled and said, 'If that's all that's holding you back, I pledge to you that if we decide Mexico is our promised land, I will return to collect Claudine's family.'

"Gaspard knew Tristan was true to his word. He decided to join his cousin on this life-changing adventure. He invested every last cent and asset he had into acquiring what Tristan knew—based on his experience trading in North Africa—would be the best items to sell or barter for a parcel of land in Mexico: clothing.

"Months later, the three sailed on a small ship from Toulon to the Spanish port of Málaga. From there, with a few gold coins in hand to pay for their voyage and incidentals, and with thirty crates of new clothes in tow, they boarded a large windjammer. They embarked on the intercontinental trip that would change their lives and mold their descendants' futures for generations.

"Their ship docked in the Mexican port of Veracruz in the spring of 1825.

"A variety of people had been on board—mostly from Spain but also a few British and some French. Some were adventurers. Some wanted to escape military conscription or were deserting. Many were idealists or peasants in search of better lives. And there were men who didn't intend to stay; they were there on a routine expedition, for the sake of trade and profit.

"In that era, when large merchant ships arrived from abroad, they remained in port for weeks. The ships were essentially pop-up malls. Locals would come on board and shop for whatever goods were available. The buyers tended to be intermediaries who would buy in bulk and then either resell the products to other local businessmen or sell the goods themselves. This meant the ship merchants would not profit as much as they might have if they'd sold directly to the public. But the trade-off was an immediate profit without the hassle of communication or labor.

"But the Martels were not there for a quick profit—they were there to stay. Everything they had to their name lay in those wooden crates. It was imperative that they maximize their gains. Luckily, Tristan had experience trading in foreign lands. He always found ways to communicate despite not knowing the local language. He quickly learned how to trade gold coins or other products for local currency and had an uncanny gift for understanding the practical facets of daily life in different cultures. He knew exactly what to do. They had paid extra to continue storing their crates and live on board a few days after docking. During the day, Gaspard and Claudine remained on board, guarding their belongings. In the morning, Tristan would procure food and water for his cousins and then go out to explore the city for the remainder of the day. His goal was threefold. One, he needed to find a place for them to stay and safely store their crates. Two, he had to get a feel for the general cost of living, as well as for products' general values, which would allow them to optimize the price of their goods. And three, he had to determine who would buy their clothes and how best to sell them.

"On the third day, Tristan came back to the pier with a handful of young men and a mule-drawn box wagon. He'd found a posada, a private home with rooms for rent, just a short distance from the city center.

"They fared well. They had a comfortable place to stay and were close to more amenities than they'd ever expected. They had plentiful food and water. Furthermore, Tristan had made sure the place was near a *tianguis*—an open-air market that operated on Thursdays, Saturdays, and Sundays—where he secured a booth.

"They sorted out their merchandise, and by noon on their first business day, they'd sold out of their first batch of clothes. Their decision to procure mostly light, casual garments made of cotton and linen, with a few more formal-wear items made of wool and silk, had paid off brilliantly. Less than two weeks later, they'd sold all their merchandise.

"Claudine, Gaspard, and Tristan were quick to observe and absorb everything they saw around them. The culture, society in general, and the economic possibilities captivated them. They knew they'd made the right decision in immigrating to Mexico and devised a short-term plan based on bigger dreams and hopes. Tristan would return to France on the same ship they'd arrived on, trek north to Paris to collect Claudine's family, purchase an even larger batch of new clothes, and return to Mexico as soon as possible. While Tristan was away, Gaspard would try to establish his medical practice, learn the language, and look for properties where the entire family could settle.

"In the days before the ship was scheduled to leave port, the three enjoyed interacting with locals, who'd welcomed them warmly. Rather than a barrier, the language became an 'in' with people eager to learn about France and about them. In turn, they began to learn and cherish Mexican culture. The unmistakable, close-knit nature of families was particularly en-thralling—children were loved and elders respected. Neighbors seemed to help each other. Above all, there was no one looking down on people telling them how to live or what to do. Food was fresh, inexpensive, and—seasoned with spices they'd never experienced—delectable. They also admired the city's beautiful white colonial architecture. In the evenings, they walked on the beach. They enjoyed the coastal breeze and relished the sounds of the ocean waves lapping the shore—in harmony with the calls of seagulls above. They fell in love with all this.

"The windjammer finally left port. Gaspard and Claudine waved goodbye to Tristan from the waterfront. They found it difficult to be separated so soon. But they put their sadness aside, knowing it was temporary and necessary to securing a future in Mexico. They went to work on the tasks they'd set out to accomplish. With so much to do, time flew by. Tristan returned four months later.

"On his return, he brought Claudine's family and an even larger shipment of clothes. Gaspard and Claudine had been diligent during his absence. They'd been able to learn enough Spanish to get along. But more importantly, in doing so, Claudine had started to become literate—something she'd never have been able to do in France.

"Gaspard discovered many of the medications he'd used in France were available at some of the dispensaries in Veracruz. He had been trained at the Hôtel-Dieu, the oldest and most state-of-the-art hospital in Paris at the time. Because of that education, he embraced the newest evidence-based medical and surgical treatments. Believe it or not, germ theory and the practice of sterile technique and disinfection were just in their infancy. Most physicians still believed in the miasma theory, which stipulated that diseases were the result of 'bad' or 'night' air. The fact that Gaspard adhered to new sterile and hygiene practices went a long way toward him helping his patients—yielding better outcomes than expected in their new community. He also owned a stethoscope, which had been invented less than a decade earlier, and which looked more like a wooden trumpet than the flexible version we use today. In short, he practiced medicine that actually worked. By the time Tristan had returned, the posada they lived in had practically been turned into a clinic."

Gaby and Sam had just finished dinner. Only a handful of other patrons still remained. Over glasses of a Sauternes dessert wine, she continued.

"Fast-forward two decades later. By 1845, a lot had gone right for them. They'd been smart about establishing a business and educating themselves. More importantly, the ideals that led them to Mexico were always in their hearts and minds. They never deviated from the basic principles of honesty, fairness, and respect for everyone—no matter their origin. And of course, they always cherished the love they felt for one another as a family and the love they'd developed for their new homeland.

"Gaspard and Claudine had three children. Claudine's siblings had also become literate, had married locals, and had children of their own. One of her brothers became Gaspard's physician apprentice and eventually practiced medicine independently. In their first decade, Tristan had continued to travel between Veracruz and Europe. They established a robust import, distribution, and retail business. And one day, Tristan returned with his own bride, who was from Spain. By then, he'd known enough Spanish to woo her.

"Tristan's adventurous spirit always stirred within him, though. He and Gaspard's oldest son ended up going west to California to prospect for gold—which they struck. Plus, they were smart enough to buy many acres of land on which the mine sat. By the way, they could do this, because California and the American Southwest were still part of Mexico then.

"Americans crossing the continent by land faced many dangers, but Tristan simply went to what is now the port of Acapulco and sailed north to California. At the time, they faced little competition from American prospectors, who didn't discover gold until the late 1840s. My family's enterprise there preceded the American gold rush.

"I mentioned 1845 earlier because it was also an important year for the Martels. The family had gotten wind of the war the United States planned to wage against Mexico, for the sole reason of acquiring its northwestern territories.

"Well, Tristan had predicted what would happen.

"He sold the rights to the California mine to an American prospector. But he kept the land and reregistered its ownership under his son's name. His son had been born in New Helvetia—the precursor to Sacramento, California's state capital. At the time, this region was led by its founder, John Sutter, from whom

Tristan had secured his child's birth certificate and land ownership documents.

"Tristan, his family, and Gaspard's son returned to Veracruz
just before his predictions came true: the United States invaded
Mexico. After that brief conflict, the US's spoils of victory included annexing the land it had set out to get in 1846. Luckily for
my family, they had capitalized substantially from their time in
California and retained a valuable commodity there. In addition
to their businesses in Veracruz, the Martels found themselves
with a sizable fortune. Gaspard and Tristan decided to move
some of their financial interests to Mexico City, since that was
the only place with a relatively solid banking system—more
like a system of credit unions, one of which my family bought.
Soon after that, some of the family began to migrate to central
Mexico. They purchased a small fleet of ships to facilitate their
trade business. They abandoned transatlantic imports. And now
with a fleet of their own, they began safer trading routes with the
United States—from Veracruz to New York, from Acapulco to
San Francisco, and many ports in between.

"So, shipping and medicine were the foundations of and
have sustained my family for generations. Over the years, many
family members have taken part in various financial, industrial,
commercial, and even philanthropic ventures. A Martel has represented pretty much any profession you can think of. Most have
gone on to work for the family in some capacity, and a few have
become independent of it. But by tradition, there has always
been this fork in the road, leading a Martel to either the medical
or business side of the family's enterprises.

"Through all this, my family has always made sure every em-
ployee working for any of the family's holdings has been well
compensated. Even from the beginning, they never took part in
the practice of indentured servitude, common up to the early
1900s. Tristan and Gaspard vowed to always give back to the
communities in which they lived. They did so by providing living

wages to even the most menial laborers and by establishing medical clinics that would serve everyone. The clinics had foundations in state-of-the-art medical knowledge—which Gaspard was able to obtain through procuring the latest texts and journals coming out of places like the University of Pennsylvania and Harvard medical schools. All that material, as well as any new medical equipment, could be brought home on their ships.

"From that handful of humble men who helped them transport their very first crates in Veracruz to the tens of thousands of people who work for any Martel entity today, treating them right and getting the best for their communities ensured the family's interests were always protected. This became particularly important during later conflicts, such as the French invasion in the 1860s and the Mexican Revolution, which started in 1910. Because the population was grateful, they never turned against—and even defended—our family during these upheavals.

"As they say, the rest is history," Gabriela concluded. "It's probably more than you cared to know. But that's why 1825 is a special number for my family."

"That's quite a background. You should write a book about that," Sam told her.

"Well, I'm not a writer. One of my uncles put together all that history from old journals, letters, and other documents. It's why I know these details. But you're right, maybe at some point a novelist will emerge from my family. I can see a book centered on Gaspard and Claudine's love story with the background examining French history and the circumstances that led them to Mexico."

"I think it's fascinating. I'm sure other people would find the romance and adventure of your ancestors' story quite engaging. By the way, what happened to the Martels who remained in France?"

"There are some stories about Tristan going back to Paris at some point to try to mend the broken bonds. Yet his and Gaspard's families were adamant they didn't want anything to do with them. In fact, since his and Gaspard's children had been born in what they deemed a savage country, the family asked he never come back to 'taint' them again. They never saw each other after that. We all consider Tristan, Gaspard, and Claudine our only ancestors."

"Wow. That's sad their parents put up a wall like that. But I can understand how back then they would've had that kind of perspective. Boy, if they could only see how your family turned out," Sam said.

"Funny you should say that. When Gaspard and Tristan left France, they never intended to pursue wealth. They just wanted to live in a free society, which, in Tristan's case, came with a bit of adventure. But fate steered them in ways that led to the present we have today.

"The consensus among us is that severing bonds with our French family was for the best. Tristan, Gaspard, and all their descendants lived by and maintained the principles that caused them to leave France. I suspect if they'd had a reconciliation, there would've been 'too many cooks in the kitchen' trying to steer the family's direction on this side of the ocean. Having only had my fourth great-grandfather's and his cousin's beliefs at the beginning has shaped my family's outlook on life to this day."

FORTY-TWO

Gabriela and Sam spent nearly every waking hour of the next few days together.

They walked around and took photos in front of the beautifully preserved Brooke General Hospital, now an office building on Stanley Road, in the Terrell Hills neighborhood. Afterward, they had a wonderful meal at the nearby Earl Abel's restaurant. This was the same place where their grandparents had gone many years ago.

On another day, Sam's military service came in handy. When they showed up at Randolph Air Force Base, they discovered it was still an operating facility—the main Air Education and Training Command. Ordinarily, the guard at the entrance would've turned them back and asked them to fill out an online application to enter the base. But after hearing their story and looking at Sam's old military ID, he asked a fellow MP to escort them to the visitor center. They filled out the application, which the attendant gladly fast-tracked, and were given a guest pass for the day. After learning the areas they could and could not go, they toured a few installations, including the Taj Mahal building Gabriela's grandfather had written so much about. They enjoyed the small military museum on the premises, where they learned more about the base and the history of the Women Airforce Service Pilots. Some of the displayed documents and old photographs endearingly referred to Sam's grandmother and her fellow aviators as "the original fly girls" and "women of moxie."

Because they were the only people touring the museum, the director noticed them and introduced himself. Gaby told him why they were there. After hearing their grandparents' story, the gentleman suggested they visit the Institute of Texan Cultures, which had a special exhibit about the 201st Squadron. He was sure Gaby and Sam would find other interesting documents in the exhibit and in the institute's library.

The following day, they visited the beautiful and expansive institute—a dependency of the University of Texas at San Antonio. The Institute of Texan Cultures served as a center for multicultural education. Through research, collections, and exhibits, its mission was to preserve the state's history and culture.

They appreciated the nicely curated exhibit dedicated to the 201st Squadron and, in the institute's library, discovered a wealth of documents regarding the unit's time in Texas. Gaby and Sam saw actual copies of the Mexican defense department's original squadron roster, a copy of his grandmother's flight-instructor card, and many photographs. They became so engaged they didn't leave until the building's closing time.

On their last full day in San Antonio, Sam arranged a meeting with Lena Sander so Gabriela could meet her. They ended up at Lena's beautiful home for dinner. Everyone had a wonderful time.

The following morning, they took a taxi to the airport. Sam's flight to Providence was scheduled after Gabriela's flight to Mexico. He had plenty of time to accompany Gaby to her terminal's security area. When the time came to say goodbye, she kissed him on the cheek. Their subsequent hug lingered longer than either of them had expected. As they pulled apart, both were smiling—the kind of smiles that seem cursory on the surface, but which hide fervent feelings underneath.

Gabriela joined the people in the security line. Once she passed the X-ray scanners, they waved one last time.

Should she have blown Sam a kiss? she thought as she walked to the gate.

Should he have held Gaby longer and kissed her cheek in return? he wondered once she disappeared around the corner.

Nonetheless, despite this goodbye, neither was sad. They'd see each other again.

The previous night, after their dinner with Lena and while driving back to the inn, Gabriela had asked Sam if he'd be interested in returning to Mexico as a consultant.

"I avoided asking earlier because I didn't want my request to color our time here. But installing our clinic's new digital information systems got delayed. It will be installed in the next few months. My cousin Alberto thought...well, we both thought to ask if you'd be willing to offer a double check, since you have a lot of experience with these kinds of networks. We want to make sure we can rely on this new system for at least the next ten years. You'd be fully compensated, of course. We estimate it would take two weeks—I wouldn't ask you to be away from your pets for longer than that."

Sam was pleasantly surprised. Playfully, he said, "Does the job come with dental?"

Gaby tilted her head and smiled. "Dental, health, room and board, cable, internet, minibar, and tons of free entertainment."

"What's the dress code?"

"T-shirt and flip-flops, if you'd like. Although you might be chilly with that attire in March."

"I'm kidding. Of course, I'd love to be your one-man geek squad."

"Sam, you're the best. Thank you."

"Don't mention it. Besides, I think it's good for Tony to be on his own every now and then."

"When you break the news to him, tell him I promise to make it up to him."

"Nah. I'll just bring him back some gear from your local soccer teams and he'll be good to go."

"Well, that gear is on me," she told him, then put her index finger over her lips. "Now that you've agreed to that...I have two other ulterior motives. One, my mom really liked you. She wants you to stay in her guesthouse during your time there. But don't worry, the Four Seasons is no match for her hospitality. You'll love it. Besides, I'll be at work most of the time, so I wouldn't want you alone in the evenings in my loft or in some corporate apartment. While you're there, I'll temporarily move back in with my parents. That way I can see you whenever I do happen to be away from work. And two, the last weekend you're there will coincide with a very special birthday party. It's not mine, but I'd like to take you to it."

That night, the last thing they did was exchange Christmas gifts. They'd previously agreed it should be something wearable, simple, and inexpensive. Sam gave her a Worcester Polytechnic Institute sweatshirt. Gaby got him two custom-made luchador masks the colors of the New England Revolution soccer team: one for him and the other for Tony. "Since you guys seem to be superfans, I thought you'd like to wear these at games," she said, smiling.

"Hell yeah! These are awesome. But I thought we said 'inexpensive gifts.'"

"Oh, don't worry. I stuck to the deal. Luchador masks are a dime a dozen and sold on every street corner. For a little more, they'll customize them on the spot."

And thus, their five days together came to a pleasant end. Despite everything they did and shared in that time, yet again, their conversations remained just shy of being truly personal. Both were hesitant to cross that line of platonic interaction. Their feelings remained bottled up—feelings that seemed ready to erupt, sparkle, and possibly transform their friendship. Perhaps more was yet to come.

FORTY-THREE

For the second time, Sam landed at the Mexico City International Airport. It was a late afternoon in March.

Gabriela and Alberto spotted him after he emerged through the large sliding doors of the arrivals hall. She walked in earnest toward Sam, waving to get his attention. Within seconds, they were hugging—a heartfelt embrace—like old friends reuniting after a long absence. Arm in arm, she and Sam walked back to Alberto and Alon.

"You know Beto. This is Alon Hernandez, our head of IT," Gaby said. The three men shook hands. "These two want to put you to work immediately, so they're here to whisk you away. But I wanted to make sure to welcome you, since I probably won't see you again until tomorrow at dinner."

They made small talk on the way to the parking structure. A chauffeur was waiting behind a parked SUV, and when he saw the group, he opened and stood by the door, waiting for Gaby.

"Sam, duty calls. Sorry for the quick hello and goodbye. These guys will try to make sure your experiences are equal parts labor and fun. I look forward to seeing you soon." Gaby hugged Sam again, as she did Alon and her cousin. The three waited until her SUV drove away before walking to Alberto's car.

As Gabriela had predicted, she couldn't make it to dinner that day nor, unfortunately, the following evening. Yet Sam was content to know that for at least a few hours each night, she was under the same roof, a few steps—well, maybe a few hallways—away.

Her presence was palpable everywhere in that mansion. Throughout his stay, Sam saw photos of Gabriela on walls or shelves. Olivia Martel filled Sam in on the stories behind many of these photographs. Sam also met and got along brilliantly with Gabriela's father, David Martel, a baronial-looking man with a stoic demeanor but a surprising sense of humor.

By the end of his first week, Sam had become well integrated into the IT group. He was able to contribute a number of helpful suggestions and had modified some applications to make the work smooth and efficient. He also made new friends. The IT group took him to a different place for lunch each day and, on a few occasions, even shared some good times drinking beer and watching soccer at local pubs.

Sam and Gaby saw each other a few times that first week, although mostly in passing. She was able to make it for dinner twice, after which they enjoyed spending time with her family playing dominoes or watching TV.

Then Saturday evening came. It was a mostly sweet, yet strangely bitter day.

No special occasion was ever necessary for Olivia Martel to organize a gathering. That day, she'd invited a number of friends and family for cocktails and dinner in honor of a good friend who was a longtime officer of the Martel Corporation. This individual had begun his career under her husband's tutelage and climbed the ranks but eventually left the family business for a position in government. Two weeks before, he'd been named Mexico's sub-secretary of commerce and industry. "It will be a smallish gathering to celebrate the achievement of a dear friend. I'm certain you'll enjoy it. Besides, I've invited a few people you already know and made sure Gaby's schedule was clear for the evening," Olivia told Sam that morning.

At the party, Gabriela introduced Sam to some family members he'd not previously met. Mario, the family friend who'd helped give him a tour of the city during his first visit, introduced his wife to Sam. Alberto and his wife were also there. Ari and Eduardo came, both ecstatic to see Sam again.

Before inviting everyone to their home's north-wing rooftop, where the caterers had finished setting up for dinner, Olivia and David gave short speeches formally dedicating the evening to their friend. After that, the nearly fifty guests, some still with hors d'oeuvres in hand, proceeded merrily toward an ample staircase that rose three stories to the roof.

Tables for eight, with artful floral centerpieces, had been arranged on circular slabs of concrete. Trimmed grass filled in the gaps between the concrete slabs and their connecting walkways. Small trees, flowers, topiaries, and benches lined the rooftop's spacious perimeter. It was both an event space and a garden. Near each table, freestanding patio heaters had been placed to counteract the modest chill that set in with the sunset. There was a buffet station with servers doling out Italian food, and a bar supplemented the wine bottles already on each table.

The food was exquisite. The conversation at Sam's table was lively and, in many instances, witty. Laughter abounded. Soft music emanated from speakers around the garden. The view of the city was astounding. And with Gaby sitting next to him, Sam could not have been happier or more comfortable—until one of Olivia's housekeepers came up to the table and politely gave Gaby a message.

She told Sam she had to step away for a moment, then stood and told everyone she would be right back.

Sam had assumed Gaby's summons had to do with work. A few minutes later he noticed Alberto look up and mutter something negative that didn't need much translation. Alberto nudged his wife, who glanced toward the stairway and sighed.

Sam turned and saw Gabriela come up the stairway.

In her black Cushnie et Ochs dress and Diego Torreblanca heels, she looked stunning. He nearly missed she was coming back with someone by her side.

Sam quickly returned his focus to the people around him. But out of the corner of his eye, he followed Gabriela and the man beside her. The pair walked to her parents' table, where Gabriela's father stood and shook hands with the distinguished fellow, gesturing he should partake of the food and drink. Olivia also rose, gave the man a hug, and pointed to the empty place at their table, which apparently had been designated for him. The man appeared to apologize and declined. Then he greeted the guest of honor and the others at that table, who seemed to know him. Gaby and the mystery man went around and greeted a few individuals at the remaining tables, grabbing a drink from the bar halfway through their rounds. A half hour later, they finally approached Sam's table.

"You know the usual suspects here," Gabriela said. Everyone remained seated and simply waved. Then she turned to Sam. "This is Sam Gleeson, our special guest and friend. Sam, this is Carlos Márquez." Sam stood and they shook hands.

"A pleasure meeting you, Sam. Unfortunately, I have a previous commitment and can't stay to enjoy this wonderful gathering," Carlos said. Then he addressed the table. "I hope you all continue to have a delightful evening."

"I'm going to walk Carlos out. I'll be back in a few minutes," Gabriela said.

Gallantly, Carlos waved goodbye, and arm in arm, he and Gabriela both walked away.

Who was this character? Sam wondered. The fellow looked to be in his fifties and sported a groomed beard and mustache that matched his thick salt-and-pepper hair. Carlos was tall and muscular. He reminded Sam of Charles Atlas, the fitness icon who'd appeared in ads in old comic books and magazines. His flawlessly tailored suit almost obscured a midsection bulge that intimated an indulgence in life's finer things.

"What do you think about the most interesting man in the world, Sam?" Alberto asked jokingly. Mario's wife rolled her eyes.

"I don't know. He seems…regal. And nice, I guess," Sam replied hesitantly.

Ari leaned across the table and half whispered to Sam, "Looks can be deceiving. That regal dude is a fucking asshole. This family tolerates him because, well, we don't have a choice. But I wish we didn't have to."

"I'd call him other things, but since we're speaking English, I can't think of a rotten enough word for that man," Alberto added.

"All right, all right. Lest things deteriorate into a Carlos hate-fest, we should at least tell Sam *who* he is," Alberto's wife suggested.

"Fine, fine. Sam, that dude is the chairman of the Central Bank, which is this country's equivalent to the Federal Reserve," Alberto said. "As much as I hate to say this, you just met the second most powerful man in Mexico, aside from the president. Now, we don't have a problem with his power, per se. To his credit, he does have a brilliant mind and has done a pretty good job with the economy. But he's an elitist who wouldn't give the average person the time of day. Unless he knows you, and unless you 'belong' to his circles, he'll literally look past and walk away from individuals—even if they're trying to address him. He's despotic. And the worst thing is, he tricks unsuspecting individuals who he happens to like into thinking he's a nice guy. A consummate professional at his job, but a prick everywhere else."

"Gaby seems to like him," Sam said.

"Yeah, not sure how that came about. But as far as I know, they're just friends. I suppose Gabriela is so busy she has not had the opportunity to see through him. Or she gives him the benefit of the doubt," Mario said. Everyone at the table had seen the chemistry between Gabriela and Sam. Mario's comment was intended to deflect attention from what he, and everyone else there, felt certain was Gaby's relationship with Carlos. "Anyway, I hope Gaby sends him on his way quickly so she can get back here and join us young, cool folk," Mario concluded.

No one said anything else regarding Gabriela's relationship to Carlos. Sam told himself it was unlikely she'd have a romantic relationship with someone almost twice her age. So, he joked, "If he's as bad as you guys say, maybe he's just trying to get Gaby to sign him up for a heart transplant to get a kinder and gentler ticker."

Everyone laughed. Despite the laughter, Sam still felt discomfort over Carlos—it gnawed at him until Gabriela returned.

A few hours later, all the other tables had emptied. Olivia and David Martel came by to bid the group good night. Some family members in their late twenties, who'd been sitting at a different table, suggested it was time to break out the karaoke machine.

Noticing the caterers were packing up the tables and chairs, Gaby asked Sam and Mario to help her bring up blankets and pillows from the main house. They set up on one of the grassy areas and had a merry time singing and drinking.

At some point Sam wondered about Alberto's kids. But he realized these folks were fortunate to have live-in nannies. Thus, Alberto and his wife stayed with them until nearly dawn, when everyone decided it was finally time to call it a night.

"If any of you are still drunk, please pick a guest room, take an aspirin, and get some rest. After we get a few hours of sleep, I'm going to try to wow Sam with my chipotle chilaquiles. You're all welcome to join us for brunch at eleven," Gabriela said. She held her shoes by their ankle straps in one hand and extended her other arm down to Sam, offering to help him up from the grass. Smiling, she said, "All right, Sam. You seem unaffected by the alcohol, but since I didn't have any, I'm technically in charge. I'll be your escort. Come on, I'll walk you to your room."

Mario laughed. Sam took her hand but rose with his own effort.

"What?" Gaby exclaimed, looking suspiciously at Mario. But all she got was a playful head shake in return.

Sam was only too pleased to be walking hand in hand with her. Therefore, he decided to forgo telling her about the optics of her "escort" comment, although they would've surely had a laugh about it. At the steps leading to the guest wing, Gaby lost her footing. She reflexively scrambled for additional support and more firmly clasped Sam's hand. As the pair walked to his bedroom door, their fingers had become fully intertwined. They each felt elated. But once they reached his room, they prudently let go and bid each other good night.

That Sunday evening, Gaby and Sam caught a showing of *Wicked*. Earlier, during brunch, Ari and Eduardo had reported they were too hungover to enjoy the show and offered them their tickets. Whether planned long in advance or more recently premeditated, their offer was an innocent yet sneaky way to get Sam and Gaby to spend more time alone.

They had a fabulous time before, during, and after the show.

Through it all, both kept thinking of last night, when they'd clasped palms and intertwined fingers. However brief, that moment had deeply—almost transcendentally—warmed their hearts. But at present, they'd reverted to walking arm in arm as friends—each uncertain about the other's feelings. Uncertain about their complicated circumstances.

Sam and Gaby connected briefly, mostly at dinner, the ensuing week. He continued to contribute positively to the IT job at the clinics, which came to a successful conclusion on Friday. That day marked the culmination of the main reason he'd flown back to Mexico City.

The two weekend days that followed signaled the transition of their relationship.

FORTY-FOUR

Saturday morning, Sam and Gaby were on the Cuatro Caminos line, part of Mexico City's massive subway system.

They could've been driven to their destination. But Gaby loved using public transportation. She'd always felt joy in being part of the city's vibrant, mainstream life and the communities just outside of it. Interacting with people from all walks of the socioeconomic spectrum made her happy. There was no better way to be in the thick of quintessential Mexico City life than to take a bus or ride the Metro. It nourished her spirit and gave her a sense of peace to be among the people she loved and the people she professionally served. It also allowed her to escape from the often unavoidable seclusion of her privileged environment.

They got off at the Toreo station. With loud music all around them, Gaby and Sam navigated through the masses of people and merchants. Delectable food aromas enveloped them along every walkway. Finally, they reached the Rápidos de Monte Alto bus station.

Gaby and Sam waited in line and then boarded their bus. They found some empty seats toward the back. Sam placed his backpack and her tote on the slightly rusted overhead rack. Within minutes, they were on their way to "Villa," as their destination was typically and affectionately called.

The municipality of Villa del Carbón was charming and infinitely picturesque. Despite being rough around the edges, it was a hidden gem. Located in the beautiful mountains about sixty miles northwest of Mexico City, it was home to nearly ten thousand people in the city proper and nearly forty thousand others living in the surrounding area. Many of its inhabitants were of Otomí origin. They still preserved their cultural traditions, which predated the township's founding in the early 1700s and had roots dating back to the thirteenth century. Most of the downtown buildings were white with red and brown tile roofs. Small family-owned grocery stores, eateries, a myriad of leather shops, delightful and inexpensive posada-style lodges, and other businesses lined its main streets. Only a few city slickers in the know, as well as the nearby local population, were aware of and descended on the town on weekends, holidays, or special occasions.

Not long after Gabriela returned from Boston and took her current position, she had found herself at an official function in this small provincial city. As part of her job's outreach program, she'd been part of the delegation there for the inauguration of the town's new rural hospital. Her brief task was to introduce and promote organ donation.

Now, as she and Sam made their way to Villa del Carbón, she remembered the moment that further connected her to this small village. Following a short presentation she'd given to the several hundred who'd gathered in the courtyard in front of the new hospital, she'd asked if anyone had any questions. Surprisingly, a number of people did, including whether they'd be doing transplants in their tiny twenty-bed hospital. She addressed each person cordially and succinctly.

The Q&A was ending and Gabriela was about to allow the emcee to take over. But she saw another hand go up hesitantly. One last question.

The wireless microphone had been passed to a short, young man in his early twenties with a dark brown complexion. His features were indigenous. The young man's overall appearance suggested a life of modest means. Despite his age, his face seemed weathered yet humble; it hinted to a vocation in the area's harsh agricultural environment. In a soft voice, he asked Gaby, "You said that a living donor can give a kidney. How about a liver?"

Gabriela told the young man yes, a living donor can give part of a liver, part of a lung, intestine, pancreas, and also bone marrow. The man, who'd appeared preoccupied, almost sad, now smiled and thanked her. She reflexively smiled in return, though curious about his inquiry. He then negotiated his way out of the crowd. Gabriela took her seat on the stage, and the function continued.

When the event concluded, Gaby exchanged a few parting words with some delegates and then walked to the parking area, where her driver was waiting. A physician in a white coat hastily caught up to her. She'd not previously met this doctor. Out of breath, he begged her pardon and asked if she'd be kind enough to go back to the hospital and see a teenage patient. She agreed. As they walked back, she noticed the young man who'd asked that final question holding the hospital door open for them. His name was Felipe.

Sonia, the teenage patient in question, had been admitted the previous night. She was in acute liver failure.

Three days prior, Sonia had obliged her grandmother, who'd wanted to teach her how to harvest edible mushrooms. The old woman had been foraging for mushrooms all her life. But in a moment of senile confusion, she'd erroneously picked a few highly toxic mushrooms. After they'd returned home to prepare dinner, Sonia was tasked with washing and cutting up the produce. By the time the toxic mushrooms had gone into a saucepan, they were mixed in with other ingredients and were indistinguishable from the edible kind. Both Sonia and her grandmother had, as they'd cooked, sampled the vegetable medley. Almost immediately, they'd both fallen violently ill.

Luckily, Sonia's father had realized what happened. He'd immediately thrown away all the food before any other family member could consume it.

Sonia's father had called for a *curandera*—a local healer—but their condition had inevitably worsened. The grandmother had died forty-eight hours after ingesting the mushrooms. But Sonia was still hanging on. She was the only person in their family to have gone to school. Sonia had shared with her brother, Felipe, her dreams of going to the national university, which offered free education to all its students, and becoming a doctor. He knew she was smart enough to pass the entrance exam and get accepted. Felipe couldn't let Sonia die and have her dreams die with her. *We have to try everything*, he'd thought. He'd implored their father to take her to the new hospital. Finally, the patriarch had conceded. After being evaluated in the emergency department, she'd been promptly admitted. But they'd been told there wasn't much more that could be done, except for comfort care. Sonia's liver was beyond recovery.

The following day, Felipe had been walking back to see his dying sister when, by coincidence, he'd heard Gabriela's introduction. He'd stood in the crowd. After Gaby's speech and after she'd answered his question, Felipe had gone into the ward and asked the physician in charge of Sonia about a transplant. He'd told the doctor he was healthy and ready to donate part of his liver to his sister. His father had been a registered worker during the hospital construction. Since the hospital was a government institution, his family was entitled to free access to the national healthcare system.

But the doctor had told him it was too late. The bureaucratic process of getting a procedure of such magnitude was too long, and his sister had only hours to live. The physician had said the procedure was something that couldn't be done in that hospital. Yet Felipe had insisted. He'd pointed out Gaby's presence right outside the hospital and begged the doctor to at least ask her to see his sister.

Within minutes of reviewing her chart and assessing Sonia, Gabriela asked the teen's doctor to run a panel of blood tests on Felipe. She got on the phone, moved a few mountains, and in a little over an hour, had a medical helicopter landing on a make-shift pad behind the hospital. The helicopter promptly took off with Sonia on board. Minutes later, a Martel Corporation chopper also landed. Felipe and Gaby similarly flew to the National Medical Center.

Sonia's operation lasted nearly twelve hours.

Sam and Gaby's ride on the rumbling, shaky bus lasted an hour and a half. After they'd left behind the concrete jungle, they admired the landscape. They saw gated communities, chaotic-appearing but actually organized suburbs, and the green countryside. Finally, the bus traveled the uphill roads leading to Villa del Carbón.

As the bus traversed the downtown area, both appreciated the quaint buildings lining the cobblestone streets. Almost every passenger had already gotten off. But the bus continued just past the city center. The rumbling and jolting of the undercarriage intensified. Sam and Gaby laughed as they bounced up and down and swung back and forth. The bus was now on dirt roads. The buildings and houses they saw through the vibrating windows were made of gray concrete blocks, red brick, or adobe. Some roofs were made of thin laminate material. Other rooftops were made of concrete, but all seemed unfinished, with rebar and cinch wires sticking up from corners. Gaby explained to Sam the ubiquitous practice of leaving homes seemingly unfinished. "By law, if a house's construction isn't complete, owners aren't obligated to pay property taxes. So leaving roofs like that allows people to argue they're planning to build another story and thus indefinitely postpone their tax burden," she said.

"Hey, if it's all kosher, I'd probably do the same," Sam replied.

At last, they approached a cul-de-sac with a small brick office building in its center. A handful of buses were parked in line by the office. There were a few erratically parked cars all over. Two small food booths were nearby. Some people came and went, while others formed a queue, waiting to board the front bus.

Their bus looped around the building and then stopped behind the last parked bus. The engine ceased to clatter. The driver stood and, with a smile, announced, *"Destino final."* Along with three other passengers, Sam and Gaby grabbed their packs and walked to the exit.

As they descended the steps, Sam noticed a small group had suddenly materialized near the bus. Gaby exited first, with Sam just behind her. Two small children ran toward Gaby and tightly hugged her legs. She put down her tote and hugged them in return. Next, she hugged a young, teary-eyed, yet smiling woman.

"Happy birthday, Sonia," Gaby said in Spanish. Then she introduced Sam to Sonia, Felipe, and their father.

They traded hugs or shook hands with other family members and friends who had all come to welcome and thank Gaby for accepting their invitation. Gaby told them she was grateful and honored to be there with them to celebrate Sonia's second birthday since her transplant. All along, she did her best to translate—especially any questions and comments directed at Sam.

Felipe grabbed Gaby's tote and Sam's backpack and directed them to a 1980 Ford Fairmont station wagon.

The car had been through a number of paint jobs and piecemeal body work over its several decades of use. None of its rims matched. The tint on the windows had faded unevenly. It was old and rickety. But it was the family's small element of luxury. The car was in working order and had been pristinely detailed as a gesture of respect to Gaby.

Gabriela and Sam got comfortable in the back seat, and Felipe and Sonia sat in the front. Their father took the wheel but

waited for three children, belonging to members of their extended family, to climb through the hatchback before he drove off.
The remainder of the welcoming party followed on foot.

One of the kids jumped over and settled between Sam and
Gaby, grabbing Gaby's hand. "You smell pretty," the little girl said.

"Thank you. Would you like to try my perfume?" Gaby said.

The sociable girl smiled and nodded.

Gaby unzipped her tote, and from a toiletry case, she produced a small bottle of Creed Aventus. "Okay, now rub like this,"
Gaby said after spraying the fragrance on the six-year-old's wrists.

Holding her wrists to her nose, the adorable child inhaled.
She was ecstatic.

They chatted with Sonia during the slow, bumpy ride. Gaby
translated back and forth. She explained to Sam that except for
the last two years, Sonia's family had never celebrated a birthday. Not even a traditional quinceañera. But that last year, the
whole family had pitched in to have a small party. They wanted to
commemorate Sonia's first birthday since the transplant and also
wished to honor Gabriela. She told him this year's celebration
was also twofold. They'd be celebrating not only Sonia's birthday but also her recent acceptance to the medical school at the
national university. It meant the world to the community to have
one of their own, for the first time, become a physician. Sam
wasn't surprised Sonia was only eighteen, since he knew from
Gustavo's journal that medical education in Mexico began right
after high school.

Ten minutes later, they arrived at the family's half-adobe,
half-concrete-block house. A hodgepodge of similar homes stood
close by. A rough-hewn enclosure that housed a few cows and
workhorses was twenty yards behind their place. Chickens and a
handful of animated dogs roamed among the dozens of people
merrily going in and out of a sizable barn in a courtyard between
some neighboring homes. They were hanging colorful bunting
and balloons within the barn. A group of men inside were laying

down a wooden surface, which would serve as a stage and dance floor. Several women paused from dumping vegetables into a large outdoor cauldron to wave at Sam and Gaby.

They walked into the house. The vinyl floors were uneven but clean. A tiny living room was composed of two handmade wooden sofas with dark tartan cushions. These were positioned around a flat-screen TV, which lay on top of an old, nonfunctioning console TV. On a corner shelf, lit candles surrounded an image of the Virgin of Guadalupe and a framed photograph of Felipe and Sonia's long-deceased mother. A low archway led to a kitchen, which had a concrete sink, a four-burner stove, and a concrete countertop in between them. An old refrigerator stood behind an aluminum table. Women came and went, politely stopping to greet Gabriela and make Sam's acquaintance. A short hallway beyond the living room held a bathroom with a metal door and two bedrooms. The two siblings walked them into the room their father shared with Felipe. The previous year, Gabriela had stayed in Sonia's room, but it had only one bed. The current plan was for Gaby and Sam to share the larger room. Felipe would stay in the smaller bedroom to be available in case they needed anything during the night. Sonia and her father would spend the night with relatives.

Felipe placed their sparse luggage on one of the two twin beds and told them to make themselves at home. Sonia pointed to a chair on which blankets had been folded and stacked. A shelf just above that held towels. Just then, Sonia's father walked in carrying a large flower arrangement, which he placed on a nightstand.

"For you, Dr. Martel. These are wildflowers we picked this morning," the soft-spoken man said.

Gaby went to smell the colorful flowers. "These are gorgeous, and so fragrant. Thank you. You're all so kind," she told the three family members, as well as the two smiling women peeking around the door. From the bed, Gabriela grabbed and opened her leather bag. "I guess this is as good a time as any. This is for you," she said to Sonia, handing her two elegantly wrapped presents.

"Dr. Martel, you didn't have to do this. You've done so much for me already, for all of us," Sonia said sincerely.

"I very much wanted to get you these," Gabriela told her.

"Should I open them now?"

"Go ahead," Gaby responded.

Sonia unwrapped the first box. It contained a Littmann Classic III emerald-green stethoscope.

"The same one I use," Gaby said.

Tears began to accumulate in Sonia's eyes as she opened the second gift—an iPad.

"It has every one of the basic texts you'll need for the next five school years preloaded," Gaby told her.

Sobbing, Sonia gave Gabriela a heartfelt hug. "You are an angel," the young woman whispered to Gaby.

Gabriela held Sonia gently by the shoulders and looked her in the eyes. "Thank you. But the real angel is standing right over there." She gestured to where Felipe was standing. "Your brother's courage, his love for you, is why we're all here. What I did for you in the operating room and even these small gifts are a reflection of my passion, my purpose, and my responsibility. Don't ever forget that. Those are things you'll soon be able to do for the people in this room, for everyone just outside your house right now, and for anyone you'll ever touch from this moment on."

Sonia hugged Gaby once more.

Sam just watched their emotional interaction. He didn't understand most of what was said but did catch a few key words. In his heart and mind, he concurred with Sonia's assessment. Gaby was an angel—an angel he was deeply in love with.

Gaby and Sam were later escorted to the house across the way, where a brunch had been prepared. They shared this meal with Felipe and Sonia's family and friends. They were then given a tour of their *ejido*—a large communal parcel of hillside land surrounded by green woods that their predecessors had received from the government soon after the end of the Mexican Revolution. Unlike ejidos in other parts of the country, which were either barren or had been stolen back from farmers, their community had made a living off the land ever since.

"It's amazing this land gives so much to everyone here. I'm certain some of what they produce ends up on our tables," Gaby said to Sam during their short walk. "This landscape is beautiful—all of it—even the patchwork of dwellings, all this seemingly incoherent infrastructure, and the general absence of the usual comforts and aesthetics we're accustomed to. Any cursory glimpse at this land might lead someone to think these people are painfully poor and this environment is undesirable. But everyone has a roof over their heads, and all the homes are as warm as the people who live in them. The air is pure, and the scenery beyond these farmlands is grand. Food is simple but plentiful."

Sam said, "And now they're also cultivating future professionals who can hopefully give back to their community for years to come."

She looked at Sam warmly. "Oh, Sam. Yes. You get it."

"Trust me. I do get it," he said.

Later, Felipe drove them back to the city center. They walked around the charming streets. Sam stopped at a leather shop and bought a beautiful handmade collar for Nic, as well as a stylish black leather jacket for Tony. The three got fruit cocktails with lime and sprinkled chili powder from a pushcart vendor while strolling around the central plaza. Gaby and Sam continued to have a wonderful time taking in the town and its people. Just before sunset, they returned to the house.

Preparations in the barn were done. Chairs and tables had been placed at the perimeter of the makeshift stage. A five-man band had set up, and the musicians were adjusting their instruments. A traditional piñata had been hung on a rope that stretched from their roof to that of another home across the way. A few people still came and went, but most had disappeared. They'd gone home to clean up and get ready.

"I guess it's time to freshen up and get dressed for the party," Gabriela said.

While Gaby used the small bathroom to change, Sam exchanged his Worcester Sharks T-shirt for a tan, long-sleeve, merino crewneck. He also traded his sneakers for his dressier but comfortable Cole Haans. Then he went to wait for Gaby just outside the front door. Sam saw a number of dressed-up people walking toward the barn. He waved to several who'd smiled and waved at him. Out of the blue, a soccer ball rolled toward his feet. Sam took a few steps forward and dexterously kicked up the ball. He was able to bounce it off his foot and knee a dozen times before he kicked it back to some kids a few yards away. The two boys gave him a thumbs-up.

"Nice moves there, Mr. Beckham. I'm impressed," Gabriela said behind him. She wore a lace BCBG Layla dress. Her shoes were sling-back, low-heel Chanel pumps. Despite the outfit's brand names, it was far from ostentatious. Her appearance was alluring yet perfect for the occasion.

"Did I miss the dudes with the professional cameras? 'Cuz wow! It's me who's impressed. You belong on the cover of *Vogue*," he exclaimed. He walked toward her and offered her his arm. "Shall we?"

"We shall. Let's party," she replied, a beaming smile on her crimson lips.

FORTY-FIVE

The birthday celebration had come to an end. Sam and Gabriela had gone to bed.

Like a movie reel, all the day's events, particularly those from a few hours prior, flashed vividly in Gabriela's mind.

The sweet, earthy aroma of the wildflowers on the nightstand suffused the bedroom air and soothed her. Still, Gabriela struggled to remember the exact quote. It had been years since she'd read Pascal Mercier's *Night Train to Lisbon*. But she couldn't think of anything else. A short passage in the book encapsulated how she felt at that very moment.

Lying on her side beneath a warm blanket, her face resting on a soft pillow, Gabriela stared at Sam. He was asleep just a few feet away on a similar twin bed. Moonlight broke through a slit between the curtains, illuminating his face and his partially uncovered torso. The pair of keys dangled from the leather string around his neck.

She contemplated him in much the same way he'd done, not too long ago, in that Uber on their way to the house by the river.

Gaby searched deep within the confines of her memory and finally exhumed most of Amadeu de Prado's words. They came together quietly in her mind but resonated soundly in her heart. The book's character had said this:

It is a mistake to believe that the crucial moments of a life—when its habitual direction changes forever—must be loud and shrill....In truth, the dramatics of a life-determining experience are often unbelievably soft.

It is thus that—softly—in a humble bedroom, surrounded by the almost mystical predawn silence of that remote mountain village, Gabriela fully accepted her profound love for Sam.

FORTY-SIX

"Wait. What? You slept in the same room with her, after a long evening of dancing to Latin music...and... you...didn't?" Tony leaned forward and grabbed the steering wheel so hard his knuckles blanched. They'd just exited the turnpike and were now driving north on Southbridge Street when Tony hastily crossed the opposite lane of traffic, drove into the City Tire Co. parking lot, and slammed on the brakes. The old Maverick's tires screeched to a halt.

"What the hell, man," Sam howled.

"Gimme your phone."

"What?"

"You heard me. Gimme your phone," Tony demanded.

"You're acting weird."

"Samuel Gleeson, hand over that fucking phone," Tony said.

"All right, all right." Sam handed over his phone.

Tony grabbed Sam's phone. "Now get the fuck out of the car."

Sam stared at him in disbelief. "Dude, it's freezing out. Come on, Tony. I'm tired. It was a long day and a long flight. And it's freakin' midnight."

"What? You're scared? You afraid of gettin' mugged? Sam, we've been walking these streets at all hours since we were in grade school. Now get the fuck out of the car. The more you wait here, the longer it's gonna take you to get home."

"Are you shittin' me?" Sam got out. "Now what?"

"Now you shut that door and you walk home," Tony replied, but with a smile. After Sam closed the door, Tony leaned over to crank down the window.

"What about my phone?"

"Nah. I took it 'cuz I don't want you calling a taxi. Sammy, you gotta think long and hard about what you did. Actually, you gotta think about what you didn't do with Gaby. And I don't just mean the pitiful and alarming lack of sex. This is a lesson. I need you to figure it out. Okay, see you at home." He burned a bit more rubber as he blazed out of the parking lot.

"You are demented!" Sam screamed behind the fleeing car. He caught a glimpse of Tony's hand waving out the window.

Sam sighed deeply. He shook his head and, with a smile, started walking home along the nearly deserted, barely lit street.

What Tony didn't know was that Sam had already figured it out.

Sam turned left on Hammond Street and walked about five blocks through an industrial area. Just as he emerged from the second overpass bridge, he saw a pair of headlights flash on and off from the loading dock at New Method Plating, a small old factory just off the road. He crossed the street and got back into the car.

"Prick!" Sam declared, playfully pushing Tony's shoulder.

"Sammy, I don't think you get it. I can totally tell there's something there—something different and good with this chick."

"Don't call her that."

"See? That's what I mean. Do I have to spell it out for you?" Tony exclaimed as he pulled out of the driveway.

"No, you don't have to tell me." Sam adjusted his seat belt. "I know what you mean. I think I've known for a while. It's just… it's just I've never felt that…felt *this* before," he said. "But it's just not possible."

"What do you mean? Next time you see her, you just gotta tell her. Easy peasy. What's the worst that could happen? If she's not into you, well, fuck—you deal with it then. But you won't know unless you ask."

"Dude, her mom told me she's been groomed to become the director of the National Transplant System—for all of Mexico. So it's not that easy. Besides, I don't think there's gonna be a next time."

"Why not?"

"I doubt she'll want to. Not after the stuff we talked about after the party last night—the stuff I told her about me, about my simple small-town, small-time life. I mean, it just all came out." He looked pensively ahead. "But in a way, it's good I got my cards out on the table. I wanted her to see me for who I am, I guess."

"Shit! With that attitude, I wouldn't want to talk to you either. Why are you puttin' yourself down? The last thing you are is a loser, so stop sounding like one, bro!"

"Can we not talk about it?"

"Fuck that. We're totally gonna talk about it. Now, how come you think she won't want to see you again?"

As they drove home and after they got to their apartment, Sam told Tony the bits he felt were most relevant. After finally getting to bed, Sam continued to rehash all the weekend's events. With Nic and Vin by his side, he eventually fell asleep.

The previous evening, he and Gaby had enjoyed a delicious dinner just before Sonia, in her lovely prom-like dress, made an entrance. The band played "Las Mañanitas"—the traditional Mexican birthday song—and a number of other special-occasion classics. After Sonia had her first dances with her brother and father, everyone else joined them on the dance floor. Gabriela did her best to lead Sam in dancing to *cumbia*, *norteño*, *sonora*, *trio*, and even rock and roll music. They also each danced with different family members and their friends. Sam was invited to try pulque, an ancient alcoholic drink derived from the maguey plant. They were made to feel like part of the family.

The cake and the piñata provided an intermission, and then there was more dancing, more food, and more glee.

It was just past midnight when the band played the final notes to La Sonora Santanera's "La Boa." Gaby twirled one last time under Sam's arm before they joined everyone else in applause.

"I'm exhausted," she told him.

"Yeah, me too," Sam replied. "Not to mention, a tad inebriated. That pulque sure packs a punch!"

They went around to thank and wish everyone a good night. Felipe escorted them back to his house and pointed out where they could find snacks, water, dinnerware, and utensils. They said good night to Felipe and went to their bedroom.

"Well, that was so much fun," Gaby said, sitting on the edge of the bed, her legs elegantly crossed.

On the opposite bed, Sam had lain down, stretching his arms out. He promptly sat back up. "Yeah, I had a great time. I really appreciate you bringing me here."

"It was my pleasure. I thought it would be nice for you to see a little bit of what lies beyond the zip codes you've been privy to while with our family and friends. I wanted you to get a sense of how most people in the greater metropolitan area and just outside the big city live. Obviously, many don't live in the bubble of privilege my family and even the middle class enjoy. As I mentioned earlier, the infrastructure and the general optics of towns like this may not be what the average American or those in my neighborhood are used to. But as you can see, beyond the bubble, there is beauty. And nature. And culture. And grit. Not to mention love and happiness. I mean, look at this incredible town. The food is simple but abundant. The homes are cozy. And there are plenty of smiles. Now, I don't mean to whitewash the circumstances in these communities. A great deal should be done—from education to services—in order to procure more comfortable lives for everyone and bring them closer to what the rest of us enjoy. People here work very hard, help each other, and with high spirits, slowly strive for better futures. Sonia is a perfect example of this. But she shouldn't be the first in their community to go to school—everyone here should have more access to education. Their labor definitely needs to bear more fruit. That's why it's incumbent upon people like me and families like mine—as well as the government—to help everyone here succeed more and more often. I don't know, I guess my point is that first impressions don't tell the whole story: yes, there is much to do in order to close the socioeconomic gaps, but poverty in most Mexican communities, in relative terms, isn't absolute. It's real, it needs to improve, but there are silver linings that may not be readily apparent. How's that for an impromptu social commentary?"

"That was pretty good. I get it. Their kind of poverty is material. A financial infusion could definitely do wonders—they are so nice and surely deserve it. Yet they make do. While they don't have much money, they have the basics. And they are rich in community, land, and most of all, love. It has been so nice to know these folks, to know about them," Sam said. "I've only spent three weeks total in Mexico. But wow. So far, everything and everyone has been way beyond anything I ever imagined. In an extraordinary way, actually."

"I'm so glad you think so, Sam. It's great to know you had a good time. But all good things must come to an end, I suppose. Time for rest now," Gabriela said.

"Yeah, I'm with you," he responded. A brief awkward silence ensued. "You know, before we came here, you asked if it would be okay if we shared this room. Which is totally cool, but I didn't quite think it through. So, do we sleep with our clothes on, or turn around while we change, or turn the light off? How do you wanna work it?" He smiled without motive or agenda, just wanting to make light of things.

Gabriela's first instinct was to thank him for once again making her feel at ease. But with a devious smile, she said, "No, no. I think we can just go on and get naked. We're both grown-ups. I'm sure I can resist you, my friend."

Sam picked up on her playful tone. "I don't know about that, Gabs. Just in case, hmm, let's see." He pushed down on the mattress a few times, pretending to test the bed's sturdiness. "This one might do just fine. How's yours?"

Gabriela burst into laughter. She scanned the beds back and forth, mockingly analytical. "Bummer! If only the beds were bigger. You see, I need a lot of room for this sort of thing. And this floor is too hard. I wouldn't want to hurt you."

"Yeah, I'm pretty fragile. I do try to avoid injury and stay away from solid surfaces."

"Oh, Sam. Your knack for making me laugh is endless. Anyway, we can take turns in the bathroom," Gaby said, standing and grabbing her bag. Halfway between the beds, she looked over her shoulder at Sam. "Would you mind giving me a little help, though?" She tapped her upper back with her index finger.

"I think I can be of service." Sam went over to assist with the zipper on her dress.

With her neck flexed forward, she lifted her shoulder-length hair with one hand.

His fingers were now in contact with her skin. Sam grabbed the dangly metal stump and slowly lowered it halfway down. The dress parted like a time-lapse of a flower bud opening in early spring. Her back's delicate midline ridge was exposed. For an instant, his thumb grazed her supple skin, just below her bra. "I think this should do it. Any more, and we may have to reconsider bodily injury on the hard floor here," he bantered.

She smiled. "I can take it from here. I appreciate your help."

"Anytime," Sam replied, gesturing chivalrously toward the bedroom door.

When Gabriela returned from the bathroom, she'd changed into formfitting purple pajamas. She looked impossibly cute and sexy. Sam could think of so many things he wanted to say—even just one cursory compliment. But he simply said, "All done?" After Gaby nodded, he took his turn using the bathroom.

She sat down on the bed and leaned back against the wooden headboard, then began fiddling with her phone. Minutes later, Sam returned from the bathroom, still towel-drying his hair. Gabriela lowered her phone and squinted. "What does that mean?" she asked, pointing to his T-shirt. It read "I am programmed to think I am human."

Sam smiled and pulled down the corner of his T-shirt. "You probably can't read this other smaller bit from there. It says 'And I have a plan.'"

"Yeah? And what is that?"

"I suppose some would say the plan is to get rid of humans and replace them with androids, aka Cylons—like myself, of course. Others would say the plan is to integrate with and live among humans," Sam said with a sarcastic smile. "You look confused. I take it you've never seen *Battlestar Galactica*."

"That kind of sounds familiar. But no, I've never seen it," she replied. "Once again, nerdy, but okay."

"Come on. You don't like space-based or futuristic shows and movies?"

"Of course I do. I like *Star Trek*. I mean, I don't speak Klingon, but I've seen some episodes and have enjoyed some of the movies."

"Phew!" Sam pretended to wipe sweat from his brow. He hung his towel on a nearby chair and got into bed. "I was worried for a second there. I'm glad you're cool with *Star Trek*." Facing Gabriela, he asked, "So, what's your favorite TV show?"

"Huh! I've never thought about it. I guess *Rebelde* is up there. I used to watch it while I was in college. It's a telenovela about a group of high school friends who, among other things, aspire to become singers. Not because I wanted to sing. Mostly it reminded me of my own experience in school, of my friends, and of a time when life was more carefree. I think it's now on Netflix, with subtitles, if you're ever interested in watching an old soap opera in Spanish."

"That's cool. Maybe I'll check it out. I suppose high school can go either way for people. It was mostly good for me and Tony," he said, smiling.

"How about movies. What is your favorite movie?" Gabriela asked.

"*The Godfather,*" Sam said.

"Wow. You didn't think twice about that. But since that's probably every guy's answer, how about your second favorite?"

"Gee. Let's see…I guess the one that holds a special place in my heart is *Summer of '42.* It's an old coming-of-age flick from the seventies. I saw it a long time ago. I must have been in junior high or high school. I was totally in love with Jennifer O'Neill."

"Funny. I know that movie. Well, I don't remember it much, except that my dad loves it. Probably for the same reason you like it" she said with a quick roll of her eyes. "Wait, isn't there a famous song or melody from it?"

"Yes, it's called 'The Summer Knows,'" Sam replied, surprised she recognized the movie and its musical score. "I know your favorite movie is *Casablanca.* You quoted Bogart's character the first day we met. So, how about your second favorite?"

Gabriela set her phone on the nightstand. She hugged her knees, now fully facing Sam. "I want to say *Citizen Kane* or Fellini's *La Strada* or *Gone With the Wind* or *Lawrence of Arabia* to impress you. But the truth is, the first thing that comes to mind is *Twilight.* Or, more specifically, *The Twilight Saga.* All five movies. There! I said it. I'm a Twihard."

Sam burst out laughing. "Well? Team Edward or Team Jacob?"

"Wow, Sam. I can't believe you know *Twilight.*"

"Of course I do. Why wouldn't I? It's not just for teenyboppers. I mean, who wouldn't be into looking like a million bucks?

Alongside someone you love? Forever? Hell yeah! I'd move to Forks or a cool place like Portland and live eternally on blood. There is a certain allure to being a vampire." Sam grinned and raised an eyebrow. "So?"

Gabriela cheerfully shook her head. "Well, I went back and forth at the beginning. But in the end, Team Edward, of course," she said, glancing studiously at Sam. "I was about to ask your *Twilight* team preference. However, more importantly, how is it you came to be a Twihard too? Did you purchase your ticket months in advance and stand in line for hours with a bunch of teenage girls on opening day?"

Sam smiled and nodded. "You laugh. But I did. Like a bunch of other nonteenage dudes there, I was dragged to it. Obviously, I ended up liking it. Over the next few years, I watched the rest of the series on my own. Just don't tell Tony about this. I'd never hear the end of it."

"So you *are* a romantic. Don't worry. Your secret is safe with me," she gleefully assured him. "I was now going to ask, in a roundabout way, who dragged you to see the movie. But since we're having a sleepover, and since one asks these kinds of questions at sleepovers, can I be totally nosy and ask if there's someone special in your life?"

He pretended to ponder the question. "Yes, of course. There's Tony, my sister, her family—"

"Come on, Sam. You know what I mean," Gaby interrupted.

"Hmm. How about you? Anyone special?"

"No, no, buddy. You're not getting off the hook that easy. I asked you first. After spending two weeks at my mom's, I'm certain she shared all kinds of silly and indiscreet things about me. It's my turn to know more about you."

"Nope. Nobody special," he responded. Almost instantly, Sam worried his quick response could've come across as if he were trying to hide something. He wasn't. He simply felt unsure about revealing anything she might perceive as undesirable. Yet he knew she deserved a more detailed and personal answer—whether as the woman he secretly loved or as the friend he openly cherished. He cleared his throat. "There *was* someone. Her name is Emma. We met at a friend's party. It was during my time in the army. I had some leave and went home for a couple of weeks. We kind of hit it off. After I returned to Afghanistan, we had a long-distance relationship. And when I went home for good, I had a girlfriend waiting for me. She was the one who dragged me to see *Twilight*," Sam said, smiling and now lying on his side to face Gabriela. His arm was bent at the elbow, and his head rested on his palm. "It was nice for a while. But in the end, it didn't work out."

"I'm sorry to hear that," Gaby said, looking empathetic.

"It's okay. In retrospect, it's for the best."

After a moment of reflection, she said, "I guess love doesn't always work out."

"That's the thing. The more I thought about it after the fact, I realized that what we had wasn't love. Or maybe just not enough of it. When push came to shove, I don't think I quite met her expectations. Although I was willing to try," he said.

"What were those expectations?"

"I don't know. More than expectations, I think she had visions of what we could be." Sam paused. "She had visions of what *I* could be. I mean, it was fairly straightforward. She wanted me to get a master's degree in engineering, get a high-paying job, propose to her in a way that would make her girlfriends jealous, have a dream wedding in the Berkshires, move to a proper house near Boston, and have a couple of kids."

"I see. And what did you want?"

"Hmm. I think I've kind of made her sound superficial or frivolous. Emma is actually really nice. At any rate, the truth is, I didn't have a life plan. The only thing I knew for sure was I had to help Tony. To Emma's credit, she was behind that, including having him live with us for as long as he needed. So I did honestly consider everything she'd suggested for us, and I was willing to give it a shot," Sam said, transiently musing—wondering what life might have been like with Emma. "I don't think I have a concrete answer to your question. I didn't want anything in particular. Basically, over time, my aspirations for the future just weren't what Emma envisioned, especially when it came to the big-ticket items. I think she realized this, which is why she graciously bowed out. No regrets, though. I'm sure it was best for us both."

Gabriela let a few seconds go by, waiting for him to continue. But he seemed done. "I'm sorry, Sam, but you're not sticking to sleepover etiquette. That was kind of vague. You're leaving out the juice!"

Sam laughed. "The juice?"

"Yes, *the juice*. You can't leave out the nitty-gritty. What were those aspirations, and what do you mean by big-ticket items? Sam, what makes you tick?"

Sam knew he was about to extinguish any possibility of being more than just friends with Gabriela. She'd be unimpressed. Or worse, disappointed. But there was no point in obfuscating the truth about what he now considered his modest hopes and dreams. He needed to communicate to her that he lived a plain life and imagined a comparatively unembellished future for himself. But that *this* made him happy.

Let the cards fall where they may, Sam thought. "Okay...well, I do want to get a master's degree. But not in engineering. In education. I want to teach high school. More specifically, I want to teach at North High, where Tony and I went. It's the kind of place where it's probably hard to be a teacher but even harder to be a student. There's insufficient funding on one side and difficult home situations on the other. It's a rough place.

"Despite it all, every year a handful of kids do graduate with decent chances of success. This is due, in great part, to a few teachers who are really good at what they do and who really care.

I don't think I would've been able to go to college without teachers who went the extra mile for me. I want to give back to my community—to the kids who are growing up like I did. I want to provide them with as much academic and personal guidance as I can. Maybe one day, I can help increase the number of students who go on to college and to better lives.

"Now, thanks to your grandfather, I can also try to find ways to assist them with some essential material things most people take for granted.

"I mean, take a backpack. A poor kid literally may not have access to one. Without it, you're much less likely to take textbooks home. That limits your opportunities to read, learn, or even just expand your vocabulary outside of the classroom. You never acquire a personal reading culture. This puts poor kids at a disadvantage when competing against those with shelves full of books at home or, for that matter, a paid Amazon account that allows them to download books onto their iPads.

"Another example is something as basic as being able to buy toothpaste and toothbrushes on a regular basis. Kids from disadvantaged homes just don't have that. If your oral hygiene is substandard, you get toothaches or worse, which then prevents you from concentrating on learning. These kids might not have school supplies, or a sweater that could keep you from shivering in a classroom with a rickety heater, or even the right socks to go with the free track shoes your coach gave you. You get the picture. I want to lend a hand to these kids and provide them with basic things that could jump-start their journeys in life."

Sam wasn't sure what to make of Gaby's observant, quiet demeanor. But he continued, "That's kind of my professional vision. Plus, on a less career-oriented basis, I'd also like to continue coaching sports and volunteering in animal welfare programs—that sort of thing."

She was in awe, processing his every word. After he stopped, she asked, "How about personally? Marriage? Kids? What's in store for you in that respect?"

With a playful smile and raised eyebrows, he said, "Those are some of the big-ticket items. After my near engagement, I haven't given marriage much consideration—a tarot reader might actually have a better idea about that." Sam transiently pressed his lips together. "With regard to kids...I'd find it hard to have any of my own. I'm not sure I could, knowing so many are in the system who could use a real parent—someone who's in it for more than a monthly check."

There was a brief interlude. Then, softly, Gaby told him, "Sam, that is admirable."

"Well, my aspirations aren't particularly ambitious and are far from glamorous. They just feel like callings. Plus, my view on having kids may be a bit skewed but also feels right. These are probably some of the reasons why Emma bailed. Not to mention, of course, that I never saw myself in shorts and flip-flops, mowing the lawn and trimming hedges around my white-picket-fenced home. That's why I don't think what we had was love—if it had been, we probably would've tried to meet in the middle."

"I don't often think of these things," Gabriela said. "I've never been in a situation of such magnitude. But something tells me the traditionally important milestones in life eventually fall into place. How this happens is sometimes great and other times not so much. When it comes to relationships, people often try to force their square dreams and hopes into the round convictions, sensibilities, and even practical realities of another. Naturally, this can lead to lifelong problems or regrets. But every once in a while, I believe people do get lucky and find their perfect fit. I don't know. Maybe perfection is not possible. But it's something to hope for." She sighed. "On that note, would you mind if we end it here? I think a little sleep is in order."

"Yeah, of course. Let me get the light." Sam sprang up to shut off the wall switch and then returned to bed. All the while, he thought, *I guess my natural relationship repellent did its job—just friends it is!*

Her seemingly abrupt request to end their conversation made Sam assume the worst.

Gabriela, though, just didn't want to diminish the significance of what he'd just shared. Logically, she would've had to share her own relationship experiences, which she felt were inconsequential and inadequate in comparison.

Silent minutes passed.

Sam glanced in her direction. Through the darkness, he saw Gaby lying comfortably on her side, facing him, with her eyes closed. He thought she was asleep. He quietly sat up and slipped off his T-shirt, then burrowed back under the covers and eventually fell asleep.

Her eyes, though, were open—just a smidge. She looked at him, her mind engaged and her heart astir.

Later that morning, a driver picked them up. They went back to her parents' house to say goodbye and grab Sam's luggage before heading to the airport.

FORTY-SEVEN

"Yo, Sam. Got your order right here. Three fried-chicken specials with rice, mac, and corn bread. One order of collards and one potato salad. That'll be thirty-two dollars even," said Axel, working the counter at Addie Lee's Soul Food. "Good to see you again, by the way. How you been?"

"Nice to see you too, man. I'm well, thanks. How's business? Oh, and how's the crew?" Sam asked as he handed over his credit card.

"All good. No complaints. Say, we heard you were down Mexico-way seeing about a señorita."

"Nah. Just a good friend. Went there for a job, actually," he said, immediately realizing who was behind the press release on his recent whereabouts.

"That ain't the word coming out of the barbershop. But good to hear it straight from the horse's mouth. How's business and your crew?"

"As usual, we could use more foot traffic in the evenings. But we're all good," Sam answered. "That may change, though, now that I gotta go back to the shop and beat the crap out of Tony for spreading rumors."

"Yeah, you do that. He can't be puttin' you at a disadvantage with the ladies around here!"

"Catch you later, man."

"See ya, Sam."

With lunch in hand, Sam crossed the street on that chilly, cloudy spring afternoon. It had been less than a day since his return from Mexico.

Two days later, Tony had gone out for poker night with some friends whom Sam wasn't too keen on spending time with. While watching TV, he felt a craving for a slice. He figured he'd take Nic for a long walk and swing by Tech Pizza on Highland Street. Once there, Sam asked for his usual: a plain slice and a slice of pepperoni.

After Sam paid, he waited near the counter. Nic sat patiently next to him, knowing some crust would eventually come his way. The older, good-humored man tending the pizzeria knew Sam well and didn't mind the four-legged customer. He went to grab the crispy hot slices, slapping them on some overlapped paper plates and nearly simultaneously shoving them into a take-out bag. "So, Sam, when do we get to meet this Latin honey of yours?"

Before he even answered, a motherly female voice called loudly from the kitchen, "She's just tryin' to marry you for a green card! Does she even speak English? You be careful, Sam. Lotta fine girls here in Woostah for you, hon."

"Don't listen to her, Sam. If she's as pretty as Tony and Lenny say, you just do what's in your heart. It's time you found someone steady again. If she needs a little part-time gig, we can probably help you guys out. Maybe she can go to beauty school. Have you thought about that? You guys could have a barber *and* a beauty shop."

Sam almost burst into laughter. He shook his head. "Not sure what they told you, but it's not like that. She's just a friend I recently met. And she's more than fine where she is."

"They didn't tell me much. Something about you going there to help her find some house and fix her computer or something like that. I guess they don't have those kinds of services there, huh? It was kinda busy in here when Tony and Lenny came by. I was just tuning in and out. I do remember they said she's a stunner. Anyway, go on home before those get cold on ya. Just let us know if we can help."

It wasn't the time to clear things up. Sam just smiled and thanked him. He walked down a few blocks to Elm Park. He and Nic sat on a bench across the street from the Price Chopper parking lot. With the headlights of cars intermittently spotlighting them, they ate their pizza.

Sam reflected on his friends' inability to keep their mouths shut. He wasn't mad. It was just guys being guys—part and parcel of what they'd always done. He understood the facts would get murky in the blender of gossip. At least Sam knew the guys were prudent and respectful enough to keep the inheritance part of his new reality private.

One day the following week, Lilly asked Sam to meet her for lunch at the Worcester Common, behind City Hall.

"Hey, Lilly, what's up?" Sam said. Lilly was already waiting for him at one of the many umbrella-covered tables in that section of the park. Despite the chilly weather, people were sitting at other tables, enjoying their lunch.

"Sit down, I got you a burrito from Talyta's across the street. I figured this would help you ease back from your two-week stint in Mexico."

"Yeah! Good call. Although they don't actually have burritos down there. These are an American invention," Sam said as he unwrapped his goodie. After a few bites, he asked, "So, what's the occasion?"

"The girls are back in school. I had some free time today, so I thought it would be nice to have lunch. And I wanted to show you one thing, and tell you about another…things you've probably seen countless times, actually. But like me, you've probably never quite fully noticed them. The second one made me cry, but in a good way."

"What do you mean?"

She sipped from her Starbucks. "Last weekend we came here for a playdate. The girls were running around over there, and then Lenny pointed something out. Take a look that way. What do you see?"

Burrito in hand, Sam glanced at the east side of the park. He scanned side to side, far and near. "What am I missing?"

"What's right in front of us?"

"Do you mean the fountain?" He asked and looked closer. "Holy crap. It's a World War Two memorial," he said after reading the inscription.

"It is. I never knew it. Even if I did, it wouldn't have meant anything to me. But now it has this personal significance. It honors both our grandparents—whom we knew nothing about. All my life, I've had this feeling of…I don't know…aloneness, I guess. I've always felt it was just you, Tony, and me. Of course, later on, Lenny and the girls came along. But even with our friends, everyone else we know, and despite having lived here all our lives, I've always felt sort of disconnected. I've felt like an outsider…like the people and the city took us in."

"I know the feeling. I think it's to do with not having had an actual family core—no house or something physical to point at and say 'there, that's where we come from.' Even though we couldn't be more native to Worcester, we've always felt shaky about our roots," Sam said.

"Well, after everything you told us, and realizing what this fountain represents, Lenny and I did a little more research. This memorial isn't everything we uncovered. Do you know the corner of Lake Avenue and Hamilton Street?"

"Do you mean Tivnan Field?"

"Yes. Across from the baseball park," Lilly said, a hint of mois-ture now in her eyes. "There's a tiny monument on the grassy knoll there. It looks like a large headstone."

"I know which one you mean. Off and on I've seen flowers and flags in front of it. I've always assumed it was a tribute to someone who died at the intersection in a car accident."

"Nope. Turns out, it's the first monument to honor the two hundred and fifty-three World War Two veterans from Worcester," she informed him. "It's much older than this one. That one was built and dedicated in 1947. Lenny and I went there last week-end." Tears now glistened and glided down her cheeks. "We climbed up to check it out, and on one of the crumbly plaques, almost immediately, we found an Evan S. Blake. We couldn't be-lieve it. I still can't believe it...your middle name? And our mom's maiden name? It's obviously our grandfather. He's enshrined in this city's history. I mean, talk about roots—about something and someone to point at to show where we come from! Not to men-tion everything we now know about our grandmother. Somehow, for the first time in my life, at that moment, I didn't feel like an orphan. It was weird. It's still weird."

"That's freaking amazing. I gotta go see it," Sam said, truly excited.

"Now that you are back, I thought it would be nice to have a picnic there this weekend—with everyone. We can celebrate that we actually have a past. We can celebrate *their* past. We'll honor that they were part of the Greatest Generation, some of the best to ever come out of this city. We can toast to them: because of who they were and what they did, we have the freedom to be and do what we want."

"That sounds great. I'm totally looking forward to it."

After a moment of mutual reflection, Lilly asked, "So, on a related note, have you heard from Gaby?"

"Yeah. We text off and on," Sam responded.

"And?"

"What do you mean, *and?*"

Lilly looked back at him skeptically—an eyebrow raised, a crooked smile.

Sam shook his head. "I guess you can't bullshit a bullshitter, huh?"

"Sam, I just don't want you to get hurt."

"I know that. I won't. I guess it's obvious that I like her. Who wouldn't? But I accept this can't be more than a friendship. For one, I have no clue how she feels about me beyond the friendship we have. For another, like I told Tony, even if she ever thought about something more, after this last trip I suspect she feels differently now. I mean, you know what I want to do professionally—not exactly up to her caliber. Plus, you know how I feel about having a family—not exactly what any girl wants to hear. You and Lenny are lucky to have been on the same page about adopting the girls. Anyway, I kind of told her these things just before I left."

"What did she say?"

"Nothing. It was just before we went to bed," he told his sister. "It wasn't weird or awkward, though. That's just how the conversation ended. I assumed the worst, but come to think about it, I didn't pick up any vibe one way or another from her. Maybe it's ingrained cynicism on my part. But I think it's best to assume she wasn't fond of my plans. So I need to shed these less platonic feelings I have for her because I want to keep her and her family as friends. They're really good people."

"Obviously, I don't know her as you do," Lilly said. "But based on what you've told me, she doesn't seem like someone who'd reject you for your outlook on life. I think she'd actually think the opposite. But a romantic relationship sure seems difficult. Give it time. Things tend to iron themselves out along the way."

Sam's life in Worcester went on nearly as usual. For the next few weeks, he continued to enjoy his electronic interactions with Gabriela—grounded to the fact that they couldn't be more than friends. In this regard, he told himself two things. One, he wasn't sure what *more* could possibly look like. And two, it was probably inevitable their communication would eventually dwindle, as it had after his first trip to Mexico.

Yet her texts and emails didn't stop this time.

In fact, their communication got more and more regular. Every so often, Gabriela even called in the evenings. Tony would roll his eyes and fake being annoyed if they were in the middle of watching TV. He'd tease Sam about it after, but he was thrilled to see his brother happy and animated when she called.

Additionally, despite the distance, the interactions between Sam and Gaby became increasingly personal. Slowly, they learned more about each other with every call, text, or emoji. Their now frequent communication and the resulting stronger connection made them happier and enhanced their days. Laughs abounded.

One day, the topic of relationships came up again. Except for Sam's one serious relationship with Emma, they both acknowledged they'd just casually dated. Realizing nearly all of their relationships had been trivial and short-lived, Gabriela playfully asked, "Dammit, Sam. Are you and I just sluts?"

Nic and Vin were startled when Sam broke into a loud and prolonged laugh. Even Tony yelled from the living room to ask if he was okay. When the mutual laughter finally abated, he told her, "Not at all. I'd call it an exploration of human...endeavors. Yes, a tour and analysis of the human experience. That's all."

At no point, however, did they reference what they ardently wondered every time they hung up: What would a romantic relationship between them actually look like?

As a result, over the next few months, Sam began to slowly shelve his love for Gabriela. He felt content with their relationship. That she never mentioned anything potentially romantic between them further corroborated his assumptions.

Then, on the first day of summer, Sam, Tony, and their friend Rathnakar caught the buffet at Bollywood Grill in Quinsigamond Plaza. Sam was away from the table, getting a second helping of food, when his phone chirped, indicating a new text message. Tony grabbed it.

"Dude, why are you checking Sam's messages? I know you two are brothers and all, but that's kind of messed up," Rathnakar said.

"It's all good," Tony replied, looking at the screen. His eyes widened. "Well, it's about freaking time! This is gonna get interesting."

"What's gonna get interesting?" Sam asked, coming up from behind and setting his heaping second serving on the table. Tony shoved the phone in front of Sam's face. After a slight head recoil, he homed in on the message. Gaby had texted, "I'm off for three weeks starting this coming weekend. Will you teach me how to drive?"

Gabriela Martel was coming to Worcester.

FORTY-EIGHT

Sam asked Tony to come with him to Boston Logan International Airport that Saturday evening.

From the moment he woke up, he felt jittery. He knew there'd be the usual pleasantry of a light kiss and a hug once he saw Gabriela again. He was sure this would send him into an instantaneous trance. But he didn't want to succumb to his emotions for too long. Because if he did, he was afraid he'd reveal his true feelings and possibly ruin her visit. At best, Sam didn't want to seem awkward. He needed his brother's presence to help him dull his angst. Sam knew Tony would help him keep it together.

They rarely drove to Boston. When heading to a Red Sox game or any other event in Beantown, they'd typically take the train. When they did drive, Tony always wanted to break his own record. Accounting for tolls and traffic, the standard drive time on the forty-seven-mile stretch was fifty minutes. With only a couple of speeding tickets under his belt over the past several years, Tony currently boasted a cool record of thirty-two minutes.

It wasn't until they hit Newton, with the Maverick going nearly ninety miles per hour, that Tony glanced at Sam and slowed down. He stopped chattering about whether to take Gaby to the Revolution's game against Seattle the following weekend.

"Dude. You haven't said a thing. Sam, what's up?"

"Nothing. I'm good. Yeah, I'm sure she'd enjoy being thrown in the van with a bunch of half-drunk guys talking smack," he responded, staring ahead.

"Shit. Does that mean you are skipping the game?"

Sam smiled at his friend. "Not at all. I meant what I said. She'd probably really like it. She's that cool. Trust me."

Tony did a quick double take. "Oh yeah? Well, if you think she'd be okay with that, then why are you having her stay at the Beechwood?"

"Because that's the best hotel in Worcester!"

"That's not my point. I think you're having some weird inner conflict. She's either cool with who you are and where you live or she's not. And I'm betting she is. I know she's this millionaire, but I'm willing to lose my left nut to bet she is exactly what you just said—*that cool*. The last thing she'd want is for you to treat her like some princess. She's coming here to visit you, to meet your family, to see your friends, and, yes, she even came here to shack up in your—*in our*—shitty apartment. Did you even tell her you got her a hotel room?"

Sam glanced dejectedly out the window. "I didn't tell her about the hotel. I thought about it last minute." He closed his eyes. Then, lightly, he threw his head against the backrest. Glancing up, he said, "Fuck, Tony. You're right."

"Hell yeah, I'm right! She'd probably be offended if you dumped her in a hotel. Buddy, you cannot be anything more or less than Samuel Gleeson—not right now, not during her visit, and not after she leaves. You got that?"

After a short silence, Sam burst into a brief, hearty laugh.

"What's so funny?" Tony asked.

"You. You giving out fatherly advice. Some actually pretty good. But it's still a little weird."

"Fuck you, man. I got no choice. I've had to dole out all kinds of advice lately 'cuz you are acting like an insecure pimple-faced teenager."

"Shit. Yeah, yeah. I know. It's just that..."

"It's just that you're in love with Gaby. I know it, and you know it. Sammy, we have about half an hour between now and when she lands. Before we step into that terminal, you gotta make a choice: either you tell her how you feel and see what happens or you swallow all your feelings for her—completely, for good. I'd favor you telling her. But either way, if you don't make a firm decision now and stick to it, you'll feel torn apart after she's gone." Tony punched Sam on the shoulder. "I only want you hurtin' when I kick your ass for no good reason...not over something like this."

"I know, bro. Thanks," Sam responded with an appreciative glance at Tony.

"So, what's it gonna be?"

Sam let out a long sigh. "Just friends, man. I've thought about it a lot, actually. We can't be more than that. It's too complicated. So there, decision made," he said with apparent satisfaction and relief.

They continued a livelier, more two-sided interaction.

FORTY-NINE

On the first day they'd met, Gabriela had politely shaken his hand. On their subsequent encounter in the lecture hall in San Antonio, she'd walked slowly toward him and they'd converged in a gentle hug. And on their last reunion at the airport in Mexico City, Gaby had walked in earnest to give Sam a heartfelt embrace.

This time, Gabriela emerged from the international arrivals doorway in a knit Balmain dress and heels—an outfit comfortable enough for a five-hour, first-class flight but still elegant. Her makeup was bold and flawless—the kind that transforms inherent beauty into captivating glamour. Gabriela had chosen her appearance for the occasion with considerable forethought and determination—like she'd never done before.

She stopped to scan the clusters of people around her, the raised handle of her roller bag providing a physical crutch for her shaky and nervous inner self. Suddenly, her eyes met Sam's. He stood at the far end of the crowd. Her heart fluttered. But after an instant, her face lit up and her anxiety vanished. Gabriela left her luggage behind, impulsively dashed nearly twenty yards through the crowd, and leapt into Sam's arms.

Impervious to the turned heads, to the many smiles acknowledging their endearing embrace, and to Tony's mesmerized expression, their lips fervently came together. The shackles constraining their suppressed emotions and uncertainties were set asunder. Their feelings were finally liberated with that rapturous first kiss.

FIFTY

Tony procured a pair of large pies from George's Pizza. He set them on the stovetop and turned on the hood light. Then he left a note: *If you finish these, there are plenty of sandwich materials in the fridge. Sam, I'll take care of everything tomorrow. Gaby, again, welcome!*

Tony scooped up Vin in his arms, coaxed Nic to follow him, and turned off the lights in the living room. Just before heading into his bedroom, he glanced across the way. He smiled as he noted the dim light from beneath Sam's closed bedroom door. Tony was certain his friend, his brother, was truly happy.

Save for necessary treks to the bathroom and nourishing forays into the kitchen, Gaby and Sam did not fully emerge from the spellbinding bliss of his bedroom until late the following afternoon.

"I wish we could stay in here forever," Gabriela said, her head resting on Sam's bare chest when they woke up that afternoon. In response, he tenderly tightened the arm he already had around her. Their eyes remained closed. They listened to each other's breathing and continued to bask in the reality of their new relationship. Sam had gladly left behind the previous evening's shock. He'd set aside the impulse to ask about her thoughts and feelings. Any inquiry would lead to complicated questions about the future. He was all too happy to defer logistics and practicalities for another time.

As if she'd read his mind, Gabriela sighed. "For a long time I wondered whether or not you liked me." She raised her head to look up at Sam. "Last night when I felt you kiss me back, when I felt your arms firmly around me, I had my answer. I came so close to asking you a few times before. But I never said anything sentimental or romantic about us because…I just didn't know how. I rationalized that it was for the better. This way, I wouldn't have a distraction of my heart conflicting with all my responsibilities. But eventually, I realized suppressing my feelings was actually worse. So I gathered my nerve for this trip." Gaby reflected silently, now staring at the bits of light percolating through the window's closed blinds. She added, "I know long-distance relationships are difficult. And I don't know how it all works out. But for now, I am happy. I hope you are happy too. If it's okay with you, can we not worry about what's next and just enjoy the time we have together?"

Without hesitation, he replied, "I'd told myself I was going to sweep my feelings for you under the rug and go through the motions of just being friends. But when I saw you last night, I knew there was no way on earth I could hold back anymore." Slightly pulling away, he looked at her. Their eyes met. "Gaby, you stun me. You make all my rational thoughts go up in smoke." With a swift motion of his powerful arm, he pulled her onto him. "I'm happy too. Yes, it seems complicated. But let's just see where the wind takes us."

One more time that afternoon, their bodies lovingly coalesced and reaffirmed the bond of their affection.

Later on, they showered together and got dressed. Gabriela officially met Vin, with whom she immediately fell in love. The sociable cat was pleased to have made another friend. Gaby played with Vin for a few minutes while Sam talked to Tony on the phone in the kitchen. Then he returned to the living room.

"Lenny came by this morning to pick up Tony and Nic so we could have the car. Are you ready to meet the rest of the gang?"

"I'd love to. Although, I don't know why I'm a little nervous," Gabriela said.

"You shouldn't be. You've won them over since last summer, when I first told them about you and your family. Everyone is really chill. In fact, they're the ones who might be a little weirded out to finally meet you."

"Why?"

They walked out of the apartment, and Sam smiled as he locked the front door. "Well, because it's hard not to use superlatives any time you've come up in conversations."

"Oh no, Sam. I just want to be a regular jane."

He shook his head. "Sorry, Gabs. That's not possible. You're anything *but* a regular jane. I mean, come on. For starters, you're on your way to being an entire country's top doctor."

"Not really. The country's top doctor is actually the secretary of health, who is like the surgeon general here. Besides, that would be way down the line—if ever. There are many, many highly trained and capable transplant surgeons in Mexico who'd be brilliant directors of the transplant system."

"According to your mom and other people I talked to, none as brilliant as you." He held the passenger door open for her. Just before closing the door, Sam warmly looked down at her. "That's just one of a ton of reasons. The most important of which is that you're special to me. And that's enough for you to be special in the eyes of everyone I know."

Sundays at Lilly's were always pleasant and low-key. The usual suspects included Lilly, Lenny, their two girls, Sam, Tony, Lenny's parents, and Lenny's sister, including her husband and kids. Friends or neighbors would also occasionally come by. There was plenty of food—potluck dishes in the fall and winter, and nicely charred meats and veggies coming off the grill in the spring and summer. The grown-ups generally talked about grown-up things or watched whatever big games were on TV. The kids and pets played among themselves or slept when their energy ran out. The house was on Mohican Road, a partially paved street facing the docks of the UMass Medical School and a short walk from Lake Quinsigamond. It was located in an agreeable middle-class neighborhood. To anyone passing by, their weekend gatherings were quintessentially all-American. But to Lilly, Sam, and Tony, they were so much more.

These Sunday gatherings meant the world to them. They represented success after their many tribulations growing up in the foster care system. The three had avoided so many pitfalls along the way and managed to stay together. Despite having had a childhood without a traditional family to pattern their lives on, they'd eventually created a beautiful and healthy family of their own.

Gaby was a hit with everyone. She eased into conversations, often wittily. The children immediately took to her. She helped the kids tackle a hundred-piece puzzle. Later, after dinner, and along with Lenny and Sam, she gladly allowed the kids to drag her down to the lake's edge to set off an armada of paper boats.

During this time, alone in the kitchen, Tony asked Lilly why she seemed a little off.

"I'm okay." Lilly leaned over the sink, looking thoughtful. "It's just...she's just too perfect, Tony. I mean, look at her. She's in jeans, a generic-looking top, and sneakers. She's not even trying. And she looks like a freakin' movie star. And she's really nice and...well, everything else that she is."

"What's wrong with that?"

"Nothing. But what happens if things don't work out between them? What happens then? Where do you go after being with someone like that? He'll feel a million times worse than he did when things went south with Emma. I don't want Sam to get hurt."

"Me neither," Tony said. "But at this point, things are what they are. We just gotta be there for him, like we've always been there for one another—no matter what happens. Let's just hope for the best."

Gaby had insisted Sam go about his daily routines the following week. "I want to see you in *your* element," she'd told him Sunday night. Hence, almost every day that week, she tried to fit into Sam's everyday life. In the mornings they jogged and ate breakfast. Gabriela got up to speed quickly at the barbershop, befriended their two employees, and doubled competently as a receptionist-cashier. She even helped sweep up hair after each customer and tidied up the waiting area. Nic got spoiled as she took him on more frequent and much longer walks than usual. Gaby used some of these strolls to explore the downtown area. She and Nic went as far as Institute Park, picking up lunch for everyone from Lucky's Cafe on the way back. On a different occasion, she went as far as Union Station on the opposite end of downtown.

Driving lessons began Monday evening. After many fun fumbles and the inevitable stripping of gears, Gaby quickly conquered the basics of the 1972 Maverick Grabber. By Wednesday, she'd graduated from the relatively empty parking lot at North High to driving on nearby streets.

While enjoying a savory *mi thap cam*—seafood noodle soup—from Dalat Restaurant Friday evening, she jokingly offered to drive the van down to Gillette Stadium the following afternoon, to which Tony replied, "Let's not get ahead of ourselves there, Miss Danica Patrick."

"Lenny, you're the designated driver. Not one drop of booze, you hear?" Lilly said, surrendering the van's keys. She pointed at Sam and Tony through the window. "You boys take care of her," she told them and winked at Gaby.

Lenny made a few stops in Vernon Hill, and later in Marlborough, to pick up their four closest sports-crazed friends.

The fans' excitement at the stadium was contagious. On the way to their seats, Gabriela stopped at a booth to get a temporary tattoo of the flag of New England on her cheek. When the guys said it looked great on her, she quizzed them on its meaning. Sam and Rathnakar knew, but they feigned ignorance and allowed her to school the gang about the red flag with a canton depicting a green pine tree within a white square.

"Really, guys? Look, it's behind the collar on all of your jerseys. All right, history lesson: it was the symbol that arguably preceded the current American flag." She pointed at her cheek. "*This* was created to unify the early colonies that now make up New England."

"Shit! Been livin' here all my life. I didn't know this. Any o' yous knew?" Paul asked.

Everyone shook their heads.

Pleasantly perplexed, Julius said, "I thought you were Mexican. How do you know this?"

"Because I lived in Boston for nine years. I picked it up along the way," she said.

"Hear, hear. To our smarty-pants friend Gaby, to the flag of New England, to the Revs, and to fuck Seattle," Ed exclaimed, raising his plastic cup. Everyone joined in the spirited toast.

Gaby had borrowed one of Sam's scarves, but it was not enough. Besides the tattoo, she also bought and changed into an official Revolution kit. She was now geared up and fit perfectly in section 142, the heart of the Fort—the team's passionate supporters' group.

Gabriela and the guys—including Tony and Sam, wearing their aptly colored luchador masks—appeared three times on the jumbotron. New England beat the Seattle Sounders 3–1. The day couldn't have been more perfect.

The following week was also wonderful. Sam made sure Gaby sampled a variety of eateries, from hole-in-the-wall joints like Maria's Kitchen and Tito's Bakery to the Zagat-rated Sole Proprietor and the Boynton Restaurant. The driving lessons progressed soundly. With Gaby at the wheel, Sam showed her most of the city. They also attended a midweek fundraiser for the Worcester Animal Rescue League. The event's keynote speaker was the founder of the Paw Project—an organization dedicated to educating the public about and advocating to end the painful and crippling effects of feline declawing. Sam explained to her that ever since he was a teenager, he'd always felt a kinship with shelter animals in need of humane care and loving homes. But because he could never contribute financially, he and a handful of friends from the system had always volunteered their time as much as they could. Except for his absence during his military service, Sam had always been part of the league's volunteer corps. He intimated to Gaby that thanks to her grandfather, he'd soon join the donor ranks too. He'd just not figured out the best way to do it. Furthermore, she learned that Sam had used only a small part of the trust fund's discretionary account to pay back his and Tony's debts associated with the barbershop. He'd soon pay off Lilly's mortgage, get his nieces college trust funds, and maybe move to a larger apartment—mostly so the pets could have more space. But Sam told her that for now, he'd decided to leave the main account intact until he felt certain of the most prudent way to make use of it. "It's weird, being debt-free. It almost feels un-American," he joked.

Saturday morning, they had brunch at the legendary Maxwell-Silverman's before heading to Union Station and taking a train to Boston. Gaby had been invited to spend the day and have dinner with an old college friend who lived in the South End.

That week culminated with another enjoyable gathering at Lilly's the next day.

FIFTY-ONE

On the Tuesday of her last week in Worcester, something deep inside Gaby changed. The inciting event was unexpected yet powerful. It was the first practice of the season of Sam's youth soccer team.

Gaby commented on the regal stone griffins welcoming everyone at the Cristoforo Colombo Park's main entrance. Once on the grounds, Sam introduced her to some parents and a few of the kids. By the field's edge, she helped set up a couple of coolers full of cold drinks. Later, she went down the roster Tony had given her and helped measure some kids for their jerseys, shorts, and cleats. After that, the kids and their two coaches hit the field. Some of the players' families sat on lawn chairs along the field. Others sat on blankets on the grass. Gaby opted to sit on the steps of the small amphitheater behind the field's north end.

A middle-aged woman in a bohemian-looking outfit and a little girl were already sitting there. They exchanged hellos. Gaby sat a few feet from them and was about to start checking her phone messages.

"You must be Sam's new girlfriend."

A bit surprised, Gabriela smiled. "Well, as of about two weeks ago, yes, I think I am."

"I'm so sorry. That came out wrong. I think I made him sound like some kind of womanizer."

"No worries," Gaby told her.

"Anyway, I saw you helping out over there. Thank you."

"It was my pleasure. My name is Gabriela." She extended her hand.

"I'm Alisha. This is Maddie. Maddie, do you want to shake Miss Gabriela's hand?" The girl politely did.

"And who is this?" Gaby asked, referring to the stuffed animal on the girl's lap. Maddie said it was Bennie the Bunny. "Nice to meet you too, Bennie the Bunny," Gabriela said, shaking the plush toy's oversized paw. Addressing Alisha, she asked, "Do you have a boy on the team?"

"Four, actually. And that's just on this team." Alisha smiled.

"Oh wow."

"Yeah, I've had so many kids, my uterus fell out." The woman laughed. "Sorry, that's a bad reference to an Andrew Dice Clay joke. But I do have a lot of kids. I'm a social worker. I work for DCF—the Department of Children and Families."

"Ah. I see," Gabriela said.

"Four of the kids on Sam and Tony's team are in the system. Maybe he mentioned that?"

"Yes, we're taking them out to dinner after practice."

"Mac's Diner, down the street. We're going, too, so Maddie can spend some time with her brother, Harry. She's currently in a group home, so Harry can't freely go see her. It's a little complicated, but we try to get siblings to stay in touch as much as possible. That's why we are here today. These two really love each other. Harry is only twelve, but he constantly talks about claiming her as soon as he ages out. Luckily, he also talks about becoming a computer engineer like Sam. But that's another story, I guess. At any rate, you've got a good man there," she said. "Tony and Sam are great with all the kids, but especially with the fostered ones and those whose home circumstances are suboptimal. Only about half the kids on the team belong to the families sitting over there. Tony and Sam understand where the other half stand; they're good role models for them. Plus, during the school year, Sam and Tony take other kids in the system on field trips, out to eat, and to the movies. And, of course, Sam helps the older ones with math and science. They've been godsends to many of these boys and girls."

Suddenly, Gabriela had many questions.

"What's Harry and Maddie's situation? Why are they in the system?" she asked.

"Unfortunately, I can't share any of that. Outside of DCF, only foster parents are privy to it," Alisha said. "Naturally, there's nothing to stop foster parents from discussing it. So I'm sure people close to the kids have some idea." She slyly bobbed her head toward the field, making it obvious that Sam could answer her questions.

They continued to chat during the soccer practice. Later, during dinner, Gaby got to know the kids a little better.

That night, just before going to sleep, Gabriela sat on the bed, petting Vin in her arms. Nic was asleep at her feet. When Sam came back from the bathroom, she hesitantly asked him about the two siblings.

Sam considered her question, climbing into bed. Then he told her, "They're amazing, as you saw earlier. But they got a raw deal. I mean, every child in foster care has it rough—not just because they're in the system but also because of the unfortunate factors that first put them there. Some of us lose loving parents forever, and others lose loving parents temporarily—for a number of reasons. And then, there are children like Harry and Maddie, who had to be rescued from straight-up abusive parents. Maddie wasn't even a year old when her parents took her to the hospital, saying she'd fallen off the bed and hit her head. She had bleeding in her brain. She's okay now, but her injury indicated it couldn't have resulted from falling off the bed."

"Shaken baby syndrome," Gaby stated.

"I don't know. But they ran other tests and determined she'd been physically abused. The authorities later found out the parents also had Harry. And this is where it gets even uglier.

They tested him too. He had old fractures and other injuries all over his body. He'd been abused all his life. He was only six at the time."

Gabriela was in tears. She put Vin down and slid over to embrace Sam.

"I'm so sorry, I shouldn't have told you that," he said.

"*I* asked you to tell me. I wanted to know. I still want to know. What happened next?"

"Are you sure?" He felt her nod. "Well, their parents went to jail and then relinquished all rights to their children. They moved out of state when they got out. Nobody has heard from them since. On top of it all, the kids actually got adopted. But those adoptive parents gave them up after a little more than a year. I mean, who does that? It pains me enough to know people return pets to shelters, like defective merchandise. But children?"

"That's horrible," Gaby said. "I feel so bad for them."

"Luckily, there's a bright side. They both seem emotionally unscathed. In fact, Harry is so mature for his age he'll be the team captain. All things considered, DCF has done a decent job helping them out."

"Alisha asked if I wanted to go visit Maddie tomorrow afternoon. I told her I would."

"That's nice of you. I'm sure they'll enjoy having you."

"I want to get her something nice. But I don't know what," Gaby said.

"Hmm. That's tricky. She's in a group home, so it's not a good idea to give her things the other kids can't have. I'd recommend something simple, like a coloring book with a nice box of crayons or markers, maybe some stickers. A LEGO set would be okay too. Basically, stuff she can share. There's a kids' store over by the Worcester airport. We can shop there before you see Maddie. We can even stop for lunch at Bushel 'N Peck on the way."

With the two pets now used to sharing their bed with one more person, the four soon fell asleep.

Gabriela enjoyed visiting Maddie so much she returned on Thursday afternoon.

On Friday, now familiar with the seven other kids in the home, she recruited Alisha to help with an errand. Together, they nearly emptied the Button Tree Kids store and went to distribute clothes and toys to each child.

Aside from the few hours she spent with the kids, nothing changed between Gaby and Sam. They continued to cherish every moment they had together. Their happiness was singular and whole and like nothing either had ever experienced before. Their bliss was evident to everyone. They felt their love for each other deeply.

For this reason, what Sam discovered at dawn on Sunday came as a startling surprise.

FIFTY-TWO

During Gaby's first few nights, the dog would wake every time she stepped out of the bedroom. But this quickly ceased as she became a normal part of the nightly routine. For the last two weeks, Gaby getting in and out of bed no longer prompted the loyal mutt to even raise an eyebrow.

Sunday was the last day of Gabriela's visit. It was still dark when Nic woke and stood by the foot of the bed. He stared intently at the closed bedroom door, his tail wagging vigorously. Even Vin slothfully turned his head, like a periscope, toward his canine mate. This woke Sam up, but he didn't make much of it. "Go back to sleep, Nic," Sam muttered.

Unlike Nic, Sam hadn't heard the front door open and close—swiftly, quietly.

A few minutes passed. Sam was dozing off when he heard a hurried knock on his bedroom door. The dog barked, prompting him to wake up and go to the door. In his morning stupor, Sam thought perhaps Gaby had locked herself out of the bedroom.

"Dude, she in there?" Tony whispered.

"What? No, I thought she went to the bathroom," Sam said, confused.

"Sam, she's gone."

"What do you mean?"

"I heard a noise in the living room. I thought it was one of you. But then I heard a car door shut outside. I went to the bathroom and noticed Gaby's luggage was no longer where she'd left it, next to the kitchen table. I went to the front door, and it was closed but unlocked. So I came to check things out."

Sam went into the living room and looked around. He walked to the kitchen and grabbed a note left on the table, folded in half. His name was written on it. Sam sat down, and Tony came around and sat opposite him. Sam unfolded the note while he gently petted Nic, who now sat by his side. He read aloud.

Dear Sam,

I hope one day you can forgive me for leaving like this—abruptly, in the dark, like a thief. It's selfish of me. But I wouldn't have been able to leave…to leave you, as we'd planned this afternoon. You, your family, your pets, your friends, and your hometown have stolen my heart. This has made everything between us infinitely more complicated. I am at a loss. So I ask that you give me space. Give me time to sort this all out. And please know this: it's the timing, the circumstance, and the reality of my obligations that confound me. But as my grandfather once wrote in his journal, "There is no confusion in my heart. There is only love."

Always yours,

Gaby

Numb and puzzled, Sam and Tony sat quietly.

Tony's thoughts were everywhere at once. *Did she just break up with him? After such a short time? Like this? Bitch! Nah, she don't seem like the type. Will she come back? Will she ask him to go there again? Will she tell him what she decides? When will she decide? Should he call her and talk? They're fuckin' rich, they can go back and forth. Don't she get that? Shit, maybe Sam was just a rich-girl fling. Bitch! Nah, that can't be. Maybe she wanted him to move down there but realized he belongs here. Respect, I guess. Sam can't move there for good. But wait. For love? Maybe he should move there. Crap! This is so fucked up.*

Sam's thoughts were more organized and simpler, yet bittersweet.

Bitter in that he felt history repeating itself. He recalled that fateful morning in the old bank vault in San Antonio, when he first read Gustavo's letter. Sam reflected on the instance when his grandmother had left a note for Gustavo, expressing her eternal but impossible love for him. "As we would surely kiss again, by the river—in another life," she'd written. Sam felt as the young doctor must have—three-quarters of a century ago as he stood next to his lawyer friend at the Greyhound bus station—with a forlorn mind and a severed heart.

Sweet in that there seemed to be a silver lining. Unlike her grandmother's, this note held no tone of finality. Sam latched on to this small hope. He just wasn't sure what that hope might mean. Sam's love for Gaby was such that he understood her decision to leave. If she loved him as much as he loved her, he empathized with the surely agonizing, tearful, and heartbreaking decision to avoid a formal goodbye. So, he'd do exactly as she asked. Sam would give Gabriela all the space and time she needed.

At that very moment, Sam believed there was nothing else he could or should do.

FIFTY-THREE

"Time is a flowing river. Happy those who allow themselves to be carried, unresisting, with the current. They float through easy days. They live, unquestioning, in the moment." Sam found solace in this quote from Christopher Morley's 1922 novel, *Where the Blue Begins,* and took each passing summer day in stride. He felt a deep-seated certainty about his connection with Gabriela. This conviction allowed him to float, optimistically, through the swift and inevitable current of time.

He felt an odd inner peace. He was convinced he simply had to wait for her to call to say how she'd decided to incorporate their relationship into her life. For about two months after her departure, Sam went along with whatever endeavors came up each day. With hope fully alive, and with Gabriela always at the forefront of his mind, Sam truly lived every waking moment, in the moment.

As the summer dwindled, Tony and Lilly were increasingly concerned his unperturbed demeanor only seemed that way. They thought Sam's indifference was just a coping mechanism. They believed their brother was suffering. After much deliberation, they'd planned an intervention. But the opportunity to let Sam know what they thought presented itself earlier.

Nic was asleep, sprawled on the long couch belly-up, with his head near Sam's thigh. Vin lay on part of his lap, intently watching the cursor as Sam used his laptop.

With an Ipswich Original Ale in hand, Tony walked up behind them and looked over Sam's shoulder.

"Really, Sammy? Surfing the web for old VW Beetles again?"

"Yeah. I think I may have found the right one. It's from 1968 and fire-engine red. It's part of an estate sale. Everything is original, including a roof rack. Plus, for its age, it's barely been used. It has seventy-three thousand miles. The only problem is it's in freakin' Palm Springs."

Tony went around the long couch and set his beer on the coffee table. "Let's see." Sam handed him the laptop. Tony went to sit on his armchair and took a quick look. "Yeah, cool car for sure." Then he shut the laptop and grabbed his beer. "All right, buddy, hear me out. I've been snooping around and keeping track of your activities since Gaby left. Let's see: You watch all kinds of stuff on YouTube about Mexico. The other day, your Netflix was paused on some Mexican teenybopper soap opera. Lately, we only order from restaurants you ate at with Gaby. And you now seem obsessed with getting an old VW. You seem fine, but me and Lilly aren't sure. Only about half of the usual Sam Gleeson is here. The rest is elsewhere."

"Dude, I know things have been a little odd. But I'm fine," Sam said with an assuring tone. "I just love her, man. That's what's weird. I've never loved anyone before. I'm really just basking in that feeling. So don't you and Lilly worry about me. I know Gaby is gone. But I have this gut feeling that somehow, someway, things will work out."

"Come on, Sam. Gut feeling? Somehow? Someway? That sounds like faith. What happened to mister logic and reason and facts and objectivity and bottom-line reality? I get the love part. But just sitting around waiting for...whatever? That ain't you. It pains me to say what I'm about to tell you. But Lilly and Lenny agree—you two belong together. This bullshit about logistics is just that: bullshit! We get that Gaby is some VIP and has to stay at her job. So, while you're important to us, to the kids, and to our friends, you're not completely tied down. We have a theory that Gaby cut out the way she did because she saw you coaching, mentoring, and just interacting with the kids, especially Harry and Maddie. Also, knowing you want to be a teacher, there was no way she could ask you to leave. That's the only thing that makes sense, and we respect her for that. But Sammy, you could easily spend most of your time with Gaby in Mexico. We're pretty sure she wouldn't mind if you came back, for some good stretches of time, a few times a year. Don't forget, you're now a damn millionaire. You can surely afford the back-and-forth." Tony stood to hand the computer back to Sam and then returned to his armchair. "Both times you went down there, you couldn't stop talking about how awesome Mexico City was. So, bro. We love you. But if you don't get on the next fucking plane to Mexico City, find her, tell her you love her and that you're ready to be with her wherever she might be, I'm going to kick your ass." Tony then pointed to the pets. "As much as I'll miss them too, we can figure out how to get those two punks down there later."

FIFTY-FOUR

Heeding Tony and Lilly's advice had been simpler than he'd imagined. It made sense.

For the better part of two months, Sam had been in a mental gridlock, trying to respect Gabriela's explicit wishes. After hearing Tony out, Sam recognized what he should've done in the first place. The moment he realized she'd left the apartment, he should have gone after her.

But that emotional impasse was in the past.

Everything he felt for Gabriela suddenly burst from his heart and permeated his being. He felt clarity of mind, which came down to one truth: Sam loved her above all else.

That evening, Sam and Tony drove to Providence. Even Nic seemed happy, riding cheerfully in the back seat. "What are the chances?" Tony exclaimed. Just as they took the exit ramp to the airport, the radio played "Are You with Me" by Lost Frequencies. He blasted the volume, and enthusiastically, they both sang about dancing underneath a Mexican sky, drinking margaritas, and listening to a mariachi band.

No direct flights had been available at that time of night. But Sam couldn't wait until the next day. He didn't care about having to travel all night—starting with a flight to Philadelphia, then a red-eye to Dallas, and then, from there, an early morning departure to Mexico City.

FIFTY-FIVE

Third time is the charm, Sam told himself when the American Airlines Boeing 737 touched down at the Mexico City International Airport.

"What brings you to Mexico City, Mr. Gleeson?" the officer asked, looking over his passport and immigration form.

Sam smiled. "I came to tell my girlfriend that I screwed up— that I never should've let her go."

"*Ooofff!* I see. Is she Mexican?"

"Yes, sir. She is."

"Well, my friend. In that case, if you want to do it right, you may want to bring along *unos mariachis*—a mariachi band, that is," the welcoming man said. He stamped Sam's documents. "I wish you good luck. Welcome back to Mexico."

Sam actually considered what the immigration official had said. He gleefully imagined himself in front of Ari's gallery, surrounded by mariachis, seeing Gabriela come out to a balcony, and having his love and the music spiral upward toward her.

He checked at an airport information kiosk and learned he could've hired a band in Plaza Garibaldi at any time, day or night. But Sam didn't know if Gaby would be home that morning. And in the end, he just wanted to feel her in his arms again. There'd be plenty of time for mariachis later.

It all happened so quickly.

The taxi came up through Orizaba Street and stopped at the south end of Plaza Río de Janeiro, a rectangular street that surrounded a lush park with the same name. Gabriela's home faced the park, just steps from that charming intersection. Given the street was one-way, the taxi couldn't turn left. Excited, Sam told the cabbie to let him off right there. As he grabbed his wallet, out of a corner of his eye, he noticed a motorcade in front of Gaby's home. Instead of giving the cabbie a tip, he stared out the car window toward her place.

His heart sank.

On the sidewalk, in front of the street-level door leading up to her residence, he saw Gabriela. She was face-to-face with Carlos Márquez.

She kissed him. Gabriela held Carlos's cheeks as her lips gently touched his. They slowly separated, smiling. They each stepped back, holding each other's hands for a second—which to Sam seemed like an eternity. Gabriela continued to walk backward, and they waved to each other. Then Carlos turned around and walked toward one of three black Range Rovers. A man in a suit held the door open for him. Gabriela was now under her front door's archway, only her waving arm was visible to Sam. The caravan passed before the taxi. Instinctively, Sam looked at the vehicles passing in front of him and then turned to look back at her. But she was gone.

Carlos leaving Gabriela's home at nine forty-five in the morning could only mean one thing. And in light of the gut-wrenching display he'd just witnessed, Sam had no doubt the mature, impossibly debonair man had spent the night. There wasn't much else to do. Sam asked the cab driver to take him back to the airport.

In the blink of an eye, exhilaration had turned into pain.

The somber part of Gustavo's story had come into play again. Sam remembered when the young doctor finally accepted that

Alessandra was gone forever and, as a result, fell into a paradoxical abyss of "rage and understanding."

Sam's dejection was just as profound. Yet he similarly accepted his fate. He didn't blame Gabriela, not for one second.

If only he'd gone after her that morning.

That heartbreaking anguish replayed in Sam's mind over and
over—when he momentarily felt lucky a direct flight to Boston
was available at noon. When he bought some magazines and a
booklet of crossword puzzles, hoping these could help take his
mind off the day's events. When he boarded the commuter train
at Boston's South Station. And even when he finally got back to
Worcester that last day of summer.

EPILOGUE

When love is lost, there's no greater solace than the certainty that—even for a moment—it was ever found. Even when love is ephemeral, it gives life meaning, hope, and profound satisfaction. Unlucky are those who never find love.

Samuel Gleeson, though, was lucky in the ways that mattered most.

Upon returning to Worcester, he didn't share his agonizing experience. Sam didn't want anyone to feel any rancor toward Gabriela. He firmly believed she was endowed with unblemished character.

But even if he'd told them, it wouldn't have mattered. His family already knew everything. Although, they had to pretend they didn't know—for just a little longer. In the meantime, they did their best to help Sam with the pain.

As it turned out, Carlos Márquez had looked out his Range Rover's window. When his motorcade passed by the taxi, Carlos immediately recognized Sam. Though a man of debatable integrity, Carlos genuinely cared for Gabriela. He called Gaby to inform her he'd just seen Sam in a taxi. Because of this, even before Sam had touched down in Boston, Gaby had already been in contact with Tony to explain everything.

Sam wouldn't be able to begin the master's in teaching program at Clark University until next May. So, it would be two years before he became licensed to teach in the public school system. But he wanted to get a jump start on classes, and that fall, he registered for a couple of courses. He figured this would also help him take his mind off Gaby.

One afternoon, a little over two months after Sam's bitter return from Mexico, Sam was walking down the apartment stairs, on his way to school. Tony pulled up. "Come on, Sammy, I'll give you a ride," he told him.

"I don't need a ride. You know Clark is around the corner. Aren't you supposed to be at the shop?"

"Nah. It's slow. Lisa can handle it. Come on, hop in."

Sam obliged. But when Tony made a right turn, Sam exclaimed, "Dude, you're going the wrong way. I gotta get to class!"

"Sam, this is a class you'll want to miss. Don't ask questions. That's all I'm gonna say. Is that clear?"

"Do I have a choice?"

Sam did his best to relax. Tony's demeanor was strangely exuberant. Sam smiled and shook his head. He felt a hint of worry, wondering what Tony was getting him into this time.

A few minutes later, Tony drove up a curved driveway in front of the University of Massachusetts Medical School. Lenny was there waiting. He opened the door for Sam.

"Come on, guys, you're late! Hurry up and park the car so you can join us," he told Tony. "Sam, let's go. Follow me."

Lenny led Sam through a few elevators and hallways. Finally, they reached a double door. They went inside. The function inside the large conference room had already begun. The place was filled with about fifty people—physicians and medical students, as well as hospital administrators and even some reporters from local newspapers. Lilly and the girls were sitting in the back row. They smiled at Sam as soon as he came in. He and Lenny sat beside them.

Sam gasped softly the moment he settled and glanced forward. He found himself trying to contain the feelings and memories suddenly overwhelming his heart and mind.

Gabriela was sitting at the long head table with a handful of administrators and physicians on either side of her. She was being introduced as a faculty member in the department of surgery, and as the director of the school's new Transplant Research Initiative. After a few other comments from the panel, Gaby answered a question from the audience.

"As Dr. Croft mentioned, UMass has a fine tradition in the field of organ transplantation—over seven hundred transplants and counting. But this center has never had a dedicated department for translational research in the field. I want to help ensure this institution not only continues its tradition but also remains at the field's cutting edge. I've secured a number of grants that, for years to come, will vastly expand this center's tissue transplant research. This will also allow us to create a fellowship program so we can continue to train transplant surgeons and encourage more scientists to join the field—right here in Worcester."

Another person raised his hand. "Dr. Martel, *Worcester Telegram* here. Your professional bio is extraordinary. May I ask, why Worcester?"

Gabriela smiled affably. "Well, there is a short and a long answer. The long one is for a particular person to hear. So I'll give you the short one. You see, not too long ago, I told someone that places are like people. They always have a heart to claim. And it seems that even before I knew it, someone in this town claimed mine. This person lives, loves, and belongs in this very special city. Therefore, because Worcester is his life…Worcester is my love."

Many years later, a young woman told, in much more eloquent terms, Sam and Gabriela's story. She wrote about it while an English major at Yale. In her paper, she discussed herself and her brother—a young doctor based in Mexico City but currently in Africa with Doctors Without Borders. "While my brother obtained his computer engineering degree from Worcester Polytechnic, he eventually decided to follow in our mother's footsteps," she wrote. "His name is Harry Gleeson, although when he's back in Mexico with our extended family, he uses his full name, Harry Gleeson Martel. As for me, Maddie Gleeson, I want to be a journalist. I want to explore the human condition and bring to light some of the common bonds, such as hope and love, that unite us all. In doing so, perhaps I can help ensure that the extraordinary stories and legacies of ordinary people transcend time."

In her account, Maddie concluded the story of her parents with the day Gabriela had gone back to Worcester for good—where they still lived, blissfully, to that day.

"But I saw you with Carlos a couple of months ago. I don't understand," Sam said after Gaby had finished introducing him to some people after her official welcome to UMass.

The conference room was nearly empty now. Standing in front Sam, Gaby said, "I'm so sorry you saw that. It was a strange coincidence you decided to find me at that precise moment. As I told Tony that day, it was nothing more than a final goodbye. I'd had a relationship with Carlos Márquez, which, for all practical purposes, had ended before I ever met you. A relationship that in retrospect was for all the wrong reasons. But we remained friends, and even in our subsequent time together, I always felt he still carried a torch for me. He'd always been forthright and kind to me, and I felt he deserved a proper, gracious goodbye. On that occasion, I had invited him to breakfast—specifically to avoid the connotations of a dinner or even a lunch. I wanted him to know his hopes for something more than friendship were futile. He understood and cordially accepted it. I then told him about you and about my plans, already in motion, to come here.

"You probably saw me kiss him. Probably why you didn't come knocking. Well, it was the kind of kiss you give someone you are fond of—the kind of fondness you feel for someone with whom you once shared a relationship of convenience. Nothing more. He was just a small part of the staggering checklist I had to contend with in order to make my way back to you."

That was all it took for Sam to bring her closer and, with a tender kiss, confirm everything he knew and felt about Gaby was true.

"Sam," she said, gently holding his face in her hands, "that first day we met, just before we went out with Ari and his friends, you may have noticed it took me a while to come out of my office bathroom. It wasn't because it took that long to put on a tank top and pair of jeans. It was because I was having a panic attack. I'd diagnosed many in the past, so I knew what I was feeling. I had that attack because being with you stirred so many feelings in me. They shook me in ways I never thought possible. The only thing that stabilized me was logic. But that unfortunate, shitty logic dictated I had to ignore what I was feeling. I thought I had to fall out of love with you. But I couldn't. I can't.

"I've loved you from the second you rose from my office chair and looked at me with your confused and beautiful and caring eyes. For nearly a year since, the matters of geography and logistics have continued to exact a hefty burden. But that's all over. I've given myself permission to freely love you now. And I plan to love you always."

Their embrace was so intense they each felt the old keys, still hanging from that makeshift necklace around Sam's neck, press into their bodies.

Forever after, he seldom took the necklace off. The keys reminded Sam of a long, sweet story—and of his perfect life in love.

THE END

AUTHOR'S NOTE

The Keys is fiction. However, it's based on the history of the 201st Squadron of the Mexican Expeditionary Air Force during World War II. And thus, I'm grateful to a small group of elite men who represented an entire country with distinction and honor at a time when human dignity and freedom lay on a tenuous balance. I don't believe any member of the 201st Squadron is still alive, but they will never be forgotten.

I found historical and factual information regarding businesses and institutions mentioned in *The Keys* on websites and using publicly available information, including newspaper articles, archived local news segments, and educational videos on YouTube. Specifics about the 201st Squadron come primarily from Lt. Col. José G. Vega Rivera's research paper "The Mexican Expeditionary Air Force in World War II: The Organization, Training, and Operations of the 201st Squadron" (1997).

Finally, for the purpose of weaving this fictional story, I've taken some liberties in chronology, as well as in portraying certain public figures—past or present.

ABOUT THE AUTHOR

RAFAEL SILVA is the author of *The Package*. He has lived in Worcester, Massachusetts; San Antonio, Texas; and Mexico City. He is a practicing physician and lives in Portland, Oregon, with his wife and their pets.

For fun facts and videos related to THE KEYS, visit

limbicpress.com

63776506R00195